Opaque Blue

11 Short Stories

Second Edition

MICHAEL G. RANIS

Publishing Coordinator – Sharon Kizziah-Holmes

Paperback-Press
an imprint of A & S Publishing
A & S Holmes, Inc.

ISBN -13: 978-1-951772-03-1

DEDICATION

To the memory of my parents who were so intent on teaching me right from wrong.

CONTENTS

PREFACE

The seeds for this book were sown almost twenty years ago. Affected by the sadness and the turmoil of a personal crisis, I needed an outlet for the overflowing feelings and started writing. I was doing so in my third language. I was bilingual at home, but English was not one of the languages. English, however, was the language of the authors I most admired and enjoyed reading. It seemed completely natural to write in English. Secretly, I wanted to "sound" like these authors! Instead I found myself writing and erasing, typing and deleting, scribbling and crumpling. Soon enough it became clear that writing "literature" was hard for me. I would only bring these stories to the general public if I could be proud of them. And if it took time, so be it.

While I was gainfully employed, and spending many hours fulfilling work requirements, these stories were just interesting muses. I would not have dared sharing these with a wider public. It was even hard to share the first story with a lover as I tried to capture her heart. Her response was warm, positive, encouraging. I expected her to point out problems as I thought that she would enjoy criticizing it. When I garnered courage, and showed it to a few other friends, the response was similar. The most common response was "nice" or "interesting." Maybe he or she would suggest an edit, or point out a missing link, transition, or a badly structured sentence; in effect, they encouraged me without sounding effusive. It was obvious to me: interesting stories but the writing needs to improve. I was not able to dedicate the time and energy to bring this about while working full time—it would have to wait till I retired.

The next hurdle was to find out if I could get editing help and whether that expense would be justified by the publication of these stories as a compendium. I was not interested in this being a "vanity" piece. I had accomplished plenty in my life I could be proud of; the stories needed to be of similar quality if they would be published.

The conclusion of this information gathering process was positive. Men and women working in the publishing industry, who day in day out are approached by would-be first time authors, read the stories and thought that they justified publication. First rounds of editing by M. Burnley and editors affiliated with Kevin Anderson Associates helped immensely, and I am thankful for their work.

To those who have inspired some of these stories, read and criticized the writing, offered encouragement: Ruth A. D. David G., Harris L., Sybil B. and a few I can't name here, I owe a heartfelt thank you for their intentional and unintentional contributions, their edits, their suggestions and above all their encouragement. To my new Miami friends, most notably Claire A., Frida B., Susan F. and David R., who more recently invested time and energy, read one or more stories, offered encouragement and suggestions, and provided all sorts of help, I am extremely grateful for their friendship and support.

Dr. Patricia Ross at Hugo House Publishers was instrumental in the last phases of editing. But, when it became impossible to correct errors in the final proof I chose to launch this, hopefully error-free, second edition.

I am very thankful to Sharon Kizziah-Holmes of Paperback Press for her willingness to expeditiously lend a hand in making this edition possible. She should be a model for what the publishing industry could become.

Though the phrase Opaque Blue appears only in one story, I chose it as the title of the book because, to a degree, it is a symbol. Many of the stories in this collection reflect on the struggle of middle-aged men in a world that gives them less and less consideration.

There is, however, a more important theme travelling through many of these stories: the difficulties modern men and women have in successfully communicating with each other. It is my sincere hope, that these stories affect readers by triggering reflection, self-assessment, and perhaps even the realization that we all can do better in how we share information, how we communicate desires, how we pass on critical thoughts.

WHEN EDITH PRAYED TO JESUS

■

E dith!" Frau Schoen's shrill thundered across the classroom.
"Wir sind ja nicht in der Judenschule!" (After all, we are not
in a Jewish schoool!) The teacher's mouth, her distorted face,
eagerly focused on that one, most common, ethnic slur: "Juden"
as she uttered her admonition. Chastising Edith had become routine,
more so now as the Nazi edicts gave Frau Schoen the impression that the
full state machinery was behind her, cheering her on. It was with great
glee that this middle-aged, rotund spinster joined in on the anti-Jewish
tirades promulgated by the regime; she was demonstrating her patriotism
and her full-fledged support for the Party. She often wore red-and-black
colored traditional clothes that were more likely to fit her Bavarian
origins than this industrial region. They were hardly the best look for this
rather plump woman, but one can guess that she was thrilled with the
colors matching the new symbol of the Third Reich—the black swastika
over a red flag. In Edith's eyes, Frau Schoen looked grotesque, but she
made sure not to show her disdain.

The tirade was in response to Edith chatting with the only remaining
close friend among her classmates; they mostly had taken their distance,
even shown animosity befitting these hate-filled times. Edith could be
recognized from afar as her brownish red and extremely curly hair was
unique. About ten years earlier it had prompted someone to make up a
limerick: "Curls no end on Edith's head, causing her never to sit still, but
maybe only when asleep in bed." Edith was also bright and strangely

1

unafraid despite the sensation that the world was closing in on her. Edith hardly let anyone abuse her—she whipped back instantly: *"Nein, Frau Schoen, dort sind Wir wirklich nicht"* (No, Frau Schoen, indeed that is not where we are). Maybe one would be quick enough to interpret this to mean, "If it were, it would be a more pleasant place." but it mattered little what Edith meant. The Jewish girl was standing up to Frau Schoen.

A few years earlier, her schoolmates had seen Edith break school records in the 110-meter hurdles and had cheered her on; more, perhaps, because of school pride, but maybe, Edith hoped, they were rooting for her as well. They heard she had earned third place in the regional contest and they were even more proud Edith represented this school. Now they were told to hate her because she was a Jewess. If not outright hostile, most distanced themselves from her—Deutschland, the Fatherland, demanded it from them.

There was a box full of trophies and garlands in the basement of her house; it used to be in Edith's room. The night after the new edicts prohibited Jewish athletes from participating in Aryan events. her father, Max, banished the box. He saw no need for his darling daughter to see the trophies and be reminded of a more glorious past. Later that night, alone in bed—his wife had died five years earlier—Max glared at the ceiling with eyes wide open. He was contemplating what to do about his four daughters. He was afraid that their lives would become impossible in this country. He may be able to survive somehow; after all, he had been a soldier during the Great War and had even received a medal for valor shown in battle, but they, his daughters, were a different matter. They were still so young. Edith, secretly his favorite, was so bright and so eager to become a physician … none of that would be possible under Hitler. Could it be that even that behemoth of a person could be brought down? Governments, after all, did fall routinely in Weimar. If Hitler remained in power, could Edith even finish school? She had managed to stay in school because in her area the laws against Jews were not fully upheld, even less so in smaller towns like Offenbach. However, this was already 1939, and the grip was tightening every day.

"You insolent Jewish girl, how dare you talk back to your teacher?" The school director, the same man who had enthusiastically embraced her as he presented her the last trophy of her athletic career, told her that she would be suspended from school for one week because of her behavior. Edith turned red with anger but knew that this time she could not quip back. She knew there was no use in protesting, in reminding Herr von Knause that this was the same girl who had brought so many honors to the school. As Edith left the school's premises, she couldn't know that she would never see the inside of that place again.

Once safely home, Edith burst out crying. Neither her sisters nor her father could calm her agitated mood. In between bouts of tearful hollering, she managed to convey the incident and the punishment. Max left Edith to be consoled by her sisters while he withdrew to his room. He acted like a man possessed. There was now great urgency in sending his daughters out of the country. Lotte would go to Holland to visit with her married sister Friedl. Herta was planning to emigrate to South America with her fiancé in any case, but that needed to be expedited. What, however, could he do with Edith? He needed help, he needed ideas. He was not an active member of the small local Jewish community. In fact he was trying hard to assimilate into the Christian society; but he had a good friend, Moritz Baum, a well-connected lawyer who could maybe help.

That night at the dinner table, Max spoke solemnly to his family. He had decided that it was time for them to leave Germany. The scheme was simple. Herta and Samuel should marry immediately and seek to emigrate to Brazil as they had planned, but sooner. Lotte would travel to Holland in the very near future, and Edith would go to England next week; a special visa he was able to organize with the help of Baum and the Jewish Agency would allow her migration. The reaction was of course emotional: "We will never be together again! What will you do, Father? What will become of us?" Max reassured them that this was just temporary. They would be together again. Germany would respect his Iron Cross medal and do him no harm.

He took Edith by the hand, like he used to do after her mom died. She was the youngest, and for him the most precious. "You will travel with your sister to Holland and from there to Antwerp. Lotte will make sure you get on the right train. In Antwerp I have a cousin you've never met, her name is Rosa, and she will take you to the boat that will see you off to England. Remember to stay calm, tough, and strong, all the time ..." He put his hands over Edith's head, said a prayer, and blessed her.

"Your name and surname?" asked the tall Englishman with the largest bright reddish mustache Edith had ever seen. "Edith Blumenwald," he repeated. "You have an English name, Edith, of course, not Blumenwald. Quite international, aren't you? Even if you come from Germany, but then you are Jewish, aren't you?" Edith just nodded; she was all too

3

impressed with this man's mustache and baritone voice to notice the sarcasm. The new world was still too confusing for her, and she was concentrating on her next steps: pass the immigration officer, pass customs, and look for the person from the Agency who was supposed to help her. The baritone voice sternly reminded her as she was ready to move on: "You must report every three months to the nearest police station. Do not do anything illegal. Remember, you are a guest in this country."

As she entered the port's lobby, she saw dozens of people looking for friends and family. She almost despaired when, with great relief, she identified a sign simply saying "Agency" (no need to publicize the ethnic affiliation) held by a stern woman with long, straight black hair and a black hat which tilted to the left. Once she took note of Edith's name, Mrs. Brass expeditiously told Edith she was one of five girls expected to arrive in the next two hours. Edith should make herself comfortable, perhaps over there, in the corner, on a bench. Edith walked over quietly and stared at the bare walls of this port facility. For a moment, she felt tears coming to her eyes, but then she swallowed hard and said to herself, "Stay calm, tough, and strong." As she said those words, she mimicked her father's deep voice and that caused her to smile.

Once all the girls had arrived, Mrs. Brass took them to her car and they drove for what seemed an eternal journey to London. No one said a word, there was so much and so little to be said. They were quiet, wondering, nervous, and sad. Mrs. Brass didn't talk either; she was doing her good deed and that should suffice. The weather was unpleasant considering it was April, damp and cold. Intermittent showers made it difficult to look outside the window and see the landscape of the new countryside. Eventually they made it to the city and Mrs. Brass ushered the five girls into a large building that looked like an old school. Indeed that was what it was during the day; in the late afternoon the Agency used it so that its personnel could meet the incoming refugees, interview them, and find them a place to stay, a new home of sorts.

"Edith, you seem rather young, how old are you?" the Agency person asked in German. Edith responded in English that she was seventeen. "Your English is rather excellent, I should say. Perhaps you have a bit of an accent, but really not bad at all," exclaimed the cheerful lady interviewing Edith. "Do you speak any other languages?"

Edith perked up as she answered with obvious pride. "I learned French and Latin in school and am rather good in those languages as well; however, my plans are to go to medical school."

"Well, well," clamored Her Roundness, "maybe later, but not now that you are a refugee." Somehow it seemed to Edith that the word R-E-F-U-G-E-E had emerged from this big woman's mouth slowly, enunciated with extra care, making sure it sank in, making certain that Edith absorbed the notion of being of inferior status as quickly as possible.

"I have the ideal place for you to stay. They are a family in central London, near Hyde Park." As she described the location, the voice was pitched very high—a function of her excitement. "The Hutchinses have a son who is having some real problems in school, especially in Latin class. You will help him and help the family with some other chores. In return you will receive room and board and a little pocket money. This is, of course, transitional, but I have little else I can offer you right now that would be better." Edith did not think this was such a bad option and went to sleep thinking positively of the new family who would adopt her. In her mind, medical school was just a few steps away from this interim undertaking.

Mr. Hutchins arrived bright and early the next morning. Dressed in a dark suit and overcoat he seemed ready to go to some important function. Edith had rarely seen people dressed up with so much care back home. He introduced himself with a handshake. In the car he told Edith that they were looking forward to the help she would be giving their son Percy. "He is not a bad chap, but a little disoriented, a little unmotivated. He must develop character, and he needs some skills if he wants to follow in the Hutchins footsteps." Edith listened quietly and nodded. It was still raining outside, but she tried to look through the drops streaming down the side window. The newness of everything overwhelmed her: the cars, the many people, the noise.

They arrived at a house that was not dissimilar to other houses on this street. The color of the narrow building was plain white, just like most other buildings in this strikingly nicer neighborhood, and yet, it appeared cold to Edith. She had not detected a single plant or flowerpot. Mr. Hutchins handed her the suitcase and watched her climb the stairs with great agility.

He opened the door and announced himself and Edith to Mrs. Hutchins. She eventually came down to the foyer where they waited. Her steps were slow, she took one stair at a time. It was as if she were measuring Edith with every step that brought her closer to the girl who would help Percy with his homework and studies. She finally came close enough to extend the whitest hand Edith had ever seen; it was also the coldest she had ever felt. "Hello, Edith, I am Mrs. Hutchins and you must remember to always call me by that name." She demonstratively looked Edith over one more time. "You are very young, and I am not sure this will work, but we shall give it a try. Let me show you to your room at once."

Edith was told that in the mornings and early afternoons, while Percy was at school, she would clean the house together with the maid who came every day. "We are rather insistent that the house, and that includes your room as well, be spotless—no dust, no dirty corners." Once Percy returned from school, she was to make sure that he did his homework and then she would practice his Latin, his weakest subject. "You must, of course, make sure that you keep proper distance from him at all times. We will give you some pocket money for your Sunday outing; it will not be much because we must make sure you do not lose your good sense, enough for a pastry or a cake perhaps. Of course, you will eat in the kitchen the same food we eat, and that will be at our expense."

Finally, Edith was left alone in her room, a small room in one part of the attic. It had just enough space for a bed and a small desk. Edith felt cold and lonely as she whispered, "I promised Dad to stay strong and calm."

Five months passed and the war between Germany and England loomed imminent. She always read the newspapers a day later than her hosts. Edith presented herself at the police station every three months as she was ordered to, and settled into her routine. On her third visit, however, she was asked to move to an interrogation room. There she heard a snappy female voice state: "Your father is still in Germany, one sister is in Brazil, the other one in Holland, and yet another has moved to Argentina. Are you a refugee or part of a spying network?" She could barely see the woman because the bright lamp shined directly in Edith's eyes.

Edith recounted the evening when her father had sent all the sisters out of Germany. The woman stated, "I don't know, and your English is too perfect for a German—Jewish or not. We must keep an eye on you."

Edith left the police station shaking and frightened. What was going to happen now that war seemed a certainty?

Indeed, England declared war on Nazi Germany four days later. Everybody seemed tense and agitated—in her home, on the street—everywhere. Edith was most concerned about her father who still lived in Germany. She received letters from him every other week, and in each one he comforted her that all would be well, but the words he used denoted that he was more uncertain, and his handwriting appeared shaky even though he was only in his early fifties.

Soon thereafter, German planes began dropping bombs over England's cities. Sirens sounded often and the sheer terror of the unknown gripped Mr. Hutchins in particular. He had developed a terrible skin rash which Mrs. Hutchins explained to be the result of a nervous condition. Mrs. Hutchins tried to keep calm and collected and decided that it was best to cheer up the household with the upcoming Christmas spirit.

"Edith," she said, "we need to unpack the nativity scene that we store in the basement and display it so that Mr. Hutchins regains his faith in our Lord and the fate of our nation. You know we are devout Catholics. I trust that you will be careful bringing up the figurines, cleaning them, and making them ready so I can arrange the display. Tomorrow, while we are attending Mass, you will be so kind as to organize that. And please do not forget to bring up the larger statue of Jesus on the cross, which is also in that same area of the storage room. I believe one should remember how he was born and how he died, and I have always added this to the display."

Promptly after the Hutchinses left the house, Edith went to the storage area, found the wrapped figurines, and started bringing them up two by two. She was well aware that they were important to this devout family, particularly to Mrs. Hutchins. She made sure to start with what seemed to be the easier pieces to handle, those that belonged to the nativity scene. She did not forget that she was to bring up the larger piece and was now ready to do so. She held it in her calm hands and began to ascend, when the impact of a shell exploding somewhere in the Mayfair neighborhood caused her to misstep and knocked the figurine against the wall. She quickly made it to the kitchen and unfolded the wrapping to inspect the damage. It was the worst; the head of Jesus on the cross had somehow been knocked off.

She panicked. What could she do? She was certain that if she told the Hutchinses, they would refuse to understand it as an accident. They possibly could throw her out to the streets. Nobody would be willing to host a German girl these days. The public was getting more and more concerned with Fifth Column spies spreading like a contagious disease all over the country. The British newspapers were demanding a resolute approach against German citizens living in England—regardless of their status as refugees and regardless of their religion or politics.

She prepared some glue from scratch and carefully applied it to the broken piece. She then lightly pressed the head onto the neck to make sure the glue held. Once Edith felt that the glue had hardened, she uttered a prayer: "Dear Jesus, please, I beg of you, keep your head up." This startled her. She had just issued a prayer to Jesus, something her father would have strongly condemned under normal circumstances, but she thought he would understand. In fact, for the following weeks she went to bed every night uttering the same sentence: "Please, oh Jesus, do not lose your head." Her prayer seemed to work well enough, for Mrs. Hutchins never commented on the damaged figurine. Edith wondered if Mrs. Hutchins noticed but decided to protect Edith, or whether she was too preoccupied with other matters to detect the crack along the neck. Edith worried that any kind of movement may cause the head to come tumbling down and worried how these objects would be wrapped and stored back in the basement once the holidays ended. She was never to find out.

On a cold morning in mid-December, Mrs. Hutchins, in a huff, shook Edith awake. The police were waiting for her downstairs. She was to pack all her belongings, two suitcases of clothes, and go with them. Edith was confused. The early morning hour, the suddenness of it all, the unknown destiny, the uncertainty was daunting to her. Why was she being forced out of her refuge? Where was she going? She had done no wrong, she protested, she had shown up regularly at the police station. Mrs. Hutchins tried to appear comforting in her impartiality. "It is not you, my dear, they are rounding up all Germans on British soil. They will put you in confinement; the security of the land in these difficult moments is paramount."

Edith looked outside wondering if there was a way to escape. Confinement sounded terrible to her. How would she stay in contact with her father? How would she survive this new, perhaps brutal, condition? Nonetheless, she had no other option than to obey; she had nowhere else to go and nobody to turn to. Certainly, the Hutchinses would not protect her, particularly after what she had done to the head of Jesus. Jumping out of the attic's window was certain death, even if she was agile and athletic. She quickly packed her things and went downstairs. She was rushed out of the house, and as she looked back she could see the nativity scene through the bay window.

At the police station, she heard German women conversing with each other in harsh tones. For a moment, she had thought that Mrs. Hutchins had discovered the damaged figure of Jesus and was revenging Edith's carelessness. Now she became certain that indeed she was being apprehended because of her origins.

8

One of those loud women approached her and asked her, "And who are you? What is your name? I have never seen you before. Are you German?
Or maybe you are a Jewess?"

Edith simply said, "My name is Edith."

As she walked away, she could hear the loud woman say, "*Jah, eine von jene.*" (Yes, one of those).

Here she was, a young Jewish woman among mostly hostile middle-aged women, interned on an island called ironically Isle of Man. She was cold, she was hungry, and mostly, she was lonely. When the German women sang their German songs, they would parody their own situation by marching like soldiers. Edith hated the sight, even more so than being caught in this situation. She was also alert enough to understand that these women were rather venomous about the Jewish women in the camp, and so she distanced herself from the women who appeared to be Jewish. It was not just out of sheer cowardice; she also felt she had little in common with the women of her own creed. She had been raised in a house that was rather assimilated; Jewish customs and traditions were mostly foreign to her—strangely more foreign than the songs those Nazi women sang.

After two weeks she received a letter from the Hutchinses. In it was only a short note: they hoped she was doing well enough to read the news in the enclosed letter. They had opened the letter sent by her father. He himself had been deported to Dachau. He felt betrayed that they did not acknowledge his military service to the country during the Great War. He hoped and prayed that the situation would improve soon, but he was unsure when. The Hutchinses never mentioned the broken statue, nor did they mention that they in effect were trying to influence the Home Office to release Edith from internment. She was a good person, a straight character who could not possibly be a spy. The letter, instead, left her sad and worried about her father's health and fate. She wondered if she would ever see him again as tears rolled down her anguished face.

The winter months of early 1940 proved difficult for Edith. She was never more than bones and muscle, but food was awful and scarce, and she suffered from hunger. Just like the other women there, she began eating roots she pulled from the nearly frozen ground. The digestion of these uncooked roots was painfully difficult. She was losing what had been the cornerstone of her survival skills, her strength of will, her confidence that she could overcome most hardships. Yes, she had promised her father she would stay calm and strong, but she began to doubt her own strength, the source of her inner calmness.

9

As the wretchedness of daylight made way to the cold loneliness of her restless nights, time fused into an undistinguishable, purposeless, and seemingly endless stream. Edith saw little sense in counting days, weeks, or months; you only count when there is a date of resolution, a final set of figures translating into redemption. Midday was marked by the lonely cigarette she would be able to smoke—and as such it was a feast. She inhaled deeply and played with the smoke she exhaled. Smoking became a habit when during weekends she met with other young women who worked in the fancy households of Hyde Park. Instead of buying a piece of cake, she would buy some cigarettes. Because she never smoked much, she took what she had left to her internment at the Isle of Man.

One morning in the spring of 1941, Edith was told to present herself at the camp's main offices. A tall, thin woman with a long pointy nose informed her that she was to return to London. "The family that hosted you has asked that you return to their house; they have spoken on your behalf. They seem to have influence. You will be free to go by this afternoon. Get your belongings and be ready in an hour."

Edith hastily packed her things; a weak smile emerged on her face. She wondered when she had cause to smile last. She could hardly believe her luck; the Hutchinses had rescued her. Was it because of their son? Was it because they did like her even if they never showed too much affection? Did it matter? She would return to their house in London at once, but it would be dark by the time she got there.

She had seen and heard the German Stukas and bombers flying over the island in the direction of London. The noise terrified her, but she could not envision the destruction they were causing. She was dropped off at Paddington Station and walked towards the house. The path to the old neighborhood was littered with the vestiges of this indiscriminate total war: burned buildings and cars, the smell of fire, the broken cobblestones, and the hard faces of terrified people. The darkness of night made for blurred images and intensified her sense of confusion. Edith had walked through the pleasant neighborhood many times; she was certain she was in the right place even if she had a hard time recognizing some of what she saw. "Down this street near the next corner is the house," she muttered to herself, but as she came closer she noticed a big gap between the buildings. She started running in the direction of the house that, she couldn't quite believe, was now missing. She hit her leg against a piece of burned twisted metal and felt the pain shoot up her leg, but her eyes and mind were fixed on the last vestiges of a building that she once called home. All that remained was the bay window she so loved. In the early weeks of her stay she had sat there quietly contemplating what would become of her life. On her way to the Isle of Man, that window was the last thing she saw—the nativity scene display holding her secret shame. Now the half-burned bay window was the stage and sole witness of war's horror.

Her loud scream of denial expressed Edith's incredulity and sadness. Her body shook uncontrollably, her eyes were red and burning, her mouth kept on saying the same words over and over: "No! This cannot be." She looked around desperately seeking a familiar face, anybody who may have been able to tell her that in fact the Hutchinses had survived the German bomb. There were plenty of people on the street, rushing away from another blast nearby, but she did not recognize anyone.

Dizzy and confused, in her bewilderment, Edith ignored the sirens warning of another imminent bombing. She half-sat with her backside resting on her calves as she looked to gain comfort by burying her face in her hands. The twilight generated by slow-burning fires in the midst of a desperately and ineffectively darkened London only created more uncertainty. Where should she go now? Did she have a home, even just for the night? Suddenly she was grabbed by the arm. The man yelled at her, "You must go to a bomb shelter now! Don't just sit there." He pointed to the familiar entryway to the Underground and she followed his orders semi-consciously.

The Underground network sheltered thousands, and amid this humanity, the man who had grabbed her hand and pulled her away from the street found some people he knew. One of them cursed in French as she complained about having lost her lighter. "N'importe qui ont un feu?" Edith handed her a box of matches without saying a word. "Vous parlez français! Merci. I am Rita, and who are you? George, did you make a new lady friend? You, insatiable man!" It seemed like Rita was more intent in declaiming than in listening to answers. Maybe it was her way to reduce anxiety. Her voice was strangely happy despite the somberness of the moment. To Edith she came across as funny and friendly. In her dark suit, she also seemed outrageously elegant considering the place and the circumstances. Streetwise, as she proved to be, Rita noticed Edith's focus on her clothes. This time she used her heavily accented English: "I was in the office when the bomb alarms brought me down to this hole—again! What do you do? Do you work in the area?" Edith did not respond. The story was complicated, there was too much explaining to do. Instead, her eyes filled with tears. Rita noticed this and grabbed her by the arm. But then she noticed that Edith's leg had been bleeding. "Quick, let me have some bandages here!" The subways had first-aid boxes at many points, and George promptly found a bandage.

Edith learned that Rita and George worked in the offices of the Belgian government in exile. George quickly found out he was not Edith's type. His advances were rebuffed politely. He went on to his next prey with uncomplicated gaiety, and started chatting up some other women huddled in the underground. Rita, on the other hand, was immediately well-liked by Edith and the feeling was mutual. Once the "all clear" alarm sounded they walked to a nearby pub that remained open despite the raid. There Rita bought Edith a meal. "I want to hear your story," Rita told Edith, "so I am going to invite you for dinner; we might as well talk over a nice bowl of soup and whatever horrible food they serve at this place."

For the next two hours Edith told her story and answered a thousand questions. She struggled between wanting to share her life story with another person, and telling it to a near stranger probably ten years older. But Rita struck her as a kind woman, someone ready to lend a hand, and she knew she needed help; perhaps more now than ever. There was another, more immediate issue: the desire to eat a good meal. She was famished. She had horrible food while in internment, and only had had a dry piece of bread on this terrible day. Rita suggested Edith spend the next few days in her flat. The sofa in the living room would be a decent substitute to homelessness. Rita also promised to arrange work for Edith at the delegation's offices. Her language skills would be an asset, she justified. Furthermore, since the war seemed to extend beyond all expectations, there was more and more work. "The pay will even be decent. And for us, it certainly would good press to have a Jewess amongst us," This last comment Rita quipped with a broad, lipsticked smile.

Edith worked for the Belgian delegation until the end of the war. As war found its denouement away from England's shores, she was able to settle down, develop friendships, and adopt a sweet-looking black Scottish terrier she named Scotty. She never heard from her father again and guessed the Nazis killed him. She often wondered about her sisters but could not do much about it while war raged. She was never able to find out what happened to the Hutchinses, her hosts. Many of the people she approached to try and find out their fate, said that they probably died in that terrible direct hit to the house. They were, she concluded, very proper and correct, even if they were not very warm. She was saddened by their sudden death.

Years later, as she was sending her young son to school every morning, she would put her hands on his head to bless him just like her father had done before sending her off to England. It was from Psalm 121: "May G-d keep you from all harm as you trust in Him. May he watch over your life, your coming and your going, both now and forevermore."

Edith reunited with her sisters in Argentina a year after the war ended. With the help of the Belgian delegation, Edith found out Herta's new address. The sisters had asked her to move to South America and she was eager to see her family. They discovered that their father had died in Buchenwald in late 1943. He apparently developed a bad case of pneumonia and was left to die. Friedl and Lotte managed to get to South America via Portugal and established themselves in Brazil. The traumas of the war, the newly emerging atrocity stories, the sheer exhaustion of the soul brought about numbness and an inability to mourn properly. The sisters shared a few stories about the last years, but Edith's story lacked detail.

Occasionally, she would picture her father extending his hands over her head, as he had done every morning after her mom died, to bless her and wish her well. She did the same with her child. Deep down, she believed that his prayers, the prayers of an agnostic, were those that allowed her to survive. She knew that in her misery she was luckier than others— even if her life had been ruined forever by the events of the times, even if she never got to taste youth's splendorous carelessness, even though she never got to realize her potential, she had survived.

As her son, I wrote this story as a tribute to a woman of great character and spirit. Some of this is fiction. I even replaced her name, Thea, or Doris, as she was commonly known to all, with that of her sister. But the essence is the true story of a hero, my hero: a woman who years later sacrificed much for the benefit of her son. The most remarkable of these sacrifices was her willingness to let me go and develop my own career by pursuing a PhD at a university far away from where she, a recent widow, lived. Her father's teachings, her life experiences, her personality, were conducive to that decision—just like they convinced her of the importance of living a worthy, positive, life.

HOME AND HOMELESS

∎

Sometimes, if by volition or fate, you happen to travel to a place where you had lived for a lengthier segment of your life, you get flooded by comparisons, contrasts, juxtapositions involving what you see today and what it was like when you were there before—what you have back home and what you find here. What you want this place to be rather than what it is. When a love relationship is thrown into this already bewildering mix, it can get a bit messy.

"Let's take a walk," she says. "I love to walk, as you know, and I particularly like to stroll around this neighborhood—my German Colony in my Jerusalem." The slightest of twitches in my heart tells me that I am happy for her but also a bit jealous.

We are two friends in our early fifties walking down this old cobbled street. We used to be lovers. At least, I was in love with her. Today, one of us is at home, and one, me, is homeless. Not that I lack a nice place, well furnished, basic comforts, that I could call home. It is that I have nearly no attachment to it. That is the case with other places and localities where I used to live. In effect, I am homeless everywhere.

We first met when we were young; in fact, I was very young. We parted ways and lost contact. Many years later, I sought her out. She said on the phone, "Come spend some days in your old country and visit me." Since I was curious and needy in my loneliness, I agreed.

That this is home for her is evident.No two steps are taken without someone greeting her, or she greeting them, and she loves to show off

14

her intimate knowledge of the neighborhood. And that it is not just streets and buildings but neighbors: the former high school teacher who inspired her to read Joyce, the dance instructor who taught her how to tango, even the lady whose store sells similar shoes across the street and in direct competition with my friend's business.

I am reminded of Weber's *Gemeinschaft*. This is what he must have been thinking of—a less rational, individualistic place. Juxtaposed to a modern society (*Gesellschaft*) with its emphasis on individualism and utilitarian behavior. The world of today, at the tail end of the twentieth century finds both coexisting with some unease.

This community is bound not only by geography and political borders, but also by shared life stories, and, to much chagrin, by the special ties brought on by the sorrow over lost lives and the daily, almost primitive concern with survival.

In fact, I sense a greater "togetherness" today than what I saw when I lived here before. It pleases me and puzzles me at the same time. I am trying to explain it to myself, to understand, and finally I conclude that the violence unleashed against them over the last few years has brought them together. They almost don't know it; consciousness is a more involved process than the basic instinct of survival. In short, the bombs that exploded last year at the café two blocks down the street have strengthened this community's ties. The almost daily threats to wipe out the political and physical existence of this community's inhabitants brings about a least common denominator covenant: to survive. Obviously, I saw nothing comparable when I lived in more tranquil places like New York or London or Zurich, where I live now. When threatened by someone it is natural to look for strength in numbers. The people at the receiving end of this recent violence of the late nineties have gelled into something more than plain acquaintances you meet on the street, more than casual friends you care about.

That survival anxiety, I speculated some time ago, too often makes people behave in a reckless manner. Otherwise the anguish is just too great, the mental burden too big. Pressure needs its release, and what is stupefying is that the outlet is often as life threatening as the source of the anguish. No wonder there are so many car accidents in this country.

She interrupts my busy silence to tell me about this couple she just had a long conversation with. They also have lived here, in this neighborhood, most of their lives. It is also truly home for them—every little alley, every tree, every house has a known and shared history whose parts they often enjoy recalling; it gives them comfort. There is beauty in this kind of attachment to a place, to stone walls, crooked-by-age buildings, the uneven pavement, recognizable trees and plants growing in arid lands with long, hot summer months and less than required rainfall. The small, funky movie theater to which you enter through a chaotic coffeehouse/ restaurant, seasonal smells and year-round smells, the particular cacophony of the local language. I recognize that there is beauty to this "home" feeling, but I am not totally comfortable with that conclusion.

My friend tugs me lightly with her hand as if to tell me not to wander away again. It is not that I have physically moved away, but that she senses that my thoughts are not right there. My absence is bothering her; she prefers it when I am more committed to the experience, her essence. She is, of course, right. I am not fully present. I guess that my drifting shows.

She continues her efforts to impress me with her expertise about this community. A couple that pass us by are the subject matter—"He was an aide-de-camp to one of the former prime ministers and she ran the new acquisitions department of the Hebrew Museum. He was caught in some corruption scandal (is that another evidentiary proof of living on the edge?), and she had a well-publicized rift with the head of the museum and so her head had to roll."

My friend knows about this, and so does everyone else, because that is the nature of this place. It has always bothered me that in such a community, everybody's story is known, the intimate parts as well as the more public parts. Everyone is Public Man. As a youngster, when I lived here, I used to kiddingly say that I was positive my neighbor knew what underwear I was wearing. It was surely the one that was not hanging out to be dried by the sun—plenty of sun around here—and since she knew all of them by heart, she had studied them in depth and could spot the missing one. There is something terribly intrusive about a community this closely knit, and I abhor it. Not that I have much to hide, but only a newborn baby can pee shamelessly all over the delivery room.

It does not matter if what she knows about this couple is firsthand information or some amalgam, bits and pieces of personal knowledge, the neighbor's chatter, the newspaper's front page, or the "gossip columnist" on page eleven. Community knowledge also has its presumptions and it gives out entitlements to those owning it. The longer you have called a place home, the more you know people, the broader your local knowledge, the higher your status. When she speaks to me about this couple or someone else, I can sense that what she is conveying to me is not only the actual story but also the fact that she "really" knows; she is a true authority on this place, she has been around for so long, what she knows *is* the real and only truth and she has cornered it, monopolized it.

I am almost certain that she does this on purpose. She wants to convey to me that this is where her roots are. As if she is trying to put up a large billboard sign that says "Don't you dare uproot me ..." In a way, this is all a bit depressing. Her struggle, as mine, is very basic: to the extent we love each other we face the tremendous obstacle that we cannot share a common geographic ground. Her sense of this being "HOME" does not come across as artificial. But that is not always the case for others. In America, where I used to live, people went to the local hardware store and got themselves a little shingle that proclaimed that this was "Home, Sweet Home." The slogan was meant to loudly, maybe presumptively, declare a fact, even if the dwellers were not as convinced. Those who wanted to make sure you believed it, hung it up at the entrance to their house; those who, instead, wanted to convince themselves, put it up in the kitchen. Magically the sign would turn the plethora of standard, "plastic" features of a house—the oak table, the synthetic leather sofa, the GE appliances—to meaningful objects. The need to feel "at home" may be shared by all of us to different degrees. But, I am certain that hanging out a sign that declares some number of square yards of walls covered by a roof a "home" does not do it by itself. Shingle or no shingle. I have a feeling that if I would call a place HOME it would be a somewhat artificial construct. Fake.

She pulls me to an alley where she wants to show me something new, and my mind still wanders. I smile so as not to be interrupted in my thoughts, as if I wish to say, "Let me be, let my mind meander." I feel suffocated by the narrowness of community. That is the truth. It all seems too parochial to me. If "x" had a scandalous affair with the head of the local hospital (she told me about this as we passed another neighbor), then it is their affair. I am totally uninterested to sit in jury and arbitrate their behavior. Sure, it may have caused some pain to the wife and husband of the adulterers, but what is it to me? I am not sure that even my friend knows the reasons why adultery germinated as a possibility in their minds. Was it sheer selfishness? Plain sexual desire? Avarice? Was it that they were heartbroken by their spouses? Was it the shared disappointment with conjugal bliss? The excessive involvement in other people's lives is a definite detriment to living in a community. If I lived in such, I would want to flee.

I have been walking with him a good half an hour, showing him all the little places I hold dear. It is supposed to be a walk of love to share these places so important to me, to my essence. This is where I grew up and this is where I will die. This place belongs to me and I belong to it. I know what he thinks, he and his darn broad world perspective, his rational mind.

Of course, I know that there is more to the world than just the German Colony. I actually was over there, on the other side of the argument, if you wish. I occupied myself with Hegel and Sartre for a while. In those days, when I was a student at the Hebrew University, we discussed universal issues: Liberty, or faceless, odorless, and colorless freedom, or the existentialist individuality of man or woman anywhere and anytime—and we even debated these matters over coffee in my little apartment well into the night, even smiling as the rising sun announced it was already early morning. But at the end of the day, these were amorphous generalities which did not speak to me. They left me as cold as the pages on which they were written. I know he has read the same things and many more, and that they mean more to him than to me. It frustrates me. There is a gulf between us, and I do not know how to bridge it.

My home, and feeling at home, makes me into a loving person, and his homeless nature makes him into this more rational, but also colder, person. Should I give up on him? I am attracted to him, to his excellent mind, to his depth, to his creativity, but I suffer because I know that he will never share my feelings for this place.

I know—I will take him to this alley and show him where I was born and where I kissed for the first time, when I had just turned sixteen. I was very shy then, so the kiss was a breakthrough. I know he will want to kiss me, and I will let him, and maybe, just maybe, he will no longer be so untouched by it all ... will there be a different breakthrough this time?

We are walking up a steeper street as we proceed to this alley. On each side of the narrow street, there are rather tall stone walls. Behind them I see houses made with the more modern, pale brown-yellow "Jerusalem stone." The alley itself has probably not changed in ages. The modern mixes with the ancient in a rather harmonious, eye-pleasing way. I am concerned about the casual car traveling this street, for there is not enough room for it and us. She quickly reveals why she led me to this place. "See that house, that one over there with the beautiful plants and the greenish plastic roof over the balcony? I was born there." Excitement

18

causes the words to come out staccato. A few steps later, she pulls me so that I am facing her: "And here, when I was sixteen, Danny, my boyfriend, came and gave me my first lovers' kiss." I wish I was that boy in his blue pants and light blue shirt, or his after-school uniform: khaki shorts and white T-shirt. I grab her by the waist and kiss her. All of a sudden, my mind is not wandering somewhere else, I am fully there, and very aroused. I also feel a couple of decades younger for a moment, at least I hope my kiss is younger and does not carry the odors of age. She smiles. For that one short moment, maybe twenty seconds long, we are united as we both want to be, by that most special glue of what we conceive as "soul mates" and (no use denying it) by the sheer desire of the flesh. She seems a bit embarrassed by the exhibitionism of our kiss, though I do not see a soul around us, and lightly pushes off; she does so with a smile which I return. She looks almost as beautiful as when I met her the first time: the high cheekbones, the flowery light blouse with an extra unbuttoned hole that allows a partial view of her bra, the beautiful brown hair cascading down to her shoulders, and those very piercing and devilish-looking green eyes. We are almost at the end of the hike up this alley and turn left to another street that leads in a downward path to her current house. This part is more modern. Could it be that the previous, older alley once ended where we just had been—nowhere? "He must have been handsome, that boy, and you were so beautiful. You showed me pictures once, many moons ago, remember?" She was always beautiful, absolutely gorgeous then. "Nonsense," she replies. "We all looked better then." She quickly resumes her tour-guide mode. On the left is the house where there used to be a small kindergarten which her son attended. "The funny thing," she remarks, "I also went there."

History is not only the recording of major events; it is also the story of individuals and their heroic acts (I think of the many signs along Paris's streets honoring the underground: "Here they shot dead Jean-Paul someone or another"), and it is also the result of common folk repetitively living their lives in a certain locality. Except, that one is not written up. We do not read: "Three generations of the Aboulaffia family went to school here." By their mere existence, these historical facts can never be wiped away by violence and attempts to negate. I want to believe that these repetitions cement reality, but then I remind myself of the Armenians, the Sioux, and the people of Oc. History is replete with communities that were erased, disintegrated or swallowed by others—in many of these cases it was done in the name of progress and modernization, in others it was pure ethnic hatred. I want to scream, "No one can let it happen here!" Of course, I am wholeheartedly behind the struggle of this community to prevail. I just am unable to abandon the other principles that, I think, should guide humanity. The survival of the human race lies within its ability to conquer its frailties, lies within the capacity of good to prevail over evil without the encumbrance or demarcation of ethnicity and geography. It cannot be that all issues revolving around us be phrased, termed, conditioned by the specific circumstances of this specific community.

All my life I have rebelled, more consciously these days, less so for the last thirty-five years, against the myopia and xenophobia that comes with the hypernationalistic perspective I so often encounter here. Facts, figures, and news are judged from a demonstratively particularistic angle, and it is the wrong perspective to boot. "Jews are so much better than the Arabs" (let's get out the list of Nobel Prize winners, quick!). "Nowhere on the globe is it as nice as here" (maybe, but the wild Norwegian scenery or the ever-changing colors of Kauai have lifted my spirits too). "Bush's reelection is good for us because he is our strongest supporter, ever!" (Go talk to them about the fact that he may be bad for the universe—no one wants to hear it.)

Seems to me that universal values too often clash with the particularistic values of a community, and it is not different here. It bothers me and I get some comfort because I am not a lonely voice. I am reminded of the criticism of some Israeli writers; I picture Amos Oz's Shenhav tangled in the barb wire fencing of a country whose overriding concern is "What is good for the country." "What is good for the individual" too often runs a distant second. I know my criticism is valid, but it pains me to engage in it. I do not enjoy being critical here. I love the country and believe in its historical mission as a home to Jews. Needless to say, I am also troubled that this puts a great deal of strain on our friendship, and probably kills the possibility of more than friendship. I am quiet and say little; I do not want to annoy. We continue our walk.

A couple of minutes ago we kissed; since then we are no longer walking hand in hand. But the kiss was nice, we love each other. He is quiet, and yet I know what he is thinking. I have always been good at reading his mind. I know he is trying to figure out how to be with me, just with me and not with me and this place together. He does not want to live here. He could, but he does not want to. When he left the country way back, in his mid-twenties after his army service, he left it knowing he would not come back. I am trying to change his mind but it does not seem to work. I cannot live anywhere else, not for a long period of time anyway. My place is here.

I want him to love my German Colony, my Jerusalem, my Israel, and not just the physical me, the attractive and a little coquette me. Yes, sexuality is important and it is good he wants me in that way. But, by knowing that he does not want my Jerusalem the way I do, I do not think he can have the rest of me.

We return to her house, where we had lunch before. There are no shingles here, but it feels like home. There is barely a thing here that you would call standard, even the furniture. Every little corner of the house has an item which was carefully chosen at the time of purchase—not for its efficiency and usefulness, but for its place in the ensemble and in the owners' hearts. Everything seems to have its place of honor in the small apartment. If ever a place looked and smelled like home, this is it.

Can I ever have a home like this? I assume the answer is negative. I do not have the attachment to a place that is the precondition for it. I am the modern man, a nomad by force. Work takes me from one place to another. Commitments make me call the moving company from time to time. I must be "schizoid," I like both sides of the coin. Like Janus, I face the past and want the warmth and coziness of the place, and I face the future and the ability to move about without constraints, to engage life as fully as I can. Without too much vacillation.

She explains, "This beautiful clock I bought in Marseille, at a fair. The decorative bicycles, so cute aren't they, at a flea market in Amsterdam. And of course, this is from the Old City." I imagine that she spent decades looking for each piece of decoration in the house. I shake my head and smile.

"Why do you shake your head?"

"I am amazed; it is really all very beautiful."

"Why are you amazed?"

"Because I could never pull this off."

"So, that means no one else can?"

"So, that means you are special in the way you do things, and that is why I love you."

The small living room has an armchair and a sofa; we occupy the blue cloth sofa and our knees are touching lightly, but we just look into each other's eyes with the tenderness of yesteryear, when we were in our early twenties. But we do not dare go beyond that.

21

That night, I am alone in my hotel room, and I toss and turn. I think about our walk and about our relationship. Can two people be any closer and at the same time so far apart? I fear that if we take this to another level it will be a recipe for disaster and a painful breakdown. I remember that as we walked down the street, I wanted to pull her over, kiss her the way she never has been kissed before; maybe even make love to her right then and there. I wanted to strip her naked. Yes, because I love her, but also to stop her from talking about this German Colony, this Jerusalem, this country of hers, of ours. Maybe, also, because what I wanted to do is to stop myself from continuing down this path of the homeless intellectual. I wanted to stop thinking altogether.

Over the years my "homelessness" has been an issue that has occupied me. Wherever I was, and not necessarily while in an amorous relationship. Occasionally I have talked to others caught up in the same misery. I am certain this unease comes with the first departure. Once you leave the place where you were born, not for a short vacation but for an extended time, you are condemned. Even if you migrate to another country because you believe you will be much better off, you become homeless (not in a physical sense, but in an emotional sense) for your whole life. End. No escape.

One indicator of this "homeless" status is criticism. You have seen this and that side of the fence, and you are always comparing, even when you don't want to. If you have walked life with your eyes wide open, you have understood that there is more than what any one place has to offer, and you are never completely satisfied.

People sometimes ask me: where do you feel at home? You know the answer, it is "nowhere." They look at you with some sadness. You can tell them that you are thrilled to travel places, see new things, relish the experiences, cradle whatever that new venture provides, and that is in fact the case for me too. But I also would want to feel home somewhere, would want to hang up my shingle, would want to make a definitive statement, and I know I can't. And I, probably never will. In order to feel at home, you must wholeheartedly belong, and it is just very hard to "belong."

I assert, with full consciousness, that this homelessness has its advantages. Some friends have often referred to me as "A Man of the World." Speaking several languages, having lived in different continents, well read—they think it all hangs together. One often calls me "*Un uomo colto e gentile"(*a cultured and kind man*)*. I say, I am just a "M.o.W." Yes, I feel comfortable in different cultures, I can easily find my way in foreign lands. It appears as though nothing can faze this "M.o.W." The jet lag is just biological, not cultural. I pick up nuances and demeanors as varied as the topography of the cities I travel. But that, per se, is my curse. I can sense that the locals will identify me as a stranger that is not at home in this Amsterdam coffee shop or that Mykonos bar. I can sense the "here is an intruder" glare and walk out. You just do not belong. Not here and not there.

I ask myself how she will react to this story, when it gets published and I am bothered by the potential answer: "You are a malcontent, a dour intellectual like Frederick in *Hannah and Her Sisters*, therein is your homelessness." I understand that the proclivity to be critical harbors the conditions that prevent belonging. Even if these days I seek out the positive in most of what comes my way, I must recognize that this M.o.W. tends to be somewhat critical. There is plenty of melancholy in this "homeless" status and it is ingrained.

At 1:00 a.m., the phone rings. She cannot sleep either. I know why, it is that walk and what was said and what was left unsaid. She tells me she must see me before I fly back the next day. I tease her: "come over now". I know she won't. "Then come early tomorrow morning." She agrees. I know the message will be goodbye, and I am saddened. I am exhausted but I cannot sleep. I close my eyes. In my head the images change rapidly, and one is unrelated to the next one as if the slide show had been mischievously messed up: Paris. I am walking alongside the Seine talking to my kids. The kids are now on the West Coast; I hope they are okay. Buses are burning in Paris. I am flying back to London tomorrow. Bombs are exploding in buses; not only here, also at Trafalgar Square. Is it proper to ask whether dying from a terror attack directed at your own people is more meaningful than being the "accidental victim" of terror in, let's say, Madrid?

Demonstrators in Tehran are going wild as they scream, "Down with America! Down with Israel!" Kids declare themselves willing to die for Palestine and they do not even know where to find it on a map; still, some of them will wear a specialized heavy belt, enter some crowded place, and tear themselves—along with dozens of other humans they don't know—to shreds. People, some like me, some carrying the local colors, are also being blown up elsewhere—Bali, New Delhi. Maybe tomorrow bombs will tear into Ibiza and Cancun; half-naked tourist women and men are dancing on stages there too, and the fanatics want to demonstrate their intolerant hate. Have I gone mad?

It is the twenty-first century; fireworks announce the new millennium. I imagine her standing there smiling, waving goodbye. I am numb and exhausted. I fall asleep.

I am sitting in the plane thinking about the whirlwind visit to Israel. I am going through one of those moments when everything appears a lot more straightforward and without the smudges of our past or the societies and politics around us. It is wonderful to share such deep feelings towards another person and for it to be reciprocal. I am sure we will retain this quality friendship for many years and despite the geographical distance and the time zone differences. Beyond the frustration and its pain my relationship to her has that quality. We will congratulate each other on birthdays and tell each other about children and grandchildren, and the joy they bring. We will share the grief of big disputes, and the mourning over loved ones. Maybe we will visit each other from time to time. It will be wonderful to have her within reach.

THE ORANGE SCARF

∎

He looked out the window of the LAN Airlines jet as it was taking off from Santiago. Soon enough he would marvel at the beauty of the Andes beneath him; this flight always gave him the wonderful, awe-inspiring opportunity to see these giants of nature close-up. They were majestic, and so near he could almost scoop up some snow off their peaks. He loved the rugged scenery; it was nature at its best.

He closed his eyes and allowed his imagination to take over. He thought of his recently established home in London. He smiled. Life had finally turned kind for him. These last few months he felt more alive than he had in years. But then he also thought of his children. Divorce had been hard on them, and because of that, hard on him too. He wondered how they would treat Celia. And his relationship to Celia was complicated too; could it last beyond the initial excitement?

The phone rang in Melissa's bedroom; it was too early for this to be anything but bad news. "Is this Melissa Zorn?" asked a voice that sounded ominously official, though the heavy accent made it clear that English was not the person's mother tongue. Upon confirmation, Melissa heard that her father was one of seventy-six passengers on a plane that crashed in Chile the day before. "There are no survivors; the airplane collided head-on with the mountain. In fact, I doubt that there are any identifiable remains," said the cold voice.

Melissa immediately called her brother, John, and between sobs told him the terrible news. John howled horribly, and quite naturally the phone conversation turned into a disjointed effort as the siblings sought to comfort each other. They were young, too young, to be orphans, in their late teens, and on summer vacation. Melissa was about to enter her sophomore year at UCLA and her brother had just graduated high school; he still lived with their mom in California, where they had moved after the divorce.

"What do we do now?"

"He can't even get a proper burial if there is no body, or am I wrong?" asked John. He often focused on technical details at a time of crisis; it allowed him to overcome emotional situations with more ease, better than either his father or Melissa could. "He always wanted to have his body cremated and the ashes thrown to the wind," cried Melissa. "Little did he know ..." John admitted that he had forgotten that his father had expressed that wish.

"Melissa Zorn?" The voice on the other side seemed recognizable. Yes, of course, it was the same policeman who had called two days earlier. "This is Pedro Aguirre again. Something strange has happened. As I had told you, none of the deceased passengers are recognizable; it is a true mess, and their belongings are scattered all over the mountain. There is one exception though: one metal suitcase that burst open with the impact of the crash but otherwise remained intact. From a receipt inside the suitcase we know that it belongs, sorry, I mean belonged, to your father. Would you like to recover it?"

Melissa saw in it a sign, a message from her father speaking to her from the beyond. She firmly believed that such things were possible. "What is it that I need to do to recover the contents of that bag?" she asked.

"As the closest family member, I am afraid you need to fly down to Santiago and claim it. Maybe your brother, John, should come along so there is no issue or delay."

Two days later Melissa and John arrived at the main police station in Santiago. They stood in front of a table on which rested a damaged metal suitcase. They dug through the predictable contents: shirts, slacks, underwear. Deeply sad and disconcerted, Melissa wondered what they were doing there. Just then, at the bottom of the suitcase they discovered a colorful package. In it was a lightly patterned orange scarf. "This is beautiful; it probably was meant for Celia," Melissa said as she held the alpaca wool scarf in her hands. Suddenly the purpose of their long trip became clear to her: it was to recover this specific item their father had bought and was intending to take back to London. But John, always quicker to get frustrated, became irritated.

"Who the hell is Celia? Why did he always tell you things that he did not share with me? I know nothing about a woman named Celia."

"Celia Bodin, I believe that is her last name, is a young woman he met in London. He told me about her in a phone conversation some time ago; I think that he fell madly in love with her, but he never conceded this much. He mentioned her many times in recent months. I would like to meet this woman, fill in the blanks about the recent period in his life. You know it has been almost five months since we visited with him in London to celebrate his fiftieth."

"I don't know, Sis. I am terribly sad about his death, but I am not sure I want to play archaeologist and dig up facts about him. I am not sure we can or should infringe on his privacy even after his death. You know he detested nosy people meddling and poking around."

"If she was important enough to him that he would get her this beautiful scarf, I want to meet her. Maybe it will be a short hello; maybe it will take a few hours talking to her. But something tells me that I need to do this."

"I guess we have to go to London anyway. We need to figure out what to do with his things there, his bank accounts and whatever else there is. I guess I must join you, Mel. When is it that you were thinking of going?"

Melissa was happy her brother agreed to come along. "How about going early next week?"

Melissa carefully put the scarf away in her big bag, looked around to see if there was anything else (a picture, a memento, anything), but found none and left the suitcase there.

The following Tuesday Melissa and John flew to London and booked rooms in a quaint Notting Hill hotel. They wanted to be close to their

27

father's apartment. The next day they went to the building and got hold of the apartment keys which were with the neighbors, John and Rosemary Preston. During the March trip, they briefly met the older couple as they passed each other in the hallway. Yes, they had heard about the crash but had no clue that Daniel was one of the victims. "He was traveling all the time ..." They expressed shock and sorrow together with the proper condolences.

Once inside, Melissa and John were surprised to find that Daniel was organized about matters pertaining to a possible death. In the main drawer of his working table he had left an envelope clearly marked: "To be opened after my death," in which he had put a legal last will that left all his worldly belongings to his children; all, with one exception—a specific modern painting he wanted Celia to have. And there was a list of accounts with numbers and internet access codes and passwords, which comprised all his financial assets. Even the name of a lawyer to be contacted was inside the envelope. Celia Bodin's phone number was on a separate piece of paper in the same envelope. Melissa and John were thankful that they would not need to spend endless months chasing facts.

The following morning Melissa called Celia and introduced herself. Celia did not appear to be overly surprised to hear from Daniel's daughter: "I sort of expected to hear from you, Melissa; your father spoke often about you and your brother. You know he loved you very much. The airline called me to tell me about the crash because he gave them my name. I am so saddened by this tragedy; I miss him a lot. I want to meet you too."

"My brother and I only have a few days here in London. When could we get together?"

"I work, but I will leave early, take part of the afternoon off. My address is Chepstow Villas 14D, not far from where Daniel lived. Chepstow is one of the side streets off Portobello Road, about five minutes from his flat. Please come by at around five and we will have some tea."

Melissa decided that it would be best if she went to see Celia by herself. The situation was delicate, and John's presence could turn out to be difficult for all; the way he reacted to the whole issue of Celia and not knowing about her relationship with Father could be a cause for animosity and friction. "Maybe you ought to get moving with the lawyer to settle the estate, and I will take that painting that Father wanted Celia to have over to her." John did not seem to mind; he was not eager to meet this woman who seemed to have caught his father's fancy.

Melissa put on jeans and a dark blue pullover that hung loose; she was slightly overweight and conscious of it. Her round face was quite similar to that of her mom, so were the glasses she wore. Her hair was a bit lighter and very curly—she often played with her curls while hiding frustration about her hairdo. When the door opened, Melissa saw a woman whose beauty was as obvious as it was unique. As she would reflect later, it was no single detail of that woman that was utterly striking, but rather the full package. Celia wore a light blue blouse, black pants, and black high-heeled shoes; she extended a hand and invited Melissa in.

Melissa's usual ability to be diplomatic and measured failed her miserably this time: "Wow! Excuse me for being abrupt, but you are so young! I knew that you were young, but not this young. May I ask how old you are?"

Celia produced an interesting reaction—she smiled; it was a savvy smile, but also one that in Melissa's mind suggested empathy and caring. She proceeded with a frank short cackle and answered the question. Melissa's response was abrupt; her mouth opened wide before she muttered: "Twenty-three years difference is really a lot."

That her father was smitten by this woman was hardly surprising. "It could well have been her eyes that captivated our father," she would say to John afterwards, "those unusual green eyes which probably changed colors with the woman's mood." She continued to describe the presumed owner of the scarf: Celia had beautiful light hair parted on the left side; she carried that shorter part of her hair behind a smallish, nicely shaped ear; even Melissa recognized that this could make her endearing. She was slender, almost too thin, and elegant. Not only did she wear stylish yet understated clothes, but Melissa immediately noticed that this woman had a peculiar, striking walk that demonstrated certitude and presence. Melissa sighed with a bit of envy as she told her brother: "You sort of figure out that your looks are amazing, and it translates into how you walk."

Melissa noticed she was still near the door and showed embarrassment. To avoid looking totally dumb she placed the small painting in Celia's hands: "My father wanted you to have this painting. I guess you had seen it at his place and liked it."

Celia's eyes became moist as she held up the painting. "Yes, I had told him that the colors were stunning, and the abstract composition was delicate and wonderful." Celia abruptly changed the subject: "Do you think he knew he would die? Why would he have written that in his will? We had known each other for less than a year."

As the conversation unfolded Melissa felt a bit uneasy. It was clear to her that Celia had well internalized the British culture of discretion. She was rather reticent to say much about herself. Her voice was calm and in control, even when it clearly denoted sadness. Without a doubt, there was warmth between the two women and the conversation flowed well enough, but Melissa was hoping for more insight about how far the relationship with her father had gone. Celia told her that her father and she had met at a benefit concert and had discovered that they had a few things in common other than their American past. They both liked bridge, jazz and classical concerts, travel, and good food.

When Melissa asked, "So, that means that it was easy for you two to find things to do together?" she did not get an answer. Celia seemed uncomfortable discussing her relationship with Daniel; she took the side of her right hand index finger near her lower lip, rubbed it lightly, and said nothing.

Melissa probed again: "But surely you have friends from work, from other activities who are your age more or less. You have been here in London for how long?"

Celia once again moved her finger to the lower lip as she said, "Yes, about a year and a half. London has been fantastic for me. To be honest, I have made more friends here than I ever would have expected before coming over. I am a friendly person and I make sure that people like me, still ..."

This confused Melissa even more; she could not figure out why this young woman would spend time with a much older man. She, herself, would not do such a thing—no way! This enigma became the primary concern for Melissa, and while she probed time and again, Celia would not cede, and the conversation continued to be cautious and controlled. It was not so much that Celia seemed to be hiding something; quite the contrary, she seemed truthful, but she was quite capable of making sure the conversation did not glide into private matters. It was quite apparent that she was not ready to disclose the nature of the relationship, neither its depth nor its content. Though Melissa wanted to ask, "Wasn't my father a bit too old to have a romantic relationship?" she desisted, well knowing it may cause a breakdown in her own rapport with Celia.

Melissa understood that this young woman was as intelligent as she was reserved, and trickery of any sort would be self-defeating. There was no way that she would manage to deviously pierce through the shell and extract more details—certainly not during this first meeting. Instead, she chose to make Celia more comfortable by telling a little about herself and how special her relationship with her father was. Though the geographical distance had been there for years, ever since her parents divorced, she had always felt close to her father.

Celia nodded and once again tilted her head to one side while producing a smile that conveyed charm, empathy, and warmth. Melissa thought that Celia's smile could disarm the most callous of human beings, even the biggest brute walking the streets of London. Most importantly, Melissa thought it to be genuine and honest; there was no apparent effort to deceive or entrap.

Melissa must have reacted in a meaningful way to Celia's smile because at that point Celia's face changed and her voice trembled a "sorry." She put her head between her hands, briskly got up, and excused herself. Melissa had a hunch that Celia had gone to the bathroom to wash her face so that the cold water would prevent the tears from flowing. Could it be that she suddenly reminded Celia of her father? Was Daniel's death such heavy a blow for her?

The emotionally packed meeting was exhausting both women and needed to end. While seemingly looking for something in her bag, Melissa asked if she could meet Celia again; maybe even John could tag along. Celia agreed and suggested they meet tomorrow at a new smallish Italian restaurant, Toscana, around the corner from Daniel's apartment. Melissa closed her bag without giving Celia the orange scarf.

Later John asked, "What is your opinion of this Celia? Is she a gold-digger chasing Father's small fortune? Is she a flake?" Strangely John was sometimes confrontational and cynical; maybe he was just having a hard time with the sudden turn of events.

"What can I tell you, John? She is young, beautiful, honestly sad about our father's death, and I don't think she was chasing him for whatever money he had or she thought he might have. That is not the sort of woman I met today. On the other hand, I really don't understand their relationship. She is so much younger than him. She seems to be bright. But she is also discreet and probably that was a huge attraction for our father—in general, her being classy, elegant, and stylish were probably major factors. You should see her walk. But then you go for the more vulgar type, don't you?" Melissa said that last sentence with a wink, hoping to get John out of his rotten mood. She had often teased her brother about the woman he hung out with. He ignored her sarcastic remark.

"Still," Melissa continued, "I don't get it. I don't understand what Father may have represented for Celia. Why, she certainly could attract the most available guys in town. In other words, dear brother, I am puzzled about one side of the relationship and a lot less about the other. I think you should meet her. Maybe you could help me solve the puzzle. She said she wants to meet you. She does not know that you are all set to hate her, and for no particular reason other than some Freudian thing you may have about your father's girlfriend."

"No, Melissa, it certainly is not that. I am a bit curious now too, and I love solving puzzles. When are we meeting her?"

Melissa did not change clothes, but John replaced the stuffy suit he had worn to the lawyer's office with some blue jeans and a white T-shirt. He was always quick to wear this combination—he called it his "uniform." He and Celia shook hands before sitting down, not more than that. The initial conversation was, as expected, pleasant but reserved. John immediately noted that Celia was charming and warm, but he also detected in her a determined, goal-oriented manner. She seemed to him like a businesswoman who was likely to go far. He challenged Celia a bit by suggesting that she was keeping her composure quite nicely as she went about talking to her friend's children. She handled the mild confrontation swiftly by saying that though she cared about their father, she had to be forward-looking and positive; this is how she responded to all of life's vicissitudes.

"In all honesty, this is just the way I am." She explained further that while she was saddened by their father being taken from her life, she was

determined to move on. Hers was not an artificial effort to be liked by his children, but the way she always was—wanting every person she would meet to like her. She just was being herself. In a way, John liked that as he remembered how much his father detested fake people.

By the time dinner had run its course, Celia suggested they go to her flat and talk a bit more. They had another glass of red, and maybe that one glass caused the apparent bottleneck in Celia's soul to burst. Melissa was sure she would recall almost every word that Celia spoke that night for years.

"You two are probably puzzled by the age difference between your father and me, so let me try to help you out. I work in the financial industry; they say it is full of smart people, but your father Daniel was one of the smartest people I have ever met. He was extremely perceptive; he noticed every change of expression and every move. But perhaps the most brilliant thing about him was that he knew he had weaknesses and could be fully introspective and aware of them. So many people can't do that. I could not be honest with myself when I met him; he taught me how important it is to know yourself in order to be truly happy—you know, as opposed to convincing myself that I was."

Melissa nodded; she knew what Celia was talking about and recalled some conversations she herself had had with her dad. "I guess you had some really heavy heart-to-heart talks."

"Yes. He in effect freed me from myself, my old self that is. He did it slowly, caringly. In every email, every talk, every get-together, he tried to be funny, to caress with words and deeds, and to provide strong arms on which to rest a heavy head."

"I guess that this is what friendship is all about, isn't it?" John's comment had a ring of sarcasm to it.

"Okay, I'll admit it, it is clear that he loved me. He was an honest and open man, so he let me know that in no uncertain terms. At first I was scared. I did not want to be under that type of pressure. I would shake my head as I read his overtures and ask myself what I should do. It was not always easy to accept his romantic declarations; they created difficult moments for me. As you see, I am a no-nonsense person and I made it clear to him that he and I had no chance of hooking up in a

romantic way, but he persevered. Early on, I was confused but blatantly rejected his romantic efforts ..."

"But later you did not?" Melissa broke in because she was coming close to finding out about Celia and her father and the suspense was getting to her.

"Well, I recognized that he was a special human being. At one point, we had an angry, frustration-filled exchange, and with the reconciliation we found out that neither one of us wanted to give up on the relationship, whatever its nature might be, whatever it might evolve into. With time, I became more comfortable with the notion that I could love several people in different ways and at the same time."

John interrupted, "That sounds to me like a lot of BS, frankly. And I am doubtful Father bought into that." He had been slouched on the sofa before, but suddenly sat erect and looking as if he was ready to pounce.

"I have no doubt that he truly loved me. He wanted me to be the happiest I could be and without concern for what it meant for him. He said being nice to me, in a certain way, was rewarding enough for him."

John was bewildered by what he heard. "I knew Father to be a romantic type. But he also was eager to be loved, to be recognized. And he hated to be taken for a fool. What you are saying to me is that he was willing to give without using a balance sheet that measured how much he got in return?"

"Well, to a large extent, that is right, John. I do not tend to utter such sugarcoated, Hollywood phrases, but he showed me what true love really is—the kind of love that is unconditional, the kind that can persist even if it is not rewarded, the kind that tears your insides sometimes and elates you to no end at other times. He would say to me, 'Until you have experienced such love, you have not lived a life.' Once I finally accepted that I could be loved in this fashion, our relationship became wonderfully easy and amazingly fun. We did lots of things together, and occasionally we would hug in public and it did not embarrass me at all. I thought Daniel Zorn was a terrific man, a unique man, and I was glad to have him around, to talk to him, to consult with him."

In a way, Celia's account of the relationship left John flattened. He thought he knew his father and he found out that in a significant way he didn't at all. He shook his head in disbelief. Melissa, always in tune with her brother's difficulties, recognized his frustration and seized the opportunity to call it a night; her excuse was exhaustion, jet lag. "But before we go, I want you to know, Celia, that you are a wonderful person and that I am glad my dad got to know you. Obviously, you brought him a great deal of happiness."

"You didn't give her the scarf," John exclaimed once they were halfway down the block.

"I know. I wanted to talk to you first and I also want to get together with her one more time. I still want to make certain that this scarf really belongs to her. I think Dad would want me to make sure that it was meant for her. I will call her tomorrow morning and get together with her one more time. You can come along if you want to."

"For me it is clear. Dad was in love with Celia and the scarf was meant for her. He always had good taste and the color suits her perfectly. Did you see her eyes? They are amazing. She is really a special person. I know I was put off by the whole story, the age difference, everything. But now, after I heard her talk about them, I really like her, and it is almost as if I am jealous of Dad. I don't think that I have met anybody like her."

"She is special; indeed, I agree, John. But tomorrow is Saturday and I imagine she will see me again. I will give her the scarf tomorrow. I better call her as soon as we get to the hotel to make sure I can come over."

Celia was dressed in jeans, a light blue turtleneck, no earrings, no makeup, barefoot. This time her naturally silky blonde hair was held back by a large barrette. By now Melissa knew that the casual appearance contrasted nicely with her conservative, reserved persona, and that this was a major appeal to her father whose preferences were similar. All the same, she smiled broadly at Melissa as she opened the door. It was clear that she was getting more comfortable with every day.

"I am sorry I am taking so much of your time. Before we head home, tomorrow, I would like to know you a bit better and get a closer glimpse at you and Dad if you don't mind."

"I understand, Melissa. But please be careful and remember that I consider these private matters. Sure, given the circumstances I will try to be as open with you as I, or for that matter, your father would feel

comfortable, but I would appreciate you seeing that little sign on my forehead that says, 'No Trespassing.'"

Melissa's first reaction was of shock. This woman blows hot and cold, she said to herself. Only last night she could have sworn that Celia seemed more at ease with every get-together, more willing to talk, and yesterday she openly talked about how much she cared about Father. And now she puts forth a stiff-arm implying, "No further"?

Celia did not give her much time to get upset: "I will not discuss with you my intimate life or things of that sort even if you are curious about them. What I can tell you is that when I met your father, I had been in a relationship with a man who lived far away. Your father helped me understand that my happiness was being compromised by the relationship and the ways it was evolving. That man put stringent demands on me and he sought to curtail my freedom; it all was very stressful for me. This is when your father endeared himself so much to me. He made sense and it was also obvious that he cared very much; knowing this made it easier to hear him criticizing my self-deception. It was harsh to hear that I was deluding myself to be happy. In a short span of time, Daniel Zorn became the closest person in my life other than my mother, the most-trusted friend, the individual who changed my life more than anyone else had. And I knew he did it out of love. And I know I loved him for that."

"But, obviously, in your own way, you were disappointing him in the process. And maybe now you are saddened that you did not get the chance to make him feel that you really did love him."

Celia looked for words as she put her index finger on the spot right in the middle of her eyebrows and lightly rubbed the spot up and down as if to extricate the pain. She looked at Melissa with a different expression than Melissa had seen before. This was not the confident, self-reliant Celia, but now Melissa saw the sad, moist eyes that sought comfort, understanding, and refuge. "My upbringing was a tough one, and I do not come from a culture that plunges into things, even less so into emotional matters. Maybe if we would have had more time ..." And with that Celia could not hold back any longer and began to cry. Melissa moved over to her and hugged her. Celia accepted the hug and embraced her, and when she remembered how she had embraced Daniel just before he took off on his trip, her whole body started to shake with pain.

off

36

As Celia regained her composure, Melissa opened her backpack and pulled out a small paper bag. "Celia, I do not know why I have been so manipulative to hold back on this. This scarf was found in his suitcase at the crash site. There was hardly anything that was left intact there ... you know, the head-on collision with the mountain. Somehow his suitcase did not get terribly damaged, and John and I found this scarf which, we suspect,he bought for you in Santiago. The color suits you perfectly. Please accept my apologies for holding on to it a couple of days longer than I should have."

Celia spread the scarf in front of her; her eyes filled as she said, "It is really very beautiful! I am glad that, despite all, you found me deserving and worthy of it. He knew me so well, and he obviously had good taste too. He told me he would bring me a present, and though I typically reject such offers, something made me tell him to go ahead. I guess I trusted him and his pure intentions. To be perfectly honest, that would not be my usual response. I know you know that I will treasure it forever."

"Yes, I know you will. But I also know that you will go on with your life. Though you have deep emotions, you ultimately will not let them get in the way. I suppose I could, should, do the same ..."

A light touch on his arm caused him to open his eyes. In front of him was a beautiful *morena* whose English was tainted by a poor accent: "Would you like a drink before your dinner?"

"I need a pisco sour. You have great pisco sours on LAN Chile, I know. I also need you to bring me some blank paper and a pen. I need to jot down some stuff."

"How much paper will you need?"

"Enough paper to write a short story."

He saw her face light up at hearing that he was a storyteller. He had seen similar reactions in other women before: "You write stories? What is this one about?"

"Yes, I sometimes have fun writing stories. It is difficult to explain to you what this one is about other than it is a love story. However, in this one I plan to praise a special woman while eulogizing a hopeless dreamer."

His broad smile collapsed as he remembered the conversation he had with Celia before boarding the plane at Heathrow. "You are asking me to write a story about you, Celia? If I write that story, with all that I know and that you know, somehow I fear it may be the end of 'us.' Is that what you want?"

He also remembered that she adamantly rejected the notion that there could be an end to their special relationship. He, on the other hand, had less faith that it could survive this much bearing of the soul.

MISGUIDED AFFECTIONS

■

He was riding the train home in the late afternoon, as he did most days. It took some twenty-five minutes from Grand Central to Hartsdale, and it gave him time to close his eyes and think. He often thought about the people he encountered at work. After all, that was his business—people management. On that very cold October afternoon, however, his mind turned to a young woman who had greatly intrigued him.

As he often did with other young candidates aspiring to become interns, he asked her whether she could be strong enough to withstand the myriad of pressures she would face in her job.

She looked at him straight on and said, "Let me tell you something about me. I ran the New York City Marathon even though my knees were pretty shot, and I had a tear in my left calf muscle—and I also finished it. I know I am tough when I want to be, and most of the time that is precisely who I want to be."

Charles Spencer had seen it all: the rare good ones, lots of mediocre ones, the real ones and tons of fakes. Pretenders, amateur illusionists whose efforts to portray a different image than their real self eventually collapse. Youngsters led astray by the mess of the daily this and that, the deeds and misdeeds, and the failures that come with small deviations from the written and unwritten codes during daily routines. And to top it off, there was the stupor of afterhours life in the Big Apple. The late night drunken carelessness was always a liability. This woman, however, impressed him as genuine. Somehow, she had grabbed his full attention.

She wore a gray business suit loosely hanging over a white blouse. Even before he heard the marathon story, it was evident that there was not even an inch of extra fat on her. As she walked in her black high heels on the end of well-sculpted leg muscles, she almost seemed more the model doing the runway catwalk than a woman applying to enter a selective internship at one of the most prestigious Wall Street houses. Initially the attractive woman caused the interviewer to wonder whether this would be another case of "too pretty to do the job," and so he was looking for further evidence that she could take the hard work involved or whether she would complain about a broken fingernail. Yes, he knew that was sexist, but inside the walls of his mind, as he was trying to make good judgments, he could indulge—the verboten thoughts just never could see the light of day. The young woman had a limited CV, but it was solid enough. Alongside the standard information about grades and three languages, the cover letter told of a childhood impacted by an early divorce but, that she was an avid reader from early on which helped her be, a solid college student despite the usual distractions. And, of course, the marathon anecdote. The honesty impressed Spencer enough to ask the woman to come back for a second interview. Though cynical by nature, he thought she was strong enough to take the pressure. Still he was a bit puzzled and his instincts made him feel confused. Was he just attracted to her beauty, or was there something else? Maybe he would get to the bottom of it in a second interview.

Other interviews occupied Spencer's attention during the day, but on the way home the picture of Elizabeth Farley popped into his mind with full force. Something in those bluish green eyes grabbed him. They were at once confident and fragile, demanding attention and begging to be understood. He wondered what makes some people so eager to succeed that they are willing to risk breaking their limbs. Is it the fear of failure? Greed? Perhaps they are stubbornly seeking praise because of their built-in self-doubt, or maybe it is some combination of all the above.

Charles wondered if that was really that different for modern women as so many like to claim. He was supposed to know a lot about human psychology. After all, he was the number two in the HR department of this renowned Wall Street firm. Yet, to this day, he felt unsure about the correct answer to such questions, for with every argument there seemed to be several counterarguments. All the same, in the case of that marathon runner, calling her back for a second interview was probably the right decision. He got goose bumps thinking about the pain of running a marathon with shattered legs.

Back at home he devoured a quick dinner and sat down in front of his computer. He liked to write short stories and he thought about writing a story about her and about the essence of being tough. As he outlined the story, the structure became clear: the reader would understand this story as if a visitor to a modern art gallery. The strokes would be broad, coarse, gross, lacking detail, as in most short stories. That would allow him to suggest more than outright depict in fine detail. He was pleased that this would allow him to conjure Elizabeth as he wanted her to be.

With the structure in place, he let his imagination run. Elizabeth, the oldest daughter of two, had been greatly affected by the bitter fights among her parents before, during, and after their divorce. She got a premature look at adult life that was not a walk through the park. She had to be tough to survive; she needed to develop a thick crust so that she would be mentally strong. As a woman, she's even more vulnerable. At the end of the day, she might wind up the sole provider, the mother, the rock, and, therefore, she better be prepared to play that role regardless of the faculties nature gave her, whether she was endowed with all the necessary tools or not.

Toughness is a reflex reaction, Charles mused, a psychological mindset, and much more ingrained than reflective. It's strategic rather than tactical, it's endemic even if it seems posturing. It is ingrained by life itself. Toughness would not necessarily create a happy person, but it could make her immune to some of the pain and disappointments that life dishes out. Toughness is paramount to survival.

Charles didn't need to know all the details of the quarrel between Elizabeth's parents to feel the pain. He didn't need to know the specific words exchanged, the accusations, the enlisting of the children to side with one or the other parent, the argumentation used for that purpose. He got a sickly feeling even without knowing that the children had become peons in this conjugal war. He also knew that these sorts of events would have a lasting effect.

His story was progressing well.

Days passed and he was still thinking about Elizabeth Farley on the train rides to work and back. His eyes closed, ignoring the chatter of other train commuters, he allowed his imagination to draw another picture, this one a more expressionist type of painting: Little Elizabeth was sitting at the bottom of a cold stone staircase, her legs bent at the knees and her feet tucked under her backside, as if she were unwilling to move away from that spot. The colors were vivid blues and pinks and greens. She wore a cotton shirt with little blue and green flower designs, the shirt hanging loosely over her jeans. In her small hands, she held a book. Most of the other children were running around because it was recess time at the elementary school. The playground was full of noisy children screaming at the top of their lungs, tossing around balls and other objects. They were letting go of whatever cramped up energies were being held back in the classroom. But this little girl's eyes were glued to her book. She ignored the commotion. Her fixation was complete. This is how she liked to spend her breaks, and when another child came and invited her to play, she smiled and shook her head without saying much. She was oblivious to the other children and to the sporadic scorn this behavior prompted. She truly did not care. There was some sadness in her face but only an observant person would notice it. Even this early in her life she wanted to project a picture of sheer perfection—she did not want to be pitied, she did not want to be consoled.

Toughness showed itself early in the life of this little girl. It is her demeanor and it lives in her single-mindedness, her goal-oriented character, her determination, her unwillingness to compromise and to do what others are doing just because it is the norm. She ignored the nasty comments of some children, the "bookworm" nickname they have given her.

Charles ached. He wanted to know more about her, did not dare ask, did not know how to find out. She seemed like the personification of his dreams, but he was not sure.

Once at home, he jotted down some notes and ideas to serve as guidelines for the story he would be writing. They were going to be about truth and deceit and how difficult it is to detect deception when one wishes to believe otherwise, how wishful thinking obscures and hazes over everything. He hopes that this was not the case with Farley. The discomfort made Charles abandon his task; he closed the notepad and turned on the radio to one of his favorite stations.

The music emitted had a relentless positive sound; Brahms Serenade no. 1 in D Major was, in his opinion, as positive as it was beautiful. It also was very much to his taste. Not like Mozart, so kitschy, tacky sweet, reminiscent of the silly laughter attributed to the composer in *Amadeus.* Mozart's pieces, lack any gray clouds menacingly hanging over the landscape—like those you may detect in a Beethoven composition, for example.

Brahms serenade prompted him to think of Elizabeth again. She seemed to be moving on in life with a great sense of purpose, with a clear notion that, while not easy, life is to be taken on with full zest, and to be enjoyed. There was no need to brood over trouble, nastiness, setbacks; those were just distractions.

Was this approach to life too naive? To draw the parallels, was Brahms unaware of Beethoven's bewilderment over Napoleon's new imperial aspirations while he abandoned the lofty causes of freedom of thought and religion? Was Brahms unwilling to measure up? Or was he unabashedly embracing the beauty of living a life of abundant smiles and laughter regardless? Surely, he must have been aware of the pain in Robert Schumann's soul, and how he, Brahms himself, contributed to that pain— how could that not be reflected in his music?

Charles muttered to himself. Maybe toughness meant to live a positive life amid all the shit that surrounds us. He still was trying to conjure Elizabeth's past life in his mind. The college-bound woman, he imagined, had already seen and suffered plenty. She was fully aware that many would consider her psychologically damaged. Her childhood difficulties and a world full of ignorant, yet arrogant, people could turn anyone into a negative person. But she had been determined to move on in life with a sure step and a smile on her face since childhood. "I want to be liked," she might have said to a confidante, "and I will ignore nastiness regardless of who is dishing it out."

Eventually the station replaced Brahms piece with a Rachmaninoff piano sonata—Lise de la Salle was playing it, and it was forceful, pedantic— every note played with insistent clarity, not insinuated as the old Arthur Rubinstein may have played it, but expressed fully and aggressively. Every note—clear as if it stood brilliantly alone in a crowd. It reminded him of the steps Elizabeth took as she approached her chair for the interview. The accentuated moves as she sat down. Every move was precise just like every note played by the pianist. He enthusiastically declared, "Just brilliant." He shook his head. For whom were those accolades? The concert artist or Farley? He did not even know Farley; he knew her almost as little as that pianist playing the sonata. It was all in his head, his dreams, his hopes, and his desires. He had been a straight arrow for his whole life, and here he was finding himself confused and intoxicated by a much younger person.

Charles was bothered by his unusual attention to this individual, by the fact that he couldn't get her out of his mind. He called Fernando, his best friend for decades, and asked if they can have coffee together the next day, Saturday. A weekend morning breakfast at the local diner had been something they did for years. "Yes, of course, the Scarsdale diner would be fine, and around 9:30 works for me too."

Charles sounded edgy; he signaled more apprehension than his usual New York stress-induced temper. It was clear that he needed to talk with great urgency. Usually Charles was more the introvert and this was unusual. Twice before had he sought advice, and in both cases the subject matter was meaningful. He abruptly stopped the platitudes and pleasantries about health, daily work, and weather to go straight to what bothered him: "I am thinking about her a lot. She is constantly on my mind, and I don't even know why."

"Who is she?" asked Fernando, and he barely could get the words out of his mouth before Charles answered.

"She showed up at one of the routine interviews for interns. You should have seen those eyes. They were not necessarily beautiful, but they spoke a thousand languages and told a million stories just by looking at you and saying nothing. She was striking rather than beautiful—in terrific shape, and a nice face. Yes, blonde, you know I have a thing for them, but I am not even sure it is natural. Still, it all worked like a charm for her."

He told the story of her running a marathon with shattered legs and how he constantly thought about how and why this woman appeared tough and vulnerable at the same time. And, once more, how he was totally bewildered by her and could not stop thinking about her.

"Are you in love with an applicant to your firm, Charles? You know this could only be trouble for you and for the firm, especially these days. But anyway, how can you be in love with someone you barely know? You know that what you see at the beginning is not what you get at the end; you are old enough to appreciate that any fantastic image you might have of her this early is just going to blow up in your face when with time you dig a bit deeper."

"I know all these things, Fernando. That is exactly why I wanted to talk to you. I feel I am going mad and I am allowing myself to drift in a direction I do not want to go. What do I do?"

"Well, to some extent this is all understandable. You have been single for a while now. You have not had a meaningful relationship for some time, and you are yearning for such a relationship. But you need to cool it, Charles … you really do. I know you can." As they exited the coffee shop, Fernando gave him a strong hug, the hug of an understanding friend, and told him he would always be there for him. He also told him that perhaps he needed to see a professional. "I do not know if that is the kind of thing a friend says, but it seems to be the best advice I can give you," he added.

"And you are yearning for such a relationship." Fernando's words came back to him time and again. In Fellini's *Amarcord*, a desperate man, perhaps insane, climbed up a lonely tall tree and shouted out, "*Voglio una donna!*" Was it the scream of a madman or the anguished expression of loneliness Charles knew he was feeling? Was the shout out begging for pure sexual gratification, or was it that this man's ego was yearning to be caressed? Charles always knew that fantasy and reality intertwine too often; he agreed with Fellini there. It did not help him resolve the problem he was facing, though.

On Monday evening, Farley played her answering machine and heard the following message:

"Hello, Ms. Farley, this is Joanna calling, the secretary of Mr. Charles Spencer; I wonder if we could advance your second interview by a few days. How does this Thursday at 3:30 or 5:00 p.m. sound? Please call us to confirm."

Farley raised her eyebrows in puzzlement but decided that this hardly could be bad news; yes, why not? Thursday at 5:00 p.m. sounded good, just as good as the original appointment a week later. She wondered why the change in schedule but couldn't resolve the puzzle, nor did she give it major significance.

Thursday morning, on his way to work, Charles saw a poster for an upcoming movie. As is often the case, it also has a subtitle of sorts; it read: "Hope comes with letting go." Yes, he had to let go, he was obliged to return to being a professional whose personal interest in individuals excluded all employees or candidates, not only because he believed in these norms but because he feared going insane otherwise.

A blue suit, high heels, legs that went on forever underneath the light fabric that covered them —it seemed to Spencer that this suit was meant to be sexy but understated, and in any case, way too flimsy for a late October afternoon, especially in New York City where it blows colder down the wind tunnels caused by streets flanked by tall buildings. As he saw her walk into his office and take the five steps to sit in front of him, he made a mental note that she still was impressive. He thought she was the vision of something that was déjà passé in the modern world: a woman with taste, control, serenity; whatever sexual fervor lived in her would be left confined to private settings. She could not be one of those loose cannons the magazines feasted upon constantly. She seemed more like a Dutch master's portrait of a woman who only displays whatever bit of sexuality in a minor curve of her lips. Otherwise appearing tranquil, holding back, completely in control, maybe even cold, and untouchable. He understood that this was a major source of her enchantment, a critical piece of his fascination with her.

Charles leaned forward with his hands spread over the edge of the desk, as if he was trying to maintain control. "As I told you during the first interview, the CV and the overall impression you have left with us strongly suggested we should meet again and confirm that we want you for the position. Have you thought about the department you would want to join after the internship is over? Obviously, you will get to see all important areas during your rotation, but ..."

"Yes. I think I want to work in either the corporate finance or investment banking side; that is where I believe my strengths are. But, as you said, I would need to get better acquainted with all areas during the rotation."

"Why Wall Street? Is it the money? Is it the prestige?"

Elizabeth now crosses her legs the other way; the moves appear precise and controlled. "It is all of that. It is making it in New York. It is being the best in the most exciting area of business these days. That is what I always dreamed of: being on top of the world. I am extremely competitive, and Wall Street seems like the right place for someone like me."

"But it also means working till the late hours at night and getting up early the next morning to start all over again. People get burned out very fast here; I am sure you know that."

"I am not afraid of working hard; you will be impressed with my endurance."

"Yes, I know, the marathon story ..."

She produced a peculiar smile, that upon reflection, he later described as "intelligent". It seemed to suggest that she and her interviewer shared a secret. He could not prevent himself from smiling back.

"You know, Wall Street is also known to be a male environment; some of these people are fairly crass types. Will you be able to deal with that?"

"I have dealt with crass types before, as early as high school and certainly in college. I can assure you that I can handle that and them."

She sounded positive, not hesitating for a second, as if ready for the question, for any question, in fact. For a second, Spencer had that recurring feeling that it all was unreal and just a well-rehearsed show.

Was he being duped by her? Was he missing things because she had produced feelings in him that had little to do with his role as a future employer?

"One last thing, Ms. Farley, I suppose Elizabeth is okay too?" She nods and smiles, as she again crosses her legs, but this time the skirt ends up revealing a bit more of her leg. Spencer notices it but wants to appear professional. "It is imperative that you understand that being discreet and honest is critical when working on Wall Street in general, and at this firm, in particular. Don't use information you have to boast and enhance your social status, don't give away trade secrets, keep utmost discretion."

At this point, he noticed a slight sign of discomfort, but her response gave him peace of mind. She stated in the most convincing voice that these were nonissues to a woman with her European roots and strict conservative upbringing.

On the way home that evening, Charles closed his eyes and two images kept flashing alternately in his mind. There was that quick flicker when he spoke about the need for secrecy, and the savvy smile when he mentioned the marathon story. His many years interviewing candidates had improved his intuition, and that hitch made him uncomfortable; on the other hand, the quick smile made her as endearing as ever. Spencer's mind turned to music once more. Like a Chopin piano sonata, she was elegant and flirtatious even while keeping a conservative, noble pose. Like that romantic Pole, she probably could be emotional at a given moment and not attribute too much meaning to it. She could, he imagined, revert to her tough, straight-back, chin-up conservative modality in a heartbeat. Like the gliding music on the piano, she was possibly bubbly and joyful, but it would be as fleeting as the sound produced by the momentary touching of a piano key. Such painless slithering protects you from getting hurt by reversals, disappointments, and breakups.

He decided he would hire her.

Fernando called Charles and explained: "I was concerned enough about you to ask if you wanted to get together again." The tone of Charles's voice suggested that he was happy with the call. It had been two weeks since they last talked.

"So, did you hire that woman, the marathon runner?"

"Yes, we did, but I committed an indiscretion when I called her to tell her the good news. I told her that she was welcome to come by my office if, at any point, she needed to discuss anything. I left the door open for her to seek a personal relationship." Charles seemed so eager to confess this.

"Oh, Charles. That is not good, but it could be construed as just being a friendly gesture of a warm HR person. Has she sought you out?" "Not really. She has not come by my office."

"But?"

"Well, quite honestly, I could not resist going to the trading area where she was getting acquainted with their activities."

"So, how was she doing?"

"She seemed to have a good time there. There was a lot of laughter. The guys seemed to have a great time with this good-looking woman in the midst. It made me quite angry and I swiftly turned around."

"What do you expect, Charles? This all seems fairly normal to me."

"I have great difficulty with casual behavior of all sorts; I guess I am old-fashioned."

"I don't think that that is what is going on at all. I don't think you are such a conservative guy. I think you want to be one of those guys on the trading desk and get close to her. You are plain jealous. You must watch yourself, Charles, get a grip of yourself. I know you as a sensitive man but also as a sensible man. Be sensible in this case and don't do anything stupid."

Charles seemed perturbed, anxious, and uncomfortable; he put $12 on the table and bolted out of the coffee shop. You could see him shaking his head as he was getting into his car. Charles knew better than to reject what Fernando was saying as nonsense. Truthfully, it all was getting messy and a bit pathetic.

A couple of weeks later, Spencer approached the head of corporate finance to ask how the trainees were doing. Youngman was aloof and said that in general they were doing well enough. Charles persisted to find out about individual interns. He mentioned a few others before he got to Farley. He needed to mask his interest in her.

"She is doing reasonably well. However, from time to time, I have noticed her being tired and a bit out of focus. I wonder if she is not enjoying herself a bit too much."

Spencer discussed a few more names, but the news he had just heard troubled him. He went to his office and called Elizabeth on the internal line to ask how she was doing. Her answers were curt, professional, and courteous, but obviously noncommittal. She thought she was doing "just fine" and she liked the current phase of her training; she was learning a lot. Spencer had a hard time moving beyond the tone and mode of this conversation but managed to remind Farley that his door was open if she wanted to discuss anything at all.

Spencer then called his "utility man," as he labeled him. He wondered if they could meet for lunch.

David Holman was a private eye who had snooped around for the firm in the past. Spencer had used him in a couple of cases when doubts had arisen about possible insider trading and problems involving some employees at the trading desk.

"David, I want you to do me a personal favor. We have a trainee by the name of Elizabeth Farley. We need to ascertain whether to keep this woman and give her a longer-term contract. She makes a good impression, but something tells me that she may be into the fun after-hours life in New York City and I want to know if that is the case. Could you just spend a week checking her out? Nothing too in-depth, just basic stuff about her, and make sure to keep it clean—nothing more than snooping around." Spencer had the right to engage Holman in such activities, but he still felt ill about what he had just done. This was not normally his style; he knew that others on Wall Street played a dirty game, but he wanted to stick to the rules and be proud of how he handled his affairs. There was that other side of him—the writer, the sensitive person—and these two sides of him had to live one with the other. On the other hand, he could always claim that based on what he had heard from Youngman, this was a proper step. Yes, the firm had conducted its basic due diligence about Farley; no police record, no major drug problems surfaced, but he knew that this standard procedure was limited in time and depth. And he could always claim that living in the fast lane and with decent money sloshing around there was potential for experimentation with drugs among young interns.

That night Charles slept poorly; he had a nightmare with predominantly gray and green colors and Munch-like figures wildly jumping around him with panic-stricken, crying, hollow faces. He woke up agitated and sat down in his dark living room. He reflected on what he had been doing these last few months. Was he losing his mind? He went to the internet and sought information about obsession. In one account, a man in search of companionship imagined that total strangers were in love with him and were trying to signal him that this was the case. The individual realized the problem; reality and imagination were becoming so blurred that he lost much of his common sense. Spencer thought that lately he was engaging in some of the same behavior and it made him utterly nervous. He had always prided himself on being a down-to-earth, rational human being.

"So, Holman, what have you found out?" Spencer wasted no time to spring the question. He was not keen on spending time dealing in pleasantries at a pizza parlor; he was generally eager to keep the meetings short. He needed to find out the information he had asked for before Holman would stuff his face.

"Well, she really does go out almost every night … to clubs, you know, dancing till the early hours: three or four a.m. Nothing too heavy is going on; she seems to hang out with the same group of friends. She is attractive, and in her black short skirt, with those legs she has, she looks very sexy. I would not be surprised if she is considered a very hot item."

"Anything else? Drugs? Did you see her consume drugs?

"No. I did not see her engage in that. I saw her flirting with a guy who suddenly could not control himself and grabbed her by the waist to kiss her. She pushed him away so hard the guy fell backwards to the floor. That's about it."

"Well. Thank you, Holman. Send the bill to my attention. I will approve it and send it to the appropriate people."

"Should I write a report?"

"No. Write out your bill as a routine checkup. That will pass."

Elizabeth Farley entered the small conference room where Charles Spencer was waiting for her. She looked a bit confused and her grey suit made her look a bit pale.

The HR officer did not mince words:

"I am disappointed in you. In fact, I am also disillusioned with myself for not being a better judge of character. You have let me down. You took the opportunity I gave you, the company gave you, and you could not restrain yourself and threw it away. Rumor has it that you've been partying every night till the early hours of the morning, that your behavior at those parties was not fitting the image we want to portray as a firm, that you were willing to do some things to ingratiate yourself with some of the men in your department. I am sorry, but we must let you go. The contract you signed allows us to do so after a six-month period unless the firm believes that its principles were violated; so, though the trial period is not over, we have decided that you do not fit our needs or profile. Please empty your desk immediately and go to my assistant before noon to settle all financial and other pertinent matters related to your dismissal. You will be escorted out thereafter."

There was not a tear in her eyes as she stood there stunned and feeling sick to her stomach. With a look that reflected her pain and hurt pride, she managed to say a few trembling words: "You are acting on rumors and not on facts. My private life is exactly that, my private life. My performance and the execution of my duties have been above reproach. You are making a mistake here, but mistakes are made all over and all the time. Still, it is highly unprofessional to act on rumors, and some of these I am certain are outright lies." And with that, she turned around and left.

Spencer was left wondering if the firm would be hit by a lawsuit. He also felt nauseated by the whole experience, by his own weakness, by his inability to handle the situation rationally.

Two days after Charles informed Elizabeth that she was being terminated he drafted a letter to his boss:

> Dear Mr. Ehrlich,
>
> I am hereby requesting a leave of absence for six months starting December 1. As you know, after twenty years of service for the firm, I am entitled to it. I feel I need a longer vacation to gather the energy necessary to service the firm with the same careful attention to detail as I have thus far.
>
> Kind regards,
>
> Charles Spencer

He then called Fernando and asked if he could recommend the best possible psychiatrist. "I recognize that I am ill; I need help. Not just so I can perform properly at work, but so I can look at myself in the mirror and not feel like vomiting with disgust. I also need to get better so I can find a partner and love."

ATROPHY

∎

*O*n the stage is a dividing wall; in one room a woman is adjusting
her dress, on the other is a man struggling to fix his tie.

She (with plenty of sarcasm): "C'mon old professor, when
will you ever be on time? You spend more time getting dressed
than a blonde having a bad hair day. We will be late for that
concert. What is playing again? Some Russian composer, right?"

He (sounding irritated): "Try just this once not to be your usual
bitchy self! Neither the fact that I am older nor that I am a
fucking college professor should cause you to be nasty. I was
under the impression that you liked my job—made you feel vain!
And are you really that fed up with my old dick? I always
thought that your wild fantasies allowed you to make anything
work for you. And the name of that Russian composer is
Rachmaninoff."

"Ah! Blasé! This is all so banal!" he wailed while crumbling the page.
Jackson sat frozen in front of the computer, holding his hands to his face
as if to escape reality. His world had collapsed and he was struggling not
to drown in an ocean of indifference, declining vitality, and sudden
loveless existence.

The smoke-filled study had minimalist décor. The computer stood on top of a glass table; next to it were some writing utensils and an empty, stained coffee mug. The only color was provided by a framed picture of his children hugging him. It was an old picture, and he would readily admit, outdated by time and the children's waning affection. Scattered all around were stacks of books providing silent testimony to this man's erudite pursuits, all centered around understanding humanity. They seemed useless to him now.

He went to the bathroom, glared at the mirror and shook his head in disbelief. Those same eyes that once projected a youthful sparkle of enthusiasm had turned a dull, opaque blue, the wrinkles around them had multiplied to exacerbate an image of utter sadness. In a way, it all seemed so foreign to him, so radically new. The white stubble on his unshaven face reflected multiple days of voluntary imprisonment, further testimony to his despondency.

As he paced up and down the large living room he muttered: "This play lacks any semblance of innovation, no great inventive plot. And it reeks of plagiarism to boot."

The idea of writing the play popped up in a conversation with his friend Art. He had gone to Art's apartment seeking solace and guidance after twin disasters had struck in quick succession. "What shall I do with myself?" he asked.

Art suggested writing something, maybe a novella or a theatre piece. "You always have written well, and I hardly know a person with so much emotional depth and intellect. I am sure you could come up with something exceptionally good."

At first, Jackson rejected the idea: "That's ludicrous! To think that I can sit down and write cogently about anything, especially right now!" But later in the conversation he yielded, "Maybe I will give it a try; what do I have to lose?" Secretly he harbored the idea that a successful completion of such a project could restore the world he recently knew. Maybe even restore her love for him.

About a week later, he feared that he was not making meaningful strides. Art's words "something exceptionally good" echoed in his head and they seemed to mock him. He needed to talk to Art again. He felt like a child in need of guidance. He considered Art one of his closest friends and the one who understood him best. Art's empathy was great. More than that, Art was an English literature professor. They had joined the faculty of the university the same year, gotten tenure five years later, and over two decades developed true affectionate kinship. At first, they would read each other's conference papers; with time they discovered other common interests. They both liked old classic movies, and because of a university group trip, the appreciation of a beautiful Tuscan summer night accompanied by a bottle of Chianti.

He picked up the phone with trembling hands:

"Art, would you please come over sometime soon. I need to talk to you."

From the sound of it, it was more a supplication than a request, and so Art assured him that he would be with him within the hour.

With the door barely shut behind him, he told Art in agitated words, "I am so frustrated! I want to write this play about my crisis. My twin crises, I should say. But I can't think straight, can't put on paper one intelligent thought. I have no imagination, and the drivel is making me mad."

"Jackson, you came to me some time ago; you were upset and irritated. When you left, the idea to write this play was pleasing you. I think you even surprised yourself—you had a new project in life. But you must be generous with yourself; it is not like you have been a playwright for a couple of decades for god's sake. After all, throughout your life, you have written nothing but conference papers and the occasional letter to a friend or family member. Moreover, you just have gone through what you call your 'twin crises.' You said you needed an outlet for all the tumultuous feelings in you. But you could not possibly imagine that this would be easy, could you? —This could not possibly be the same as writing about the aborigines in Papua New Guinea."

"Yes, Art, I know all that. Here is the problem —it all has been written about before. Older man, younger woman, impossible romance, disaster. Saul Bellow, Philip Roth, Coetzee, Houellebecq; they all have written about this. It is almost as if this is a genre in literature. What could I possibly add to it?"

"Well, if your recent relationship with Sylvia emulated art, as you had told me when you were involved with Sylvia, so be it. Maybe you can add a different viewpoint to that literature? Maybe some sort of critical perspective? Maybe you could stress the exploitation you may have been gone through. Sylvia did use you, didn't she?"

That last sentence was hurtful to Jackson, but he ignored it, as if it never was said. He was not willing to allow it to ignite a multitude of doubts and misgivings of his own. "You know, Art, I want to achieve a couple of things. On the surface, I want to evoke the same exuberant feelings, the excitement and exhilaration that reading Roth elicited in Sylvia. She often talked about how sexually stimulated she felt when she

read his books. To think that I was the one that suggested Roth to her."
The memory of Sylvia made his voice sound high strung. Art held
Jackson's arm, fearing trouble. His touch calmed Jackson.

"I want to emulate the masters and try to put the same motifs (older
man/younger woman/experience/beauty) to good use in the play.
Stripped down, the basic ingredients of the play are obvious—or is it just
trite? The male character is a modern Faust: significantly older, and thus,
desperate to salvage the essence of life (that excitement) by way of, what
ends up being a tumultuous, relationship. The female, as I will have her
blatantly confess in the play, 'gets wet' whenever the two have a 'heavy
discussion' that stimulates her intellectually. She accepts her inferiority
in this regard, wants to be challenged, and, by her own admission, gets a
high from what she has described as the sadomasochistic overtones of
the disparity.

"Her trump cards are her youth and beauty; she will not have any
compunction in using them, flaunting them, and shifting the power center
of the relationship in her favor. Her power over the man is
quintessentially— sexual attraction.

"My life with Sylvia replicated the same motifs and now they serve as
material for the writing of the play." He smirks cynically and shakes his
head.

"But I also want to go beyond the story. I want in some way to be
critical of these other writers and their male chauvinistic ways. I want to
make sure this point comes through loud and clear. But I have a horrible
time trying to figure out how to do that. Take for example the language
used in the play—if it is to mimic those writers, the male character's
language should be coarse, profane, using crass expletives aplenty. The
only problem is that I really hate that crass, vulgar language. It is as if
saying 'fuck' all the time makes the character more 'real'—or perhaps a
'true intellectual,' whatever that means. "Worse, it is as if being less
vulgar would make the character's words less genuine and more
conformist. All the same, I am not sure how to be critical of this
vulgarity other than to be sarcastic about it. Will the audience get the
rebuke, the criticism? Will the sarcasm come across at all?"

Art smiled knowingly, as he realized that Jackson was looking for
some direction and advice in the writing of the play. That was a lot more
benign than the alarming call an hour earlier which sounded like life and
death.

Jackson persisted: "The protagonist of the play, an anthropology
professor, surely would avoid the crass language in his writings on the

Guatemalan Maya, but he will be as profane and overt in his dealings with friends and, most of all, while conversing with the female sharing his bed. But the difficulty is in passing along that dichotomy as a critique."

"I am not sure, Jackson, how you solve the problem." Art answered carefully. Even if you would have the protagonist express himself differently to his academic audience than to his personal interlocutors, I am not sure it would be clear enough that you are being critical of the use of crass language. I am not sure I can come up with an answer, but I promise you I will think about it. In the meantime, please don't get discouraged and get on with your writing."

Almost as if he was trying to reclaim his play as a worthwhile pursuit, Jackson half-mumbled, "I think that the love scenes on stage should be quite graphic. Because of the shock effect that the over-sexualized world frenzies about, I think it will help make the play successful."

Art was a bit puzzled by that comment, but he believed that Jackson would be okay now and his presence in the smoke-filled apartment was no longer necessary. "Maybe it is best if I give it some thought on my own and we get together again tomorrow; shall we say around four in the afternoon? I am not teaching tomorrow."

Once Art exited the apartment, Jackson felt the solitude overbearing. The energy emanating from discussing the play was gone. Instead he had to contend with bouts of self-doubt. More than anything he was obsessed by the question whether this play could get a good reception by critics and audiences. That way it might lead to a rekindling of Sylvia's admiration and love.

He wanted to regain his stature in her eyes. To Art he had said that he needed this play to be a success because he wanted to vindicate himself, he needed to prove his worthiness. But there was more than that—the play had to provide the magical elixir that would rescue his relationship with Sylvia and prevent depression. It was not just about the sexual contact, he admitted to himself reluctantly, but the fear of growing old alone.

He had described the crises to Art in rather vivid emotional terms: "It all happened so abruptly," he said as he shook his head in disbelief. "One moment I was king of the hill, stood on top of the world; I even stood stark naked in the middle of this room, held up my fist as if I had won some great sports event; I was momentarily drunk with vanity. I suddenly realized my posture mimicked the outrageous exclamation by James Cameron as he got his Oscar for *Titanic*; I let out a huge laugh because I was totally embarrassed by my act. But I was experiencing such boundless euphoria; how childish was I?!"

"And then it all came tumbling down."

"I thought I was well-respected at the university, or at least until I was summarily asked to exit. That was the first shock, but more importantly, my love life which had taken a brisk, unexpected turn for the better about a year earlier, was snapped by one curt statement from Sylvia. And so, both pillars of my existence collapsed in quick succession."

It was a Sunday morning little over a year earlier when he realized that he had run out of coffee, and since it was a day of leisure, he strolled over to the neighborhood coffee shop. There she was. He was immediately stung by her looks—a brunette with a perfectly oval face and beautiful blue-green eyes. She wore tight jeans and a light pink blouse. She knew how to enhance her looks with simple but tasteful clothes.

Though generally quite shy, he decided to strike up a conversation. He was surprised by her willingness to engage. What unfolded thereafter was fantastically easy, quick, and sweeping. The conversation flowed, the common ground surfaced despite the obvious age difference. Sylvia was easy to talk to. She asked intelligent questions, and was at ease telling about her preferences, describing her position on matters of taste, religion, and politics with lucidity and no indications of self-doubt. She seemed to be eager to elicit a positive reaction from her counterpart and he was all too willing to respond. She also seemed to be impressed by his credentials. "Finally, someone with class," she quipped after an hour-long conversation, and that phrase stuck with him forever.

Remarkably, the early affinity led to a torrent of affection and rapidly evolved into a more profound relationship. After seeing each other three consecutive evenings that week, they planned a long weekend trip to some beautiful place in the countryside, some secluded inn away from town. Though they stayed in separate rooms, they enjoyed the passionate kisses of those early stages. After another couple of weeks, they were yearning for each other, and it seemed to him that it was as much about physical attraction and passion as it was because of the real and intimate conversations they had. There were times he was so swept up by romance that he even fantasized about a more lasting future, even marriage.

There were instances when he was reminded of other disparities beyond the obvious age gap: disparate circles of friends, different professional pursuits and levels of achievement. All these produced plenty of difficult moments that kept him apprehensive and cautious. Often enough, though, he let go of his better sense and wrapped himself in a most pleasant dream colored with sexual overtones. He built on her occasional statement about love and a common future. He ignored any negative remarks and the trouble they suggested.

And then, literally within one week, it all came shattering down like some cheap crystal vase violently crashing to the floor. The university demanded he accept early retirement. A couple of days later, his world shook again as Sylvia told him that his theoretical worries, which he had voiced in alarming fashion lately, were dead on: she did not love him anymore In fact, she had met a new man. So much for feeling on top of the world, for announcing to all who cared to listen that these were the best days of his life.

And now, all he was left with was this biographical material. But memoirs are for the dead or dying. Falling out of love does not lead to great theater, does it?

He was unsure and nervous about the future of his play. What possible reactions would be voiced by the critics? He feared they would go after him for employing the worn-out formula? These days, the fantasy of an old man lusting after a young woman seemed almost as ubiquitous as voyeurism and lesbianism.

His pacing around the room was a true reflection of the inner struggle. He had bouts of enthusiasm about the project followed by a great sense of despair about its success, and it was all wrapped up in the confusion created by the twin dismissals.

"So what if the play is not genuine enough; the world thrives on repetition!" he shouted out, but of course, that was just a cop-out, and he knew it. "So be it!" he exclaimed. It is true that in the past he would not have been willing to compromise, to conform. He was proud of his integrity. His academic publications were never a work of plagiarism. He always was striving to be honest, logical, and above all, an excellent academic. But now, he needed success more than he needed to be at peace with himself. He wanted the applause more than any old aspiration to excel. His badly hurt ego needed refuge and solace. It would come with the public's acclaim of his play, he decided, "and to hell with the critics."

It was already late at night and he was exhausted. He finished his whiskey and headed to the bedroom and another difficult, sleepless night.

The following morning, he sat at his desk seeking to write again, but the words were not coming easily. It was fortuitous that he could head over to Art soon.

Unlike the chaotic disorder in his apartment, Art's place was comfortably set up, but because it was an unusually warm day, they sat on the porch with gin-and- tonics. Jackson lamented to his friend that he continued to struggle with the play. It was good to talk to someone, sort his thoughts out loud, get some clarity.

"The plot of the play may not be terribly inventive, may not include some brilliant new tack on a world with established confines and set parameters, but it will garner strength from the fact that it will mimic my own personal tragedy: a passionate and turbulent relationship gone awfully sour when the ultimate incongruence involving two individuals living on two different generational planets proves too big of an obstacle, when the incompatibility engendered by a huge age gap could not be accepted by her.

"I remember that only six weeks ago, she was sitting in my living room telling me how we are kindred spirits in a thousand ways, how I knew what she was thinking most of the time. I agreed and returned the compliment by admiring her great intuition. I always would go a step further in my adulation, and this time I told her that I adored her more than I could recall loving anyone else. She smiled with an air of condescension as she told me she knew that.

"Even then I sensed that she could not live with the public image of walking next to a man who was so much older, that she was unable to tell her friends that this is the man she wanted to live with. I was certain she knew that I was special, different; she had told me so innumerable times. I was a 'more giving person than any man she had ever known,' nevertheless, I also knew that she still could not bridge the gap, take that conscious leap. All the same, I harbored a tiny hope that she would realize the value of me despite it all. I guess I was intoxicated by fantasies of a joint future.

"And then, bam! It all went asunder with incredible speed. It destroyed me completely: emotionally, spiritually, and even physically. I started having chest pains, sleepless nights, my face shrank, my body ached. Art, my total self shriveled. I have to be able to pass on this tragedy in the play. Even if the play ends up being less creative, at least it will have the force of personal pain."

Art nodded in agreement. "It is a strong story and I am sure your deep feelings will find their way to paper. Take your time, be confident, and you will be able to transmit those emotions well. You have to get yourself together and continue ..."

Jackson interrupted him. It was as if he hadn't heard a word his friend had said. "I have given some thought to the ending and am keenly aware that while the most powerful element in the play would derive from my personal tragedy, on stage the drama would need to be personified, tangible, and tragic. Especially the ending, the finale.

Art let him continue because there was a passion in Jackson's voice that he had not heard in recent times

"How should the play end, Art? Will she die—reminding us of *La Bohème?* Or will it be a Hollywood-like happy ending resulting from rediscovered love and her somehow overcoming a disease?"

He paused, somewhat dramatically, and then said "I know she will be stricken not by cancer (because it would be too similar to Roth's *Dying Animal*), but by a deadly sexually transmitted disease. It is entirely plausible. She is a woman whose sexual appetite for adventure is a sad truism, after all. And towards the end of the play, Christina—that will be her name—will seek out the old man (I decided on the name Ben) for comfort, as fears of an imminent death obsess her."

Almost as an afterthought, he murmured, "It is not that I wish death on Sylvia; for god's sake, I still love her, yet it all makes sense ..."

For quite some time he had surmised that Sylvia would never be content in a relationship with any one man, and so it made sense to throw a parallel and have Christina moving on from one partner to another until she meets a man who gives her the disease. Eventually, Christina, feeling the need to cope with the news in some fashion, would return to that one person who can perhaps help her— or at least comfort her.

Art told him that he had given some thought to the issue of the famous authors' vulgarity. "How about if you have the male read out loud a conference paper to the woman; he interjects vulgar language here and there, but immediately corrects himself deleting those interjections? This clearly would highlight the disparity." "That could work", exclaims Jackson as he thanks his friend. "Beyond that, Art said, I have nothing other to add, no other idea." Jackson sipped on his drink, considered this last comment and felt lonely and somewhat sour. He thought to himself: Why can't Art help this along; can't he see the importance of this project?

Atrophy

On his way back home, while walking through the almost empty streets of Holland Park that early afternoon, his thoughts reverted to Sylvia. He replayed her announcement bolting from the relationship. When she had asked him to meet her at the bar they often frequented, he had a premonition that she was about to call it quits. All the same, he was taken aback by her announcement. His initial, knee-jerk reaction is to tell her to go to hell. It was as much the content as the coldness of her tone that shocked him. She looked grim, unusually pale, and a good deal less attractive than her normally striking self. All the same, at the end of the brief conversation, far too short for the immensity of the event, he thought, he felt hurt and betrayed. He was certain that it showed in his face. His lips were quivering, his head was throbbing, and his eyes filled with tears.

Once at his desk, back in the apartment, he continued to reflect on the recent past. He had often feared that the relationship would eventually collapse, that it could not survive all the strain, but he expected her to prepare him, to talk to him, to ease out of the hopeless entanglement. When he worried about the impending breakup, he fantasized that they could find some sort of arrangement that would allow them to enjoy time together and maybe, just maybe, even some of the physical affection he so desired.

Instead, he had to admit to himself, she was being a self-centered, inconsiderate bitch (how he hated her sometimes!) when she did what was practical and obvious—she blasted the news at a moment that was convenient to her. She told him that she had dragged this along for longer than she could bear and that it was time to face the music. There was no sugarcoating and no postmortem arrangement either. He then had a fleeting flashback of the smile she gave him when she agreed they were kindred spirits. It had a distinct air of condescension.

The confusion created by all this rehashing was too overpowering to attempt to do some writing. He decided to give it a rest, maybe it was temporary, maybe it would be forever.

Two days later, he decided to put an end to his misery. He either ended his own life, something totally unimaginable heretofore, or he needed to find a way back into Sylvia's life. Convinced that he could not live without some contact with Sylvia, he called her and asked to meet—"Let's go to the Three Foxes." She agreed.

The encounter was tense, his hurt feelings, her defensiveness, made it stiff and difficult. In the end, she indicated a willingness to rekindle some sort of friendship:

"We can have a cup of coffee or a beer and talk about the most recent issue of the *New Yorker* anytime," she said coldly, He recognized that she was highlighting what was of interest to her, but chose to appease her.

During the next three weeks, they got together once or twice a week, usually a Monday or a Wednesday when her work schedule was lighter. The conversations had a regular pattern. They would start off by talking about this or that literary event, a new movie or play. Soon they would glide into discussing her new lover and the frustrations she was experiencing with him. Jackson was careful in his response—he wanted to tell her that she is not handling well this guy's phlegmatic reactions to her sexuality and her "live on the edge" approach. Instead, he listened quietly, provided comforting words about a better future, and carefully avoided saying things that might upset her. He, of course, would have rather compared and contrasted. He would rather have told her that while they were together she rejoiced in the electricity and tension around them, even in the actual weirdness of a couple so disparate in age. Yet he knew that this would come across as self-serving and, most certainly, push her away.

Throughout this period, he continued to be besieged by self-doubt, moments when he pondered whether his sanity was being impaired by any kind of relationship with her. He realized that the rekindling of the relationship was in fact a disaster—it was nice to see her, but she was giving him nothing! No love. Not even much affection. His hopes for more were squashed time and again. The kiss on the cheek when they greeted each other was cold as that of a fish. He wondered if it would not be best to completely cut loose, this time for good. He called Art with the intention of telling him about his feelings: "I wonder what this would do to her; despite the breakup, she has shown that she still has plenty of feelings for me, so maybe calling off the current friendship would inflict pain, maybe even devastate her, maybe cause her to reconsider." Even as he spoke those words to his close friend, he knew that he was painting reality pink! He made her look so much better than she was. Was it so he would look less used, less worthless?

But he continued the phone call. He pleaded with Art: "Should I punish her for that awful pain she had caused? Would it be okay to lure her into a false sense of security about our friendship and then do the "eye for an eye" (or is it more 'a blast for a blast'?) and drop her? After all, she probably trusts me to be the same old giving friend I had always been".

Art questioned whether Jackson could be that manipulative. "The current situation is sending your mind in wild directions, Jackson. You need to maintain your sanity. The pain associated with the past and the uncertainty, confusion, and lack of resolution in this messy situation of the present is causing plenty of heartache and anxiety, but you cannot become the manipulative bastard you have never been before."

For two weeks, he had not written a line in the play, spending his day with minutiae, watching TV and wondering about Sylvia. When he finally reverted to the play-writing, it was a struggle—he was impotent and weak.

On a casual walk around the nearby park, where the leaves were turning yellow and falling off the sugar maples, he met Roger, an old, but not very close, friend. Nonetheless, Jackson opened up and told him about what afflicted him.

"There is little to nothing that is exhilarating, uplifting, or even minimally acceptable regarding my general condition. I wonder how I will get out of the morass. Other than the play I am trying to write, is there anything else that could trigger a change in my life?"

The puzzled look on Roger's face revealed that Jackson had gone too far, talking in that fashion to a distant acquaintance. He stopped abruptly, excused himself with a handshake, and walked away.

Back in his own flat he reflected on what just happened. He feared he was gradually going mad. Self-doubt assaulted him again. He called Art and told him about the bizarre encounter with Roger. "My return to a depressive state is framed by a grim understanding of the confines in my existence," he confides. "I am old and that puts limitations on what I can do! When you reach a certain advanced age, the options narrow and the opportunities to turn a new page become much more limited. The chances of suddenly making your life less miserable become smaller, particularly when work and love have just fallen out. Yes, if the play would turn out to be a great success, I would feel that life still is meaningful, but right now, I fear, I am clinging to an improbable outcome. On the other hand, what other path is available to me?"

Art patiently listened to Jackson's diatribe and tried to encourage him to write. "You have not written much lately, you say. You must keep on going. Therein lies a path to recovery."

Loneliness affected him terribly. It was the most difficult aspect of his depressive state. From time to time, he hoped that Fortuna, lady luck as his mother would call it, would smile on him again. After all, that was exactly what happened when he met Sylvia.

Could he press his luck? Go down Portobello Road on a Saturday afternoon when the crowds pour into that street to look for bargains, and, totally by accident, bump into a new Sylvia? He could, theoretically that is, charm her, cook dinner for her, eventually kiss her neck, jump in bed and caress a beautiful pair of breasts, just like it had happened with Sylvia. But he immediately dismissed the option. Be realistic, he mused. I am too down and unmotivated to even try and bump into anyone—by accident or not. And even if I would, I could not imagine seizing the opportunity to best effect.

Is it possible that a friend would come to his rescue? He had a few close friends to whom he has confided about the breakup; in part, he did so because soon after Sylvia appeared on the scene, he had boasted to them about how wonderful life was; he felt the need to also share with them her disappearance. He did not need their pity, but they probably cared enough to want to know. In fact, a couple of them had indicated that they knew of women who may interest him. He rejected these offers.

He called Art once more and asked if he would care to join him in one of their customary walks in the park. The wind was blowing lightly and the trees were advertising the coming of winter with their barren branches. Jackson told Art how fed up he was with his life. Art stroked his beard pensively as he listened, his pale blue eyes seem to be smiling with empathy. Art tried to put matters into context and urged him to take control:

"What do you do when you walk down the street? Do you look at the changing color of the trees, do you look around to observe the people passing by, or do you focus on your path, concentrating on the pavement to make sure you do not trip over a misaligned cobblestone, a protruding tree root? There are three types of people in this world, and you can distinguish between them by looking at how they walk. The dreamer will be looking at the trees. He does not care about the humans passing him by, and he does not want to concentrate on the path because it is too boring. The opportunist will look around to spot a friendly person in the moving crowd, and the cautious guy will always focus on preventing the fall." Jackson confessed he was a dreamer, paying more attention to treetops and birds than other people, and occasionally stumbling because he ignored a bump in the road.

"That is your problem—how can you find a person to live the rest of your life with when you are looking at the wrong part of your surroundings?"

"Art, your attempt to get me to seek out other women is well intended. But I am not going to go to Portobello Road, to a bar or coffee shop. I fear that the most likely, poor outcome, would only exacerbate my misery. No. At this stage, no Sylvia replacement seems likely or even desirable. Even if I meet the most wonderful person walking the face of this Earth, I will be too consumed by my sorrow and too depressed to cause some sort of positive reaction in a woman, any woman. So, it is, in fact, best to drop the female partner issue, or at least relegate any preoccupation with the theme to the realm of fiction, toying with ideas and linking them to the play. Yes, I will avoid the Hollywoodesque ending and have poor, sick Christina die in Ben's arms. He will be reading to her lines from a poem published in the *New Yorker* as she takes her last breath. The poem will be about eternal love and commitment. Softies will be leaving the theater and a few tears will roll down their rose-colored cheeks. It is a much better ending for sure. Any notion that the play must end on an uplifting note is just pure nonsense."

Momentarily, the resolve in Jackson's words made both friends produce a little smile as they said goodbye. Back in the flat, Jackson wrote a few pages, but eventually, exhaustion claimed the best of him. It had been a long and difficult day.

His memories tortured him, he bemoaned the inability to revive the better times with Sylvia—if the laughs were still there when they were together, the physical touch was totally missing. He missed her hands squeezing his as they listened to a violin concerto; he repeatedly played back scenes in which they showed wild sexual appetite for each other. His eyes filled up again while his heart pounded and his hands trembled with anxiety. He knew he would not sleep well no matter what, but Scotch would, at least, make him fall asleep. He poured from the half-empty bottle of Black Label (he rarely ever had whiskey before the crisis); soon he emptied the glass and closed his eyes.

On stage is one sofa and one armchair and a coffee table.

Christina (sweetly): "I hate you for telling me this! I hate you for knowing me so well! How is it that you can figure me out even when I disclose so little? Okay, I am unhappy with him, maybe I will be unhappy with all lovers after about two months; maybe I just get tired of them quickly. How soon before I will become an old maid and no one will want to look at me anymore?"

Ben (proudly): "The only reason I know you so well is because I never stopped fucking loving you, because I bothered to understand who you really are. And as to him, that bastard friend of yours, he seems to want to squelch the fire in you, and it will cause you to rebel sooner or later."

The writing had progressed at a decent pace. Four months after the initial plunge, he had managed to finish the first draft of the first act and was into the second act centering on the relationship after the breakup.

Early in the morning, before he went to the university, he would listen to a Brahms concerto and pound the keyboard. He felt that the play still exuded a stench of dullness that bothered him. But he could not figure out what he was missing, what it was lacking. He had yet to find the magic touch, the gimmick, the trick that could turn things around. If only he had an inspirational moment! All the same, it was the only thing that gave him hope and he kept going, continued to write, hoping that it will somehow come together at the end.

At least he was moving on with his project, quite unlike his daily routine at the university. His end date was six weeks ahead. He was drifting in a sea of indifference and apathy. From the moment he was asked to put up his name for early retirement, he had lost interest in students, colleagues, and everything else. He harbored deep-seated resentment for the way he was treated. He concluded that he had been betrayed, he was not appreciated enough. When students came over to ask him a question, while certain that they did not know what had befallen him, he looked at them with a sarcastic, bemused look, as if to say, "What on Earth are you coming to me with that for? Don't you know that I have been labeled a washout? Don't you know that I am considered passé?" For as long as he could remember, he had striven for excellence. He wanted to be recognized as the one teacher whose classes made the time spent at university worthwhile. He wanted to be recognized as the scholar whose research shed new light on fundamental questions about the societies of yesteryear and guides for what was going on today. None of this mattered anymore—it had vanished into nothingness overnight.

Thoughts about putting an end to the "neither here nor there" relationship with Sylvia had become more frequent lately. As he became more convinced that hanging around was futile and a finite breakup could only ameliorate his state of mind. He had seen her regularly once or twice a week (her decision), usually at their favorite bar. During the get-togethers, he tried to act normal, caring, interested, and attentive, but increasingly he was having a hard time putting up the façade of the concerned and attentive friend while detecting zero improvement in her feelings towards him. She, at one point, told him: "Don't hope I will kiss you or go to bed with you." He had dismissed it as just talk. Now, he got increasingly convinced that she meant it. He continued to crave holding her, caressing her backside, as he restlessly turned from one side to the other in bed—alone. It was tough to follow that with a sympathetic "I am your friend, no matter what" proclamations. He wondered if Sylvia noticed his opaque, somber, drab appearance and whether she was reliving, having flashbacks of the more animated man he used to be. He was unsure how successful he could be in pretending that he was all fine, that he had overcome the pains of their breakup and moved beyond it. But, in any case, he did not even want to make the effort to appear someone he no longer was.

On a rainy Monday, he decided that he had the necessary strength to pull the plug on the relationship, and he became more determined to do so with every step he took towards the meeting point. To make the split last, he decided, he has to say things forcefully even if they are far from being totally honest. He had to tell her that he was totally frustrated with their relationship, that he was embarrassed to be perceived as an old bastard sitting at the café with a much younger beautiful woman, that passers-by ogling them may consider him a salivating old fool. He did not want that anymore. He had to tell her that he had little in common with a woman whose life revolved around alcohol and clubbing, that he easily got ill listening to all the fondling-on-the-dance-floor stories. He was going to be totally honest with her and state that their intellectual conversations were inane. He would say that on purpose to hurt her because she enjoyed them so much, she was so keen on them. He would say they were rather banal and boring to him. She probably was going to look shocked and sad; he may even relish the moment. Yes, it would be over, but at least this once he was going to be the one using the sledgehammer.

Of course, that persistent nagging emotional load that had been hanging over him throughout their relationship, the yearning for her at all hours, would not disappear with the breakup, but somehow, he was just going to have to get over that. The certainty of what he was about to do and say made him feel strangely liberated, stronger. He was taking control over his life. As he exited the subway station he said to himself, "I think I finally got the strength to speak my mind! Thank you, Amy, my dear daughter, for that phone call last night!"

He had experienced a strange but also wonderfully uplifting moment the previous evening. Amy was sobbing because her heart had been broken by a boyfriend of two years; she said she was in need for some good counsel and only he could provide that to her. He was really surprised when he heard that. His first inclination was to tell her that he too was in bad shape, but he could not inject his own misery into this call for help; he just had to be there for her. He tried his best to remain calm and to listen attentively, to give some good counsel. Apparently, he did well enough, or at least Amy told him that she was calmer now and that she would follow his advice.

Lately, he had surmised that he was no longer significant to anyone; suddenly, he had been reminded that he still had a role to play. It was not that he fooled himself about his importance, or that this would massively change his view on life at its current decaying stage, but he was emboldened by the mere fact that he was needed. At the worst moments of his recent sullenness he had wondered if there could be anything, or anyone, that could trigger a return to the more animated person of yesteryear, or whether his fate was to gradually, hopelessly, inexorably decline into an old morose character, or worst yet, nothingness. Strangely, his children did not enter the possible permutations since they were so much more independent and distant these days. Other than showing some awareness and occasional gratitude for the financial help he consistently delivered, they seemed to have little interest in him.

In one relatively short phone call, with his sobbing daughter on the other end of the line, he gained a renewed sense of purpose. The mere fact that he could muster some clear thinking and show compassion for another person, brightened him. Instead of dwelling on his own persona, on the darkness around him, on the hopelessness of his own future trajectory, he had reverted to being the rational human being that had been such a source of attraction to his students, and yes, even to Sylvia in the early days of their relationship. This was, of course, before he had lost his mind in a whirl of emotion and fell into his constant, desperate attempts to bring back the past.

He sensed a flow of energy that he had not felt for months. He was invigorated by the rediscovery of his old qualities. He was nervous and unsure how long this burst would last. Could he rely on this renewed empowerment, or would he relinquish the logical stronghold for the easier road, the crutch of alcohol and sadness, of defeatist thinking? Right now, though, he could leverage the momentary lift and greater confidence and do what needed to be done, and undo what needed undoing.

As he took the last few steps to the café where Sylvia awaited him, he noticed his pace to be firmer and faster, less vacillating. She sat outside enjoying a rare sunny early-spring day, wearing the customary light pink blouse and tight jeans and looking as beautiful as ever.

"How is it going, Sylvia?" he clumsily used as a greeting. His voice did lack any emotion. He was eager to move on with his plan.

He stalled when he noticed that her eyes showed tremendous sadness. He suddenly was overwhelmed by the same old feelings of tenderness— overpowering feelings he could date back to the early days of their relationship. With one look she had disarmed him.

She told him about the troubles she was having with her current beau and the horrendous fight she had had with her father. He was stricken by feelings of sorrow and empathy, and all thoughts about his prepared speech vanished. He counseled her, comforted her about the troubles with her father, stretched out his arms to offer a hug because she seemingly needed it more than ever. She embraced him lightly, not the way a lover does. This soured him for a short moment, but, he continued being warm and friendly. Just as with his daughter, he was the one giving rather than receiving.

He recalled what his plan was for this meeting and he thought his expression may have shown it. He imagined his look was tough, his eyes getting smaller, no tenderness there. Indeed, she asked him what was wrong as she sensed that he was acting different. She has always had a knack for figuring out his moods.

Maybe it was the memories of his hand resting on her young, tight behind, or the doubts whether he could ever find anyone comparable to Sylvia, but the intended "cutting loose" never occurred. He shook his head as if he was waking up from a deep dreamy sleep and mumbled, "No, nothing." He mentioned the conversation with Amy as an excuse. Her light pink mouth was small and, when slightly open, exuded sensuality; it produced a halting, shy smile. That forced smile seemed to speak a thousand words of gratitude. He would never know whether it meant, "Thank you for being there for me," or "Thank you for not unleashing on me what you had planned to say when you came over here."

About a week later, while in the shower, Jackson felt an acute pain in his left arm. He was aware enough to call emergency services and he was rushed to the hospital. They confirmed that he had suffered a heart attack. He had had huge blockage in his main artery and a stent had been inserted. It nearly did him in, but he would be fine now.

Once the doctors stabilized him, he called his children and Sylvia. He told them he would be okay. He was asked to maintain a calmer routine at home —no more alcohol, but some sedative pills if he felt anxious and could not sleep.

He felt that he had escaped death. He had been gifted with life and had to be thankful. This also needed to be reflected in his lifestyle, his work and his personal affairs.

He applied himself to his writing, and over the next months he was able to write the second and third acts of the play. While searching for something that would make it unique, lightning struck, he had an idea. "Harris, my friend, you can do it! It just needs to provide the right ambience. You have composed beautiful music before and you can do it again! It will be unconventional; I am not sure if it is a first, but it will sure be unusual. It will make us, you and me, pathbreaking, innovating contributors to the arts. When I write the play, I am often listening to Beethoven, or Brahms, maybe some Rachmaninoff. And the reason is obvious: they all provide me with the emotional strength to write. Introducing the novelty of classical music accompanying the play in the background, soft but 'there' and in sync with the mood of the moment, will give it an additional, magnificent component. You know? Some Liszt- or Chopin-like, tender piano music for the softer moments and a fiery Rachmaninoff-like piece when it turns turbulent."

"It probably will be too expensive to have an orchestra performing during the play, so we could have a series of tapes that a technician would play. Not too loud so the actors can be heard, but noticeable and grabbing the attention of the audience. What do you think?"

"An opera without singing?! A concert played as background to a theatrical piece? It is an outrageous idea, but I like it. What occurs to me is that it should be a series of études, each reflecting the center theme of what is happening on stage. That would work much better than a symphonic composition which may end up overburdening a varied audience."

"The études idea is great, but we can't make it too monolithic, and it certainly should not be overly light. Let it be a masterpiece of yours."

They both smiled broadly as they embraced to celebrate the collaboration.

Harris had been teaching music at the university when they first met, and because both had classical music as a shared love, they quickly became good friends. "This is a man with a great deal of empathy who understands me," he had said of Harris as he introduced him to Sylvia about a year earlier.

Two years after they first met, Harris left the university in anger; he had been denied tenure. The strong sense of indignation was shared by both. How could they do that? The students loved him, area orchestras performed his compositions, and his teaching record seemed impeccable. The only problem he had was his overt antagonism to the chairman's crass manner in running the music department. It was striking how perceptions could deceive: Harris had a heavy, not particularly appealing physique, his large belly threatening to burst open the shirt buttons at any moment, but he also owned the kindest and most sensitive soul. Meanwhile the lanky chairman, dapper on the outside, was obtuse and self-centered, cutting corners wherever he could, and easily turning into a despot regarding all matters concerning his fiefdom. After the denial of tenure, a disgusted Harris left academia for good and became a lawyer. However, he never abandoned music and continued to compose. His works were occasionally performed by regional orchestras. Lately, his music had turned a bit more violent and loud, but surely, he could be convinced to soften it for some of the more tender moments in the play.

Yes, Jackson could have looked for some other, more recognizable name to compose the music for his play, but it would be much more meaningful to collaborate with a friend. This friendship had been a remarkable source of comfort over the last six months, ever since the heart attack. A few days after it occurred, the large, bearded face peeked into his hospital room; he was carrying his usual broad, friendly smile while his eyes said, "I am so sorry!"

In the following weeks, Harris visited him often and the friendship grew deeper. He patiently listened to the long story about forced early departure from the university and the trouble with Sylvia, and how his friend had become so disillusioned by all of it that he started smoking and drinking heavily so he could somehow get through the day and get some sleep at night. Harris showed concern when Jackson relayed how on a given day in late August, his chest pains, frequently visiting him lately, had become worse than any felt before. They both laughed about the fact that Sylvia was probably the cause for his heart attack, and yet Jackson felt the urge to call her as soon as he was out of surgery.

It was also Sylvia who called his friends to make sure they knew what had befallen him. Jackson had suggested that Harris and Art be contacted because they were closest to him and because he did not want Sylvia to be obligated to spend all her time at the hospital.

"I still wonder if she called me so that she would not need to care for you by herself," Harris maligned her. He had no qualms about disliking Sylvia and voicing his dislike.

Jackson admitted, "I know she almost always acts first and foremost out of self-interest. In my more malicious moments, I am willing to guess that this is the reason she decided to return to the United States—she did tell me she was overpowered by a strange sense of culpability ever since that alarming call in the morning; she said she had a hard time dealing with it."

"Ah yes, geographic distance! Such an expedient thing! You can claim a girlfriend in Togo and be gay, you can say you did not think to call because you were in the Patagonia, and, in her case, you can escape any responsibility by just removing yourself from the scene."

"All I know," Harris said, "her leaving London had to be good for you. She seemed to be exploiting you time and again, and you were a willing collaborator to your own detriment."

Jackson nodded and said that he often wondered if, strangely, the heart attack had acted like a cleanser. There were times he was almost sure that it finally eradicated the emotional turmoil surrounding Sylvia. On occasion, he wanted to believe that the heart attack had violently purged his strong feelings for her. He would say to himself that she was just trouble and if he wanted to survive, for his children's sake and so that he could complete the play, he had to forget about her, give up, and relinquish any hopes of reviving their relationship. That she moved overseas was, in fact, a stroke of good luck. The obsession with Sylvia and, as he recently called it, "his disease," had seemingly dissipated with the broken heart.

Once he left the hospital, he dedicated most of his time to finishing the play, feeling focused and strangely calm. They say that people become different after a serious heart attack. They are scared, panicky, and self-absorbed. He was rather the opposite in the sense that all the anxieties of the last months seemed to be of less significance. He just wanted to get done with the project, have it be a success, and whatever would follow, would follow.

Once he returned to the university, his students got wind of his imminent departure from campus, and several came to him to express their gratitude, to acknowledge that for them he was "a terrific addition to their student experience," a "living legend," one even said. Several showed youthful anger, and stated their disgust and lack of understanding for what the administrators were doing. While not too long ago he may have responded with more vehemence, virulently voicing his own frustration, he now just smiled and thanked them for their kind words. He had accepted his fate and was ready to move on.

He met Harris twice a week to discuss the musical components of the play. Harris seemed eager to make this a success. His engagement, his commitment to the project, was total. They were pleased by their progress and figured they would have it finished within the next two months. Then they would have to see if they could bring it to the public. Harris had some thoughts about this. A producer he knew indicated keen interest in the end-product. They felt good about where it all was going. "It probably will never play in the main theaters of London or Broadway, but it will get some attention," said Jackson. "I am okay with that" His friend nodded in agreement.

The strange calm, after so much turmoil got disrupted by a surprising evening phone call. It was Sylvia, who, after some small talk, pleasantries, an inquiry as to his state of his health, announced her intent to come for a visit:

"I love you and I want to see you. Can I at least come and stay with you for a few days ...?"

His heart missed a beat. His mind told him to suggest it would be better if she did not come, that he needed peace and that he could not afford to get hurt again. What came out of his mouth was different: Of course, he also loved her, and she was welcome to come anytime. As he hung up, he shook his head in total disbelief. What was it that he just heard? What did it mean? What was this woman up to? On the face of it, he thought, the tumultuous story of a couple of years was about to have a happy ending; however, he had an eerie feeling that this was not necessarily the case. Was she exaggerating when she said she loved him? She often said that her words do not always have the weight that usually gets ascribed to them. Was she coming for a few days to probe the terrain before coming back to London for good? This woman continued to be as enigmatic as ever, even while he claimed to know her, he often was utterly perplexed.

Three days later, the morning of her arrival, he went to Heathrow to pick her up; he intended to surprise her, to please her as he had done in the past. It was in his nature to be there earlier than necessary. The flight was landing at eleven and he was already there a good thirty minutes before the scheduled arrival. He paced up and down the dirty corridor and noticed a woman who may well have intrigued Ben, the Guatemala expert; she had dark skin, black hair, and striking green eyes. She seemed impatient and edgy, her eyes turning from her watch to the swinging doors that opened from time to time, to let confused and dazed passengers pour out into the London experience. He turned his back on the doors, hoping to get a better glimpse at her beautiful eyes. He followed that with a sympathetic smile that was meant to calm her down. He hoped the expression would not look overly forced and artificial. To his surprise, it seemed well received and enough to induce a conversation. He learned that her son was coming back from Colombia and that she had to rush back into town, make sure he was settled in before heading for her afternoon date at the bridge club. He acknowledged that he had played the game a long time ago as a student and this prompted her to suggest that he pick it up again. "It keeps the mind in good shape, and it is not a bad way to socialize." He was surprised to hear her say, "In fact, if you don't mind my directness, I would be happy to play with you at a club sometime soon."

Jackson saw a twinkle in those beautiful eyes and a glimmer of hope entered his life. She gave him her mobile number, and as he entered the last digit, he was jolted by the sound of a familiar voice. "Hey!"

That diminutive sound, that short greeting, had sent shivers down his spine so often before. Momentarily, it struck him once again.

Later that evening, Sylvia and Jackson had dinner at a restaurant they had often visited before, as if to rekindle past feelings. But it was not to be. The conversation was stilted and limited, their eyes reflected ambivalence, doubt, and fear. They silently walked back to his apartment and she quickly retreated to the guest room. Sitting in the living room, Jackson felt an odd feeling of relief; lucidity, clear mindedness struck him in almost the same way it had months before when he spoke to his daughter. He concluded that there was no worthwhile content in his relationship with Sylvia. His vanity and a wild imagination filled it with glory, but reality emptied it out and only a mixed bag of confusing memories remained.

As to Sylvia, he finally was capable of admitting that, for the most part, she had just exploited the relationship. By doing so, she also exploited him. He, as Harris, had noted, was a willing collaborator. As such he was being self-destructive, a masochist of sorts. He could not allow it to happen ever again.

And then it struck him. Here was the critical revelation that his play needed so badly—the one thing that Art had been hinting at all along. That element he sensed intuitively but could not, did not have the valor, to write about. His life was anything but a cliché and he needed to tell the world. The third act needed to be rewritten. He sat down at his computer and started writing. As he typed, he vowed he would look up Maggie (Magdalena was her original name, she had said) the following week.

YOU NEVER KNOW...

■

The scene in this house in Schaumburg, a Chicago suburb, on this wintery Sunday afternoon, was not atypical: a football game on TV, the Bears losing badly again, a few empty beer cans on the family room table, and this man, George Chambers, watching the last ten minutes of the game despondently.

His wife, Bridget, had handed him a magazine and told him, "You must read this, this is unbelievable!" George was puzzled, even somewhat annoyed by his wife's excitement. He did not read these "fancy" literary magazines she subscribed to. He thought they often published "pseudo-intellectual" short stories. This was sissy stuff for those who did not care about the real world, the world of business and money. But she had insisted, "You will be surprised by what you will find here; you better read this story."

The football game was almost over, and it was a bore. His team was getting slaughtered, so George turned the TV on mute and switched his half-drunk attention to the magazine. At the very least, he could score some brownie points with his wife. The relationship had turned crisis-prone, and coming across as more sensitive and touchy-feely, the way she often asked him to be, could be a good thing. Maybe he would get lucky and the story would have some sexy vignettes that would get his attention. He began reading out loud so as not to lose the story's thread:

Daniel Fruggis walked into La Bella Italia, asked for a table for one in the nonsmoking area, and waited for the young

76

waitress to figure out where best to seat him. He was a smoker but abhorred mixing food with smoke, the clash of smells of fresh spices and the stink of tobacco. He wondered why "civilized" Europeans were willing to mix the two with such equanimity; after all, most of them considered themselves, merely by being Europeans, the arbiters of good taste. The waitress offered him the choice between two tables, and he opted for the one near a young couple. He had caught a glimpse of the female, and she looked interesting enough to be "screened" while engaging in what had recently become for him the utterly boring affair of consuming food.

The restaurant, on a side street of well-known Mayfair was rather well visited considering the early hour. It seemed to be a popular place and Daniel chose it for that reason. He had to fly back to the US the next day, and he was not keen on getting food poisoning in a riskier hole-in-the-wall. More than half the tables were already occupied, and the waiters, young and for the most part foreign, dashed about with their trays of pizza, pasta, and drink.

His short trip had been reasonably successful given the tough economic times post 9/11, but then times are never too difficult when it comes to selling medical products. His customers had been glad to see him, and he even had gotten some new orders. The trip's expenses had been paid for and then some. He was going to relax and enjoy the end of this journey.

As he watched the young pair nearby, he was pleased not to have been seated in some dark corner of the restaurant. He had gotten that treatment too often in other European cities like Paris, Zurich, and Frankfurt. It always seemed to him that he was being ostracized for coming into a restaurant alone, and he resented this. The stigma of his loneliness was made apparent and a cruel reminder of a truncated love life; it accentuated the pain he bore during his waking hours. He wanted to carry his cross with some measure of dignity, but by being placed in "the corner" he was being denied even that. Only bad children are sent to the corner.

No sooner had Daniel chosen some items from the menu than the young pair began a conversation with him. It was the young woman who leaned towards him and stated rather than asked, "From the US as well?" Daniel nodded, half surprised and two-thirds apprehensive. "My name is Elizabeth," insisted the woman, trying to put her counterparty at ease, "and this is my fiancé, Trevor." It seemed to Daniel that she was quick to add this in an attempt to declare possession over another person's existence. They always do that, thought Daniel. Isn't it curious how a relationship based on feelings quickly evolves into a relationship of ownership? Daniel was philosophizing whether "my friend," "my fiancé" was language that turned feelings into possessions. Or were these mere reflections of a reality: relationships essentially being grounded in specific material interests, as Gary Becker, the Nobel-winning economist, would have asserted. He also wondered why the woman was showing such friendliness. Was this a ploy to tease some jealousy out of the lad? Hardly possible considering he was at least twenty years older than this couple. Daniel, feeling somewhat confused by this unrelenting effort to chat, acknowledged by way of a slight nod, and stated his own name.

It seemed that the young man could no longer sit by and stay silent, so he chose to provide some old-time WASP formality. "Trevor Bluff, nice to meet you, Daniel." "This is Elizabeth Bloch and we are here, in London, on a pre-engagement trip."

"Yes," she added, "we are getting engaged in six weeks."

Young and silly, Daniel thought to himself. Being older, he was likely to see things in a jaded vein anyway, but all this joviality and naïveté was getting on his nerves. His impatience, he realized, had something to do with the fact that his own life had turned sour on him, particularly his love life. He tried to maintain a measure of restraint and aloofness and was thankful when his salad came. He could busy himself with the leaves and tomatoes that would justify the silence. Still, he would carefully "spy" on the couple since they were irritating and intriguing at the same time. He was not sure whether the couple noticed his voyeurism, but he concluded that whether he was getting caught or not mattered little; ultimately, this was the prerogative of a lonesome stranger in a foreign place.

Elizabeth was bouncing her crossed leg; there was some background music playing, but to Daniel it seemed that the leg was syncopating to the pace of her inner nervousness rather than to the melody. Her pretty pink, sheer summer dress was intended to make her look more mature. Given the hour of the day and the place, it was clearly too elegant and too formal. Youngish women always want to look older, thought Daniel, fully ignoring that many men seek to do the same. She had white skin and plenty of freckles. Daniel recalled that he used to call such skin "chicken skin," for it resembled the unsightly scene of a plucked, still to be cooked chicken. Her hair was black, extremely black, which unfortunately also left clear signs of the existence of body hair on her arms and, more lightly, above her upper lip. Hair bothered Daniel. She is cursed, he said to himself, the world is too focused on looks. Still, Daniel himself was attracted to her. Why was that? She was slender and her arms exhibited signs of routine gym workouts with weights. Good that she exercises, thought Daniel; chicken-white skin tends to get flabby faster. Her breasts were small, and probably even smaller when she stood naked and without the benefit of padding. But the main attraction was her face, perfectly oval, with a nose that matched the perfection of her face, not too straight nor too large, and just simply pretty. Beyond that perfect shape, a person looking at Elizabeth would immediately notice that her eyebrows and lips were often working together conspiring to convey a clear message: "I am smart, clever, and have a sense of humor." To Daniel, ever the cynic, it appeared that the facial expressions were the result of some careful orchestration and abundant practice in front of the mirror. Such are the ways of affluent American youth, Daniel thought. They go to a good liberal arts college, spend tens of thousands of their parents' dollars so that they can sit in front of the mirror and practice looking "cool and sophisticated."

It occurred to Daniel that he was so intent on figuring out the young woman that he had barely paid any attention to the young man, when Trevor resumed the conversation. "Here on business?" he asked, trying to sound like a man of the world. While girls were learning to move their eyebrows and lips, the college training of boys prepared them to talk like businessmen, thought Daniel, who felt perturbed by the infringement on his thought space. He really was happier ruminating in the realms of his mind, figuring these two out on his own terms, rather than talking to them. The voyeuristic position was much more comfortable to him. However, he could not ignore Trevor's question.

"Yes, I sell medical equipment to European clients. I travel a lot." As he answered, Daniel was forced to focus on the young man's features: blond, with smallish blue eyes and a face that yet had to experience daily shaving. He looked just like so many young men he had taught many years earlier when he was an economics professor at Dartmouth. This youngster, like so many others, had the good looks of a mediocre Hollywood actor whose name he had forgotten. But the young man seemed soft and lacking traces of great character. A second glance produced the conclusion that the "pretty face" was imperfect, for the area between his nose and his eyebrows was unusually narrow. That added to the image of aloofness or even outright boredom. He wore a typical outfit: khaki pants, a blue shirt, and a blazer all purchased through a name brand catalogue. The outfit was also chosen by design: portraying the fiancé as an up-and-coming business success story. Daniel smiled to himself as he thought, so long as Daddy and connections help, he will reach VP at some Wall Street firm pretty fast; the rest of his career may be less obvious. Daniel noted that Trevor was seated with his legs well parted and hugging the outer limits of the chair, as if he were a cowboy riding a horse. In preparing him for success, the parents had not been able to inculcate on their son proper table manners, thought Daniel, and yet he was annoyed with himself for being so harsh in his criticism. Trevor, after all, was no different from many of his peers.

Elizabeth provided another interruption in Daniel's appraisal of the two, as she cheerfully commented, "Traveling is fun and exciting. You get to see interesting places and meet interesting people," And then she blurted, "Even people you do not want to meet or talk to," and as she said that, her eyebrows and lips

*produced that "I know more than you think" look that Daniel
had noticed earlier when she spoke to her boyfriend.*

*Daniel felt trapped—trapped in a conversation with people
that he was not sure he wanted to talk to, but whom he would
love to examine with a critical eye from some safe distance.
Observing people and making up stories allowed him to be
critical of society without engaging it. Here he was forced to
engage, and this alone was cause for resentment.*

"I just don't get it," George Chambers yelled across the room as he
faced the kitchen. "What am I supposed to be looking for? So, this guy
meets this young chick and her boyfriend at a London restaurant; the
author obviously would like to go to bed with the girl but can't. And you
get excited about this? Maybe you have not enjoyed our sex lately … Is
that it? Are you insinuating again?"

Bridget turned angrily at him. "No, that's not it. Well, maybe, maybe
that too … But in any case, it is not about that. Perhaps you, this once,
should show some patience and read on …" She approached the sofa,
leaned over, and asked, "Where are you anyway?" George pointed to the
page and Bridget erupted in the kind of accusative, wordy cascade she
would use when she got excited. "Well, if you are here, you should have
gotten it already … You just are not imaginative enough, George. Don't
you see? This story is about us."

George looked at her as if he did not understand a thing she said. The
tone of his voice louder now, he said "Us? Where? What are you talking
about?" While replying to her, he thought: "Here we go again! I am put
on the defensive; again!" This is usually what he would do when
confronted by his wife. He knew how to handle co-workers and bosses,
but this was different. With Bridget, he was gripped by powerlessness,
the sensation that control was being snatched away each second, a great
feeling of frustration that escalated with every twist and turn. "Stop
making that all-knowing face, Bridget," he said, and as soon as he
uttered the words, he realized what had caused her to be so excited about
this story: "Holy shit! That is the expression this guy is talking about.
Maybe it is about us. Holy Toledo! But that cannot be, we did not sit at a
restaurant with anyone like this story tells." Yet, the description of a
cowboy's straddling his chair at the restaurant was also the way he would
sit. He was truly confused and upset. "Maybe I will read on after all, but
let's not jump to conclusions, okay?" He felt that he had regained a
smidgeon of control by offering these manly, corporate-sounding words

of calm; they may not help him solve the puzzle, but at the very least they would give him back the upper hand.

There were some reasons to continue talking to the young couple, Daniel thought to himself. One reason was that they did not have any tattoos on any visible part of their bodies, and they were unlikely to have pierced breasts or penises, since their lips, tongues, and eyebrows seemed to be devoid of these new symbols of decay in Western civilization. Their hair did not get fixed up to resemble the head of a crane or some other weird bird, and it even was lacking the sticky substance that was being used these days to make it look adorably messy or, in Daniel's eyes, just plain idiotic.

Another reason was that considering the alternatives, it would be better to talk to them than to stare semi-consciously at the television in his room. He had already spent the past two hours doing that, after his last meeting was sealed with a "business completed" handshake and the appropriate paperwork. Loneliness haunted Daniel everywhere and all the time. Life was almost unbearable these last few years, going through the chores of mundane living without being loved and without being able to love.

Yet, at the same time, he surely wasn't going to engage in congenial platitudes. These "kids" were going to benefit from his wisdom. After all, at forty-one he had experienced the ups and downs of life, the laughter of happiness and the sorrow of unreciprocated love. So Daniel decided to plot a fanciful strategy; he would engage the two, charm them, and then educate them about love and marriage in the new era. He would prepare them for real life in the twenty-first century. He would enlighten them about the viciousness of sex under the new rules of sex equality. If they still wanted to go ahead with marriage, maybe they would also be prepared for the vicissitudes of their undertaking.

With this in mind, Daniel set out to ask some factual questions that were going to set the ground. "When are you two getting married?" he asked.

"The engagement is in six weeks; the wedding is next spring, but we have not set the date yet," they responded in almost perfect unison as if this had been rehearsed and performed at least a hundred times. The humor of the situation, different though it may have been for the two generations, caused everyone to laugh. All three faces smiled because

laughter had broken the ice and brought them closer together. Maybe he was too eager to impose his world-rage on the couple. Maybe his acerbic nature had made him unable to deal with some young, naïve, but inoffensive people. Maybe he was searching for individuals who tried to provide real meaning to their own lives on a continuous, constant basis, just like he sought to provide content to his own self—in extremis. Life just was not going to give him that unrealistic opportunity to meet like-minded people. But as he mellowed in his criticism of them, he was overpowered by the melancholy of his own self-destructive search for perfection, the sullen depth of eternity sought but not found.

His mind raced through dense realms of epistemological thinking that had caused him to take a leave of absence from his new acquaintances. He apologized abruptly and wondered as to how to continue the dialogue. "Will it be a big wedding?" He tried to descend to their level of excitement. At the very least this would open the floodgates of unwanted detail and allow him to ruminate in his own subconscious. Indeed, so it was, for over the next few minutes, he heard, mainly from Elizabeth, about family and friends, best man and flower girls, pink (of course) dresses and purple flowers, a rabbi, a priest, a quartet first and a band later, Connecticut and the need for limousines carrying guests from LaGuardia and JFK.

How closely this resembled the satirical embroidery of the threads wandering through Daniel's mind. Critical thinking had once been a routine process for him. The salesman had once languished in the halls of Northwestern University; it represented to him the Temple of Wisdom and he was prepared to prostrate to it all his life. There he had seen thought as close to perfect, imagination as wonderful as the horizon, and criticism in its purest crystal form. It had taught him to think, to think critically, and this endowment was to be a burden for life. It made light of the mundane and despised the search for material pleasure that did not involve at the very least some authentic human feelings. It was perturbed by the chitchat of banal conversations about the weather, the shape of dresses, or sports statistics. It sought constantly the heights of the give-and-take about meaning and civilization. It sought to find Bellow's "Eternal Men."

George got up to relieve himself, and on the way back stopped near the kitchen where Bridget was still working on dinner. "Aside from the physical attributes that resemble us, there is nothing here that points to us being the couple in the story," quipped George. "Why, no one ever talked to us about our wedding while we were in London."

"But we did eat at that restaurant," responded Bridget, "and you do sit like a cowboy." She had the power of bringing painful satire to the fore; she knew how to annoy him. "Anyway, read on, because it might get interesting."

"This is a bunch of hogwash," complained George. "Who cares about this Frog's 'epistemo ... whatever' thoughts?" He knew the word "epistemology," but he was relishing the opportunity to deride his wife's more intellectual tastes. "You ought to quit subscribing to these fancy magazines; we could use the money to have some fun," he added.

"Typical George, only cares about stock quotes, football, and some fun ... Where is the George I knew in college? At least you pretended to be interested in the finer things of life."

"At least then the sex was good and frequent," responded George while thinking that the conversation had taken its typical, recurring, snowballing cycle of complaints. He did not want it to go any further, at least, not this one time. "Okay, I will read on, but this Fruggis better stop with this consciousness stuff ..."

Daniel had finished his salad and he could no longer pretend to be absorbed by the greens. Either he quit engaging the young couple which triggered such an outburst of melancholy, or he would have to resume the conversation with its falsehood of pleasantries. They were not ready for his philosophical ruminations, not at their age and not at this stage in their life experiences. He decided, however, to be more aggressive in his questions: "How long have you known each other?" The question was simple and factual; however, underneath it was the less benign implication that these two were not ready to make the leap. Marriage had lost its sanctity in the previous century, and psychologists and friends were advising whoever wanted to listen that if you are unhappy you might as well get divorced. So divorce rates were vying for equal rights with marriage rates. Yet, Daniel knew that it was never that simple. Divorce was unmitigated pain, nights of interrupted sleep culminating in red-eyed mornings surrounded by the heavy crust of dried tears.

They had known each other for three years ("college sweethearts," she actually used the phrase), and it was love at first sight. During the last year they had lived together off campus and this had caused parental turmoil on her side, perhaps less because of the implied sexual graduation of their daughter than because of the fear that this meant a break from the nest, coupled with issues of ethnicity and religion. "The intermarriage of Jewish daughters could be a good dissertation topic for a graduating psychologist," said Elizabeth, showing some surprising depth. They were planning on living in Manhattan; he had gotten a job as an investment banker ("bingo" Daniel thought to himself), and she was going to work for a publishing house that was trying to start a new department devoted to books on tape. Technology had made it possible for people to become even lazier than before, even if it is at the cost of reflection.

Daniel was about to get daring and poignant: "Have you had other serious relationships before?" The young couple looked at each other in astonishment. How dare he ask? What nerve? There was silence, and then the server showed up to Daniel's table with a dish of pasta. He muttered a short "Excuse me" and pointed at the plate, as if saying, "Let me eat, you do not need to respond."

Maybe that's the reason she wanted me to read this, George thought. What if we would have known other people before getting married? This guy Daniel had it right. He and Bridget got married too young and they got bored with each other too fast. George felt like he was trapped: if he went out with the guys, or screwed his co-worker, Bridget would be all over him and threaten divorce. If he tried to be a good boy, his frustrations would cause him to boil over at least twice a week. There was now a one-year-old boy in the house, things were not that simple anymore. His parents had taught him that there was nothing more important than accepting full responsibility as a parent. If he crossed them, his father would no longer support his career aspirations on the Street. The whole thing was a mess. He almost wished that Daniel of the story had persuaded him not to marry his wife. How foolish that he never met that guy. Things were getting mixed up in his mind. George grabbed another beer and returned to the story.

With his main dish almost finished, Daniel turned back to the pair. "Let me tell you a couple of stories. I know this fifty-four-year-old woman, just an acquaintance. She woke up one day, looked at her husband, the 'slob' as she calls him these days, and decided she had had enough with her current life. Within the span of an hour, just one hour, she found a flat in the city and announced to the poor guy she was going to live her own life away from him. Not divorce, not yet anyway, but independence. The poor man was in a state of shock; weeks later he told

85

her that whenever she wanted to come back to him, she could do so. She's still on her own, and he is still waiting, in limbo.

I also got to hear a story from another woman who is sixty-two. Her husband informed her some time ago that he would like to make new connections, have new relationships, experience new adventures. They were married for over thirty years, could not have children, but now he wanted to explore. Nice to meet you, Mr. Livingston! It's a new world out there. If you think that marriage is about embarking in a joint venture as full partners who discuss and plan the future, be prepared to be surprised. It does not work like that anymore. On the contrary, marriage seems to be viewed as an oppressive institution that men and women want to overturn—get rid of these shackles of expected behavior and set norms."

Daniel lashed out: "How are you two planning to deal with this stuff? When you feel the nausea of loneliness conspired by treachery, and you resist putting an end to it all just because it may impose an unbearable burden on your children, will you be strong enough?"

The two youngsters were clearly agitated, but they were mum. The agitation could only be seen in their perturbed looks. They were visibly shaken. This man was saying some nasty things, but it almost sounded like he was doing it out of concern rather than scorn or sadistic pleasure.

Bridget was looking at George from the distance of the kitchen. She was nearly finished preparing dinner. The previous exchange with her husband left her troubled, and while she tried to calm down, she wondered where her marriage was going. Her current situation bothered her; she felt like she and her husband had truly parted ways, and it created for her an unacceptable state of affairs which needed to be resolved. He still was handsome enough, but he had turned into a bore. Man world (his drinking, football, abusive behavior) and woman world (her search for refinement) had gone their separate courses and while doing so had created an ever-growing schism between them. Just as it was the case with so many of their friends, the gender gap had developed into a divorce monster. She resented the situation; she had hoped that their story would end up being a different one.

When they were still dating, he had been willing to go to galleries and the theater. They had discussed matters of the heart when they sat at the campus pub or the nearby pizzeria. It was not just sports and business and stocks at that time. She wondered whether her fate was to be the same as her mother's, who, disenchanted with the mediocrity of marriage, had chosen to turn her back on sex first, and on the marriage later. Even if her parents stayed married, it was in name only for divorce was too expensive. In fact, sex had already become a lot less intense and even more infrequent for Bridget and her husband. The child, exhaustion, and her new dedication to work had taken their toll. She knew that George was complaining about her preferences, about becoming much more interested in work than anything else, but she refused to see a fault in that. It was frustrating that she was not being recognized at work, the salary stayed about the same, and there was no advancement of significance. But this was her way of finding a new meaning in her life, and damn if she was going to be just another mom and housewife like some of her old college friends. She was the product of a generation that taught women to demand their fair share, that was their mission and their historic calling. They would climb the corporate barricades to bring down male domination at work and in every other domain as well.

She was so trapped in her thoughts that she barely heard him say, "Why are you staring at me as if I were some strange, never-seen-before monster? What have I done now?"

She did not want to explain herself. She could have told him what she was thinking, but that would be like reporting to the captain of this ship. And particularly at this moment, that was not the kind of concession she wanted to make. She sputtered, "No, nothing, never mind." Even though she understood that such an answer was nothing but a dismissive additional irritant, she was not able to produce more.

Daniel felt bad about lashing out. He turned to them with a smile of reconciliation: "I am so sorry. I shouldn't have said that. Let me make it up to you and invite you two for a drink. I have heard about this nice bar two blocks away. It is not a pub with drunken Englishmen slobbering over warm beer, it's a cool place—modern, slick furniture, a mixed crowd, the music is not too loud ..." The young pair looked at each other, confused, bewildered, wanting to put an end to this encounter on one hand, but being attracted by the blunt and "deeper" conversation offered by this semi-stranger on the other. Daniel decided it was best to wash his hands and allow them to decide on their own.

When he came back, they had ordered dessert and said nothing. It seemed like they wanted to buy time. He also ordered a scoop of ice cream to alleviate the aftertaste of his pasta. He decided to turn down the voltage on his new relationship with a joke: "A man gets on a bus, he looks awful: dirty, drunk, smelling terrible. Without much ado, he sits down next to a priest, and after sipping on the last of his vodka bottle, says: 'Tell me Father, why do people get arthritis of the joints?' The man of the cloth, realizing his opportunity to chastise, responds, 'Well, I suppose it is a result of living a life of drunkenness, of womanizing, an unhealthy, dirty existence.' The drunk returns to his empty bottle and the priest feels bad about his words, so he asks the drunk, 'How long have you been suffering from arthritis? To which the drunk says with a smile, 'Me? I don't have it, but I read the Pope does.'" And as they burst into a healthy laugh, he added, "Maybe I have been like that priest." This joke broke the ice, and the youngsters nodded to each other and accepted the offer to go to the bar after paying their bill.

Bridget had finished her chores in the kitchen and moved over to the den. The baby was sleeping and her husband was reading the story with greater interest than before. She was puzzled that he could show the sensitive side that had been so lacking recently, and it endeared him in her eyes. She moved behind the couch and leaned over. She started by caressing his neck, and then she stretched out her hands and fingers, those pale long fingers with beautifully manicured nails, and she slid her hands down his torso, her breasts purposely touching the back of his head. Sex had become less frequent and less innovative. She attributed this to his state of mind. He had become obsessed with advancement in his firm and the more he wanted to move up the ladder, the more difficult it seemed for him. She knew that he was turning melancholic. They had a terrible fight a few nights back over this. She had suggested to him that he was depressed and he reacted poorly to this. He argued that he was not depressed, that he had kept his sense of humor, and that she was building a case against him and creating insecurities in him in order to get her wishes. She responded that all she wanted was for them to be together more. She wanted him to spend less time watching sports, drinking, and pursuing those abhorrent late-night outings with his friends. The fight had become a shouting match culminating in George picking up a piece of crystal, that was a wedding gift, and smashing it to pieces. Bridget turned to her bedroom and wept for a long time. George had fallen asleep in the den in front of the TV watching some cheap sex movie, and stayed there after he woke up and the movie had been long over. They chose to ignore the incident the following morning, but it stayed with them, in their personal memories, a remembrance of breakdown that refused to descend to the mental chambers of ultimate oblivion.

She put her arms on George's strong chest, one on each side of his head, fingers extended, and gradually dragged them down his chest, over his abdomen, and beyond. She was trying to lure him into passion, and she knew how he always reacted to her hands, to her touch, to this type of provocation.

George had had too much to drink and was frustrated by his inability to react to the tender moment. He jumped up and forcefully separated himself from her hands. "What are you doing Bridget," he yelled. "Why are you making me feel impotent?" "You know what happens when I have had too many beers." He took the magazine with the story and threw it at her. "I am fed up with all of this! Your silly magazine, this story, your attempts to make me look bad any and every way!"

The alcohol, the story he was reading, the last couple of years of irritation, all converged into this moment of brutality. He had not done this with premeditation, but all the same, it was not what she wanted or needed. She ran to the kitchen, put some food on her plate and ran to the bedroom sobbing. She picked up the phone and called her Mom. "I would like to come over for a few days with the baby. Will you be in Evanston?"

In the meantime, George sat on the sofa, stupefied at his behavior of the last fifteen minutes. What had caused him to be so ornery, so violent? This behavior was almost foreign to him. He nearly had hit her with his fist. Thank goodness, he stopped himself. How easily we can become estranged from our own selves, he mused. He grabbed a plate and ate dinner in the den. He decided he would not go back to the bedroom that night. He was afraid of the consequences of what just happened. He would sleep on the couch.

"The point I was trying to make earlier," said Daniel to the youngsters, "is that marriage should be a constant dialogue. If a relationship between two human beings is like a dance, then dialogue is essential for those who do not want to trip over each other. If the conversation is solely an exchange of statements, and that is normally the case these days, the marriage will eventually turn sour. When one side produces the typical: 'I think that the world is blah, blah, blah and my position is this, and your position is that' you are already on your way to the divorce courts. You have to converse, but you also need to constantly adjust so as to produce a match between the expectations of your partner and those building, developing, and changing in your own mind. This is

all hard work, and yet being aware of it makes it easier to survive than stumbling on her when she is dancing the tango while you are trying to rock-and-roll."

The youngsters liked that. They rejoiced in the free advice and nodded as they heard these pearls of wisdom. And Daniel, ever the skeptic, knew right then that they were young, naïve, and impressionable. They agreed because this all sounded not only good but easy to achieve. They did not know that one arrives at these conclusions after painful soul-searching and after being defeated in the quest for marital bliss.

The waitress brought their respective bills and they headed out the door. Daniel pointed in the direction of the bar, and they walked the busy streets of Mayfair to their new rendezvous.

Trevor decided to get even. "Have you ever been married?" he asked.

"I am a statistic on both sides of the fence," answered Daniel. "Early this year the courts declared my now ex-wife and me joint custodians of our young children, a quick doubling of her yearly income-no small amount of which granted her a quick passport to wealth she had never had before- and the stamp of defeat on our marriage of eighteen years. When I talk to you, please bear in mind that it comes from experience," —genuine sadness could be detected in his voice—"and I am just glad that I still have my work and a few friends. Otherwise I would be calling myself Warren Schmidt. Have you seen that movie, "About Schmidt"? I think it was concocted by the Society for the Promotion of Middle-Aged Male Suicide."

The youngsters were getting uncomfortable again. They were on a pre-engagement fun trip and he was dampening their spirits with too many sad stories. Maybe going for a drink was a bad idea after all.

Daniel sensed that uneasiness in the air that comes when people are with each other but would prefer to be alone. He usually had excellent antennae to catch the unspoken feelings of those around him. He tried to cheer them up by telling them about his two kids ages sixteen (the boy) and fourteen (the girl), how proud he was of them, how well they had adjusted to divorce, how wonderful the encounters with them were. But as he gave the account of these positive aspects of his new life, he felt that the youngsters were ages and miles away from him. Middle age was not just a generational statistic, a biological fact, a definition of a particular state of mind. It also was the realm of sadness that drew a

90

wedge between itself and young adults whose experience, hopes, and outlook prevented any kind of true empathy or understanding. Daniel abruptly stopped, and they silently walked for a few minutes until they got to their new refuge from the street rush.

When George woke up it was about two in the morning. He still felt confused. The stupor of the alcohol, the story Bridget made him read, and which he had not finished yet, and that strange act of violence made him feel nauseous. He was not sure what to do. Should he head to the bedroom where his wife was, hopefully asleep? Or was it too risky— maybe she still was awake and irate by his unloving behavior. Maybe he should just stay on the couch and let time pass and hope that time heals the wounds of disconnection and discontent?

It is at that moment that he saw a note from Bridget:

"George. I am taking little Joe and moving to my Mom's house in Evanston. I need to think about what happened this afternoon. And you certainly need to do some thinking and make some changes if you want us in your life. I am not getting a divorce. Not yet anyway."

He was in shock. His wife was not in the bedroom, he checked to make sure, and her car was not in the garage either. This was, indeed, true. She had left him. He did not want this. He could possibly lose wife and his baby son. But how was he going to turn this around?

He could not go back to sleep. He went to the bathroom, took a shower to freshen up and become sober. He had to finish reading the story. Maybe there was a further message that she wanted to pass on when she handed him the magazine.

The fancy new drinking place had purple walls and dim neon lights, posh sofas, and lots of pillows. The staff was forced to wear very tight clothes; the women's uniform consisted of blouses that were cut to show the better part of their breasts, and very tight pants highlighting the shape of their posteriors when they walked. The message, further enhanced by some decorations around the place—female, bare-breasted statues, phallic floor lamps, and a large phallic structure in the middle of the room—was clear: sex sells better than anything else these days. Daniel noticed all this but kept his thoughts to himself. For the youngsters with him, it was part of a noncontroversial reality. They had not experienced the prudish fifties or the turbulence raised by the women of the seventies who were irate at the sexual exploitation around them. Instead of fighting it, women these days used sex to their own advantage—they were both sexually aggressive and used sex aggressively to achieve other goals. These were two sides of the same coin. Daniel took the armchair while the lovers took the sofa. The place had somehow brought smiles to all of them: she loved to see the newest places, he had discovered already that the waitresses were nice looking, and Daniel saw this as a great place for new voyeuristic expeditions on his next trip. Nearby was a group of friends in their late twenties. Two men wore T-shirts that announced in different ways that they were well-equipped to fulfill female sexual needs. One of the women wore a T-shirt that stated, "I am blonde, speak slowly." Daniel asked his counterparts what they thought of the T-shirts. Trevor spoke first: "They are kind of funky." His girlfriend took a different view: "They are stupid." Daniel rushed to agree. "Why would anyone walk around with a billboard around his torso anyway?" he began. "Labels on T-shirts and other clothes started sometime in the eighties, and these days it is hard to find any that are without them."

Daniel noticed the bitterness resurfacing in Trevor's mind and prepared himself for the expected confrontation. "Why are you so bitter, Daniel?" Trevor asked point-blank.

Daniel thought for a while before he responded: "I suppose I am more upset than others, but I think life is getting to be a sad affair for those who have some sensitivity left within them. The learned had said it in the past: it is not good for an individual to be alone, yet the yearning for companionship quickly makes room for the driving egotism of modern society. I suppose that there are many individuals who care little about true companionship, but for those who care for authentic relationships, this is not an easy world ..."

After this additional exercise in melancholy, the three sat and turned silent. There was hardly anything anyone could say. Daniel was uncomfortable with his own sadness and with imposing it on these youngsters who did not need this barrage of unpleasantness. Trevor was quite willing to have his eyes wander around the place and leave things as they were, and Elizabeth, though sorry for Daniel, was unable to find things to say that would cheer him up. She also was feeling uncomfortable by the conversation, by the place, by the wandering eyes of her fiancé.

Fruggis's flight was leaving at 10:00 a.m. and he still needed to deal with that awful mess known as Heathrow. He went to the breakfast room, grabbed a newspaper to glance at while eating. He had slept badly because of the unrest triggered by the conversation with the couple. The newspaper was one of those rags that had gained popularity in the UK. On the front page, there were pictures of a murder and the headline read: "Young tourist murders his girlfriend." At first, he gave this little attention, but then he caught the insert picture of a man being arrested by the police. It looked very much like Trevor and it stupefied him. He frantically searched for the full story in the inner pages of the rag. He found the piece after some fumbling around. His head pounded and his hands trembled. Apparently, Trevor had wrapped his handkerchief around his girlfriend's neck (the paper salaciously stipulated that it was to accentuate the pleasure of sex), he had pulled tighter and tighter, and finally he had choked her to death. As the police arrested him, he mumbled something about not wanting to kill her, just having a bit of fun. There were traces of cocaine in the blood tests of both the victim and the perpetrator. It had been the fifth case of this type of murder in the London metropolis that year. Daniel ran to the bathroom and threw up. Tears were rolling down his cheeks for most of the flight home as he was overwhelmed by guilt, memories of his divorce and what it had done to his children.

Upon finishing the story George felt his heart beating harder and faster than ever. The ending clearly demonstrated that it was not about them, and he was relieved by that. The sexual aggression that ended in murder, however, reminded him of his own violent act the night before.

He needed to call his wife as soon as the clock struck eight. He needed to tell her how sorry he was about what had happened, that he wanted to make it up to her. He would promise that he was going to be what she wanted him to be. That he would not drink more than two beers on a Sunday afternoon. Maybe they could go on a Sunday morning to the Art Institute or the park. He really wanted to be the man she wanted him to be. As he was jotting down all the promises he would make, he kept wondering if it was not too late. What if she would reject his words because she no longer trusted him? He puts his hands over his face and started sobbing inconsolably.

THE CLOWN'S DEATH

■

I f you would have been able to take a glimpse at Vladimir O's weekly schedule, you would have had a hard time finding a spare moment, an idle hole.

You also would have been amazed that every minute of his day was dedicated to the perfect balance between work and fun. You would have to conclude that he had made a conscious decision, a full commitment to a busy schedule, and that the decision took place at some critical moment in his life. Perhaps it had to do with not allowing his mind to wander to unwanted places. The fact that he killed himself last Thursday begs us to reach that conclusion.

They say that if you saw him in the classroom (I never had that chance), adored by his teenage students attending New M. High, you would take note: there is one happy man. If you observed him as he was playing basketball or battling it out at the bridge table or over a chessboard, you would say, "There is that clown, once again having the time of his life." I always saw him as a clown; in all his leisure activities, he made weird faces and strange noises, purposely exaggerating and eager to accentuate his monkey-like facial features. He had thick black hair and a black beard that surrounded a perfectly oval face. When he smiled broadly, he looked a bit like an ape, and when he made the sounds of a chimpanzee, you could not help but laugh with him. That is why I called him the Clown.

It is natural under the circumstances to recall the past with sadness. The tenor of conversations I had with him in private, or even in a group, were hardly all fun and laughter. If a joke was told, he typically was the listener, not the teller, and while he was entertained by some jokes, he rarely let out a loud and exaggerated laugh. His comedy was subtler, and he seemed mostly amused by the strange actions of people around him, be it the principal of the school where he taught, the bridge players who competed against him, his colleagues at work, or teammates on the court. He would recount strange occurrences with that broad smile that flashes through my memory. But because this clown did not wear large colorful ties and buttons, or utter boastful, attention-getting exclamations, you surmised that he was not acting the clown to earn accolades. He was just being a happy-go-lucky man, a man whose life was blessed by the calm enjoyment of what his world had to offer.

His suicide was a shock to all who knew him, and all of us are still stupefied—of all people, him? I think I am a good judge of character, and yet I would never have guessed that this happy man would pick up a revolver, place it against his temple, and fire one deadly shot.

Three days after his funeral, we gathered; foremost to try to understand why, but also to try to recover from the shock by being together, to understand what had happened, and to look into each other's eyes to find some comfort and support. It was a gathering of friends, and of course, Sylvia, his wife. It, perhaps, was odd that she was present, but I can speculate that she concluded it would have been even stranger if she was not there. Sylvia often paid attention to what people thought of her, perhaps overly so.

Only a week before, while having some inane conversation about "how time flies," he realized that he and Sylvia had been married for almost ten years. They met in New York at one of those strange cocktail parties organized by the local Mensa chapter. Both had the same instinctive reaction: to run away from each other. To her, he was odd looking and unsophisticated; to him, she was a typical Manhattan brat. Weeks later they accidentally met at the local bookstore as they both attempted to grab the same book off the shelf. This time sparks flew as Vladimir made some funny noises that provoked hearty laughter from her. At that time, she thought that this guy was cool as a cucumber making such weird, apelike noises in a public place that normally is quiet. She endeared herself to him because her laughter was frank and without inhibition. Together they looked for the store clerk, found one more copy of the book, and went to a nearby coffeehouse to find out if those positive instincts could lead to a stronger connection.

Six months later they went to city hall, got a piece of paper declaring them husband and wife, and spent the next two summer months hiking through New Zealand. Ten days ago, I was certain Vladimir loved Sylvia even if one could detect the signs of wear and tear that come with years of dealing with the same person.

There is probably no better way to honor a person than to dedicate a moment of one's life to sharing thoughts about him in a gathering of fellow friends. Marie, Sylvia's best friend and feeling a strong sense of empathy, invited ten people to her townhouse in the city. There were two sofas, a loveseat, and several chairs forming a circle of sorts. We picked a spot and tried to stay as serene as possible. Many voiced the same thought: "Sometimes you think you know someone but you are so far from truly knowing him." We spent time telling anecdotes that honored Vlad, while playing psychologists (none of us were) as we tried to figure out the "why." At certain moments, it seemed like we were gliding into the question of whether any of us would commit suicide and, if not, why not. Even under such grave circumstances, we seemed inclined to turn self-centered.

I was one of the last participants to enter Marie's house and waved hello at those I knew best. Shortly after I arrived, the hostess greeted us briefly and excused herself for not actively participating in the conversation. She stated that she was going to be busy preparing food and drink. In all honesty, she noted, she was too sad to say something coherent.

It is normal for people to seek to hear and tell the history of a dead man at a gathering such as this one, and so it was that we asked Boris to tell us about Vlad's early days in Moscow. There were hardly any surprises in his story. Still poignantly burdened by pain, he said the boy had been raised in a small apartment together with three brothers and one sister. Their mother was widowed when her husband, a lower-ranking officer in the Red Army, commanded a tank that was blown to pieces near Kabul. Because financial support from the government was meager, the mother had to work hard to support the family. She was used to it; she worked from the first days of her adult life and throughout the married years. That was normal in the USSR, but she complained all the same.

Before becoming a widow, she worked at an energy plant; after her husband's death, she switched and became part of the cleaning staff in a small hotel in the center of the city. That work allowed her to earn badly needed overtime money. Her long hours as a chambermaid precluded her from being at home much, and when she was home, she was exhausted. As a result, Vlad, being the oldest, had to devote much of his time to performing the functions of a housekeeper. He cooked for his siblings four times a week, sometimes snatching a morsel from the pan or the pot to try to allay his hunger. Still, he often went to bed hungry.

He was bright, and since school was a breeze for him, he was thankful that he had the extra time to take care of his obligations at home. He enjoyed sports, but such activities were limited to whatever he could do during gym class. He had no free time to play except on weekends when his mother was not at work. At age eleven, his mother asked him to get part-time work to help support the family and he worked as a packaging clerk at a small plant. He would play basketball in the schoolyard on the late afternoons of summer weekends to satisfy the teenage urge to move around. He had little time for friends or girlfriends. Boris asserted, "Vlad knew he did not have it easy, but he did not think of himself as unlucky. After all, he had no way to know that his young life was harsher than many others'."

After moving to America, in retrospect, Vlad could have felt sad about his childhood that deprived him of so much. But, he was much more stricken by the treatment he endured from his jealous siblings. Once he left the country, his brothers and sisters treated him as a stranger. When he went back to visit the family they refused to see him. Boris thought that they were jealous of Vlad because he was brighter than them and managed to extricate himself from the mediocre life in Russia through his excellence in math. "They punished him for this by turning their backs on him. All that Vlad did for them during their childhood was forgotten. At one point, they accused him of having stolen food from them," Boris added. "I think he kept his sorrow to himself, and the story only came out one night when the third bottle of Rioja brought Vlad to an unusual state of openness."

While Boris spoke, I recalled Vlad's tall, slim frame, his long arms, his big hands. When it was my turn to say something, I mentioned that at times I thought he looked like a large vulture ready to devour whatever his eyes saw in front of him and his long arms could fetch. I always admired his ability to stay trim despite his huge appetite and the quantities of food he inhaled—what a fantastic metabolism! I also recalled his grunts and grimaces, the little displays when surrounded by friends at a dinner table in his house. I added, "I will miss the guy a lot, even though I now think I hardly truly knew him. After all, if I had known him better, maybe I could have helped him out of his own crisis and his ultimate demise. Most people I sort of know and understand reasonably well. With him there was always a wall, a place that was reserved and private, as if a big DO NOT ENTER sign hung in front of it. I enjoyed Vlad's company tremendously; I had serious and funny conversations with him, but I could not invade his private space, and shame on me, ultimately, I did not try to break through and perhaps prevent what happened." The words were honest. I needed to apologize to all, especially to Vlad, but he was not there anymore. I felt confused and despondent, and I wanted everyone, especially Sylvia, to know how I felt.

By the end of the evening I concluded that Sylvia did have opportunities to know him in ways no one else in the room did. She was, after all, his wife. At some point, surely, that concealed space had to have been opened for her, and she got a chance to at least peek into his soul. But I am not sure she bothered to make much of that privilege. I always had the sense that she looked down on him even though he was the brighter of the two. Some of it had to do with money. She had met him when he was poor, but they lived comfortably a couple of years later because of her inheritance. Though he earned a decent living teaching and editing books, their standard of living was enhanced because of that inheritance. She was a big help to him in the early years of their marriage when her parents supported them financially. "He seemed a confused Russian immigrant," she had said in front of others while giving him an apologetic peck. Later in life, she also complained vividly to him that she had to tolerate his grunts (they were "no longer funny" to her), particularly when he uttered them in a large social gathering.

At this wake of sorts, she told us that she had become even more outspoken recently, letting him know that although she enjoyed his sexual prowess and affection and she admired his intellect greatly, he had to grow up as a person. My interpretation when I heard this was that she was confessing to looking down on him as this forlorn foreigner whom she saved from the tentacles of the city. Maybe he just got tired of it, she said, and sobbed. She spoke at length about him having been an immigrant and that led me to wonder if she had peeked into the secret chambers of his soul and hurriedly exited, dismissing the darkness there as the product of the foreign culture of his early upbringing.

"Perhaps I just was unable to understand well enough how his childhood affected him," she stated as she buried her face in her hands. Some of us looked a bit uncomfortable with Sylvia's honest disclosures. We shifted from one position to another in our seats. Maybe we just expected that she would give us reasons to shed a tear, rather than find her at fault.

After her long discourse, Sylvia said little more for the remainder of the evening. Sometimes she sat quietly and listened, sometimes it was like she was not there at all. Occasionally, a tear would roll down her face. She always looked kind of New York gray, but that evening her mourning accentuated that color. Her ashen face spoke quietly of pain.

It was intriguing to me that Sylvia showed more emotion when Boris talked than at any other moment that evening. I was wondering whether she had been crying about the sadness that had caused her husband to commit suicide or about her own loneliness in its aftermath. I always thought that she was a selfish person, but at this moment I was not sure. She did say that Vlad always wanted to have children, and it had saddened him that they could not conceive. It was good that she did not lay blame on him and his proximity to that nuclear disaster that had affected so may in the area where he got posted for military service. We all knew that Vlad thought that was the cause of his infertility. She reminded us with some eagerness that he had rejected the possibility of adoption, thinking that it was simply an unnatural situation he did not want to face.

We all were quiet for a while after that—the official story of Vladimir O. had been presented and we owed him this moment of silence. Marie gave an indication that it was over when she passed around a tray with canapés and a cart with alcoholic drinks and sodas. Boris mentioned that for Vlad, vodka reminded him of Russia and that is why he abhorred it. He often stated he would rather drink wine.

Peter had always been the jokester in the group and broke the waves of sadness filling the room by telling the following story: Vlad was having a heated discussion with another guy whose typical demeanor was to be argumentative and difficult. At one point, Vlad heard this person state in a confrontational tone: "As I see things, these are the facts and this is what matters." Vlad coolly responded to him, "In my view, you are cross-eyed." It was typical of Vlad, used to the rough-and-tumble streets of his childhood, not to buckle under pressure, not to concede an inch—not on the basketball court, or in any discussion about this or that. It was not that he was so intent on being right, on having the correct view of things. It was that for him losing meant letting circumstances force you to your knees, and his formative years taught him that surrender meant less food on the table, humiliation, maybe even a worse fate. Life was a war, and either you won or you lost.

Stella was Russian, as were many of Vlad's friends. She was a redhead who demonstrated the full-bloodedness of her character that evening. She started weeping at this point and spoke of him as a handsome, wonderful person whom she adored. To our shock, she then pointed at Sylvia and said, "He should have divorced you and married me."

When you don't know a person well, you also don't know about possible indiscretions, a flirtation, a night away from home, a moment of weakness turned into a one-night stand. Yet, I (and later I found out that others agreed with me) hardly thought it possible that Stella and Vlad had anything going except for what Stella may have imagined in her lonely late-night hours in bed. Even her adulation was a surprise until that outburst. Had she demonstrated her passion to Vlad, I doubt that he would have responded positively or acted on it. In all the occasions, together when Vlad could have seized on the opportunity to flirt or betray his wife, he stayed the solid husband. You know if a man is ready to jump off the married ship or not. He was not. So, if for a moment, we may have thought that there were clues in Stella's outburst to explain the suicide, a second, more sober thought told us that we were barking up the wrong tree.

Sylvia's response to this outburst was remarkable: she sat quietly, as if she were deaf, and a single large tear rolled down her cheek. She was tough all right, even stoic—*noblesse oblige* she seemed to be saying in her demeanor. The hostess approached Stella and quietly suggested she leave the house, and Stella did so muttering loudly enough for anyone to hear, "He should have married me ..." As soon as the door closed behind her, I simply stated that there are always people who turn an occasion into their own. I had the urge to express what others were thinking about Stella's uncouth behavior, and it seemed to have done the job because no

100

one mentioned her or the content of her outburst even after we left the house.

One of Vlad's best, non-Russian friends was Robert. They shared two passions: basketball and bridge. They had met at the neighborhood basketball court and eventually Vlad taught his friend to play the card game. They often played tournaments together. Robert tried to refocus the gathering away from the tumult created by the redhead. For him the explanation of why Vlad had committed suicide was simple: he was, despite all appearances to the contrary, a person with a deep sadness, a sadness that had been pounded into him by the harshness of his upbringing. His outward gestures and his fun-loving activities were for Robert a mask and an escape.

Robert confessed that he was saying these things with the benefit of hindsight. But now, knowing what he learned about Vlad's past, everything had become more obvious. Robert blamed us all (himself included) for not being able to extract the sadness out of Vlad. We, each one of us, would have proudly called ourselves Vlad's friends, but did we truly bother to know him? Did we sense his sadness? Did we bother to dedicate time and effort to the deeper friendship that might allow you to see the dark corners of the soul? Robert was convinced that we all would have rushed to Vlad's help had he asked for it. But Vlad was proud and he made extreme closeness difficult. The clown wore his mask, prevented proximity, and we, his crowd, were apparently all- too-happy to accept the state of affairs. "We are all too busy concentrating on our lives to open our eyes," he concluded.

Robert's hands shook as he blamed us all for Vlad's death. It was a difficult moment. We knew he was right, and we knew he was wrong. Yes, we took the impermeability into Vlad's heart at face value and did not try to force our way past it. We readily accepted that privacy is a cherished value and did not perceive the need to doubt its worth. Yet, can man in modern society just bumble around looking for lost, abandoned souls? Must we invest so much of our valuable time on Earth to comfort our friends? Those were the debating questions posed by Victor, Vlad's closest friend. When Vlad migrated out of Russia, he embarked on the venture with Victor. They had not been close in recent years, but back then they were jokingly referred to as "the pair." As Victor became a capitalist entrepreneur, he found less and less time for his friend.

Diminutive Linda sat on a low chair behind other participants. She spoke softly about abandonment. She had read recently in *Psychology Today* that certain people sense abandonment even if this is not a visible, physical situation available to the outside world (for instance, his friends— us—to see). They sense abandonment, and they fear it. Maybe Vlad had felt abandoned by his father's untimely death, maybe by his mother's long absences from home; surely, he felt some abandonment by his siblings who turned their backs on him. Somehow this little person with her soft voice and calm sadness portrayed and engendered greater wisdom, and by doing so managed to bring down the level of agitation that was building inside me, and, my hunch, in many others. Their faces looked tense before she spoke and slightly more at ease now. "When you described him as a private person who did not find it easy to open up to others, I remembered that article. What was the link? As I think about it, abandonment and this excessive privacy could well feed upon each other to accentuate a vicious cycle of ultimate loneliness. Maybe Vlad was afraid of being abandoned again, of suffering the pain of such solitude, and that's why he closed himself to others. Maybe that conscious effort to leave a large part of himself shielded created further feelings of abandonment." Linda tried to make it clear that these were just speculative muses. She had no reason to think that she had understood why Vlad committed suicide, nor was she implying that this entourage (which included his wife and best friends) had given him a sense of abandonment.

Hank was an odd figure in this group. He had spent many years as an academic in Latin America (Colombia, I think) and then decided that that life was not for him. He had become a devout Jew and spent endless hours studying the scriptures in a yeshiva thirty miles away from town. He was also the one who had spent the least amount of time with Vlad, but because of his fascination with chess, he had met Vlad and had become good friends with him despite the great differences between the two. "Vlad," he began his comments, "was an atheist." Not surprisingly he concurred with Linda, but his angle was idiosyncratic: "If we do not turn to God, we all feel abandoned."

As an agnostic, this irritated me. I thought that his words were self-serving and haughty. He had chosen to return to his God and chosen well for himself, but his attempt at generalization was reaching too far. My negative reaction stayed within me, and I said nothing. Relatively late in life, I had learned to look at things from many angles and contemplated the possibility that Hank's words were well meaning, that he wanted to come across as humanistic rather than have this be a proselytizing effort to turn us all into believers. Hank realized that he needed to explain that the world is complex and difficult; he stated: "We need to be able to rely on some outside force that helps us live our lives in a meaningful way; we need to gather strength from a deity who gives us explanations of why the world is the way it is; we need to develop inside ourselves the faith that allows us to understand and answer existential questions and prevent us from succumbing to an ultimate denial of existence."

Linda, trying to be helpful, chimed in: "In essence, are you saying that we need to surrender our intellectual meandering to religion to survive?" Hank nodded with some unease because it was not exactly what he meant, but it would do for the occasion.

Simon was a large person; he towered over most of us by at least one head and he was at least twenty pounds heavier than any of us. He also was a basketball player (with his height and bulk, obviously, a center) and that is how he came to know Vlad. Simon was a factory worker and his friendship with Vlad had opened the opportunity to occasionally belong to a different milieu than what he saw every day in his working-class neighborhood. He had always made it clear to Vlad that he was thankful for embracing him despite their obvious differences. Despite his outward fortitude, Simon was deeply shaken as he spoke of his betrayal of Vlad. Last year they had decided to join a team playing in the regional league, and at the last moment Simon backed out. Here he had been given friendship and an opportunity, but for reasons of his own (which he did not divulge) Simon told Vlad he would not play. When others at the gathering chimed in that such things happen, Simon's voice rose, "I betrayed him, just like probably many of us, in some fashion, betrayed him in the past."

This idea of basic, primordial betrayal was a powerful one. I assume that each of us did some quick inventory for a time when we had betrayed Vlad. I, for one, recalled my own instance of betrayal. From time to time we used to have coffee on Saturday mornings, and having agreed to do just that, I cancelled on Vlad at the last minute the Saturday morning before he left us. I was too lazy to get myself organized—was it a good enough reason? Had I thought about whether he would see that as a betrayal of friendship? Maybe he needed to talk and I was not there for him, maybe my casual acceptance of the appointment and subsequent cancellation signaled that our friendship was not important enough.

Helena was Boris's long-standing partner (though they never married). She had been listening to all of us but had not yet spoken. It fit her personality, for she was usually quiet. Some had mistaken that for stupidity. But I had learned to distance myself from calling her such many months back when she stated something in such a wonderful, sensitive way that I had thought highly of her ever since. She spoke then about the complexity of life experiences and the difficulty of understanding motivation. We were talking about a well-known but not very bright sports star who was running for political office. Strangely enough, she used the same angle to talk about Vlad: "At the end of the day, this perfectly 'normal' person, this 'fun-loving' individual, was also a complex person with great strengths and well-disguised weaknesses. Who are we to be able to enter all the intricacies of his personality? How can we possibly fathom what was going on in his head when he pointed the gun at himself? Maybe the cause was some chemical imbalance rather than 'betrayal' or 'abandonment,'" she said, her voice more matter-of-fact than excited. She clearly felt that while Vlad's demise was good cause for sadness, our efforts to understand it were an exercise in futility. She seemed to understand better than the rest of us that the ultimate picture that was emerging probably was some combination of a large myriad of factors and any single explanation just a contortion of the truth. The psychological, sociological, and physiological explanations would produce a cubist-like Picasso painting with its pieces out of place and the focus blurred.

Helena's words came out staccato and with a clear sound that made them sound metallic. It was as if our passionate discourse throughout the evening had met a modern and emotionless robot. But there was more to what she was saying than just rational, cold thinking: she was telling us that perhaps our lives are too complicated to understand by others. That we may as well replace the efforts to understand Vlad with a conscious effort to live our current lives with some clear purpose and enjoy the moment. My predilection was to reject such a negative perspective of what humanity, with the help of science, can achieve. But, I had a little sympathy for her philosophical stance.

Her comments were not meant to put an end to the evening, I am sure of that. But what else could we say after that? Besides, we were all emotionally drained. Suddenly I felt the urge to say something. Maybe they were a bit authoritative and pompous. Maybe they hit upon the only truth we can muster in this tragedy:

"I get the sense that we all are ready to get up and leave. We are having a difficult time figuring out the 'why' and we also know we will not be able to fully agree on any answer. But, we can do something positive right now. We can conclude that we all were enriched by Vlad being part of our life. We can honor him by pledging to contribute to a charity that seeks to help those with a propensity to commit suicide. I think there is a 'suicide prevention hotline' that perhaps would be a good recipient, or we can decide upon another worthy organization. But, most importantly, we can—in fact, I think we must—also make a commitment to be better listeners when we feel that someone aches to speak to us in confidence."

I saw a lot of positive nods by those around me; maybe some thought that it was just a good way to get out of there, and maybe some really felt that I had released the tremendous psychological pressure that had been building up. I am sure, for some this was just a good practical, positive outcome.

We used the usual courteous words to remove ourselves from the gathering, and while we walked down the stairs to the entrance of the building, some of us promised that we would make the effort to keep the friendship together despite Vlad's departure.

If Helena's words had one lasting effect on me, it was that she reminded me that in this world we all are attracted to the elixir of selfishness, and we have great ability to excuse it as utilitarian, rational behavior. Strangely I remembered Scarlett O'Hara's line: "After all, tomorrow is another day." It produced an ironic half-smile —thankfully it was hidden by the weak lighting of the staircase. Robert interrupted my ruminations: "I never knew how much sadness was in Vlad's inner person." I nodded but could not find anything further to add.

ANDREAS WÜRMLE

◼

With swollen, bloodshot eyes he looks in the mirror and angrily applies the index finger of each hand to a reddish pimple on his left cheek. The blemish tells the coming of yet one more ugly expression of age and decay. Andreas knows that there is no turning this process on its head, reversing it. Still, as he squeezes his fingers, he stubbornly wants to force the relentless biological course into reversal. Even though he knows he will only make it worse, he applies all the concentration he can muster to explode the boil. It has happened before— in fact, he has done this for years. He even remembers the admonition of his parents fifty-some years back: "Take your fingers off your face," and he remembers how he defiantly ignored their advice.

He is amazed that despite the liquor-induced stupor and the constant headaches, he still can recall childhood incidents. He speaks to himself; it is not a mumble, his words are loud enough to be heard by a random bystander: "I thought the whiskey would bring your brain cells into submission, Andreas, gradually and consistently, until there is no memory left. But if you can remember that far back, you must still have plenty of gray matter up there."

No one is there to listen. There hasn't been a soul there, in his hundred-meter abode, for years. If you could peek through his living room window, you would see him sitting in the same chair, day after day, watching TV, reading a newspaper, and dozing off frequently. What you never see is another human being come over to take the newspaper out of this man's hands, turning off the TV, making sure he would not wake up to the horrific news of a gruesome murder in some distant place, or of a plane full of people being shot down by some terrorist group. There was no daughter who would bring him, however infrequently, a piece of chocolate cake to sweeten the day, no son who would share his life adventures with him over a cup of coffee, not even a several-times-removed cousin who would invite him to take a walk.

Once in a blue moon you could see a bit of animation in him as he talks on the phone to the estranged daughter living across town. Is she okay? And how are her kids, his grandchildren?

Scotch, he believes, helps him disguise everything. His voice, he wants to believe, is not reflecting the sadness in his heart; his clouded mind is shielding him from the full impact and contemplation of his solitude.

Of course, the daughter on the other side of the call would be hardpressed not to notice the liquor-induced slur and conclude Father is drunk again, a state of mind she had gotten used to and accepted without much further thought.

Würmli goes about shaving his face and it hurts. With every touch of the blade, his face turns bloody and the cuts sting. He had gone to a skin doctor who told him that this rash may be a reaction to either some bad food or to excess alcohol. The shameless bastard said that with a wink. Of course, Würmli knows he smells of alcohol. He never was stupid, not even during these blurred days. He knows alcohol will bring him to his ultimate demise. He has been warned about the gradual erosion in his body, the eventual inability to control his needs, the mood swings (well, he already has a good inkling about those), and the mental breakdown (which has yet to reach its peak). In a moment of half-sobriety, he talked to himself: "Assuming I could quit, I would be sitting on this same sofa watching TV and feeling awfully sorry for myself—GIVE ME THAT BOTTLE!"

Würmli bangs his toe as he climbs into the bathtub, and he curses the tub for growing too tall on him and his back muscles for shrinking so much. Simple tasks are sometimes inordinately difficult on him. He takes a quick shower instead of a bath since he is pressed for time. He must immediately get dressed and get the *Tages Anzeiger*.

Maybe there is some news about the upcoming visit of the new Pope. He wants to see this new Pope when he comes to Zurich. It is a German Pope and there haven't been any German Popes for so long. Actually, he hates the Pope and he hates religions, all of them. They are all bloodsuckers and they give so little back. Even when they try to be supportive, it smells fake. Spending money on your church is a waste of each franc but the government makes you do it; the tax form requires you to declare your religious affiliation and a special tax goes to support those bastards in their religious shrines. Still, the coming of the Pope is causing waves in Zurich and he feels this urge to know all about it.

As he steps gingerly out of the bathtub, to avoid hurting himself again, he almost slips and that worries him. What would happen if he would fall and hurt his head, become unconscious and, lie there dead for days undiscovered, like a dog that did not deserve to be buried properly?

He exits the building and sees Dr. Karamanlis. He has been trying to make friends with this younger neighbor. In the past, he had accepted delivery of packages for him while the doctor was out—perhaps working at his office or who knows where. He later would bring the package to the young doctor looking for a word of thanks (which he would receive) and some human contact (which he would be denied). Würmli also had tried to establish more meaningful conversations with him. He even had suggested that they get together for dinner one time. Then, he learned from a neighbor, that this foreign doctor is actually not a physician but works for some public opinion research institute. Still, he muses to himself, one must give respect to doctors even if they cannot extricate you from your pain, even if they decline the invitation and the rejection hurts.

Karamanlis is not hostile, but he always gives the impression that he wants to flee. Würmli greets him and asks how he is doing. Karamanlis says he is okay and asks Würmli if he is well, but as he does so, he is already two steps ahead of him.

Würmli reaches out and grabs his coattails. "Why are you so angry with me?"

Karamanlis is surprised and annoyed, it shows in his voice. "If I am angry, it is with this darn building. I got stuck in the elevator for over fifty minutes last night. What a disgrace this building is, and so expensive!" Würmli desperately wants to be helpful. "You know, it's the window of the staircase; it has not been fixed. I am sure the elevator got stuck because of that."

Karamanlis looks at him puzzled and seizes the opportunity to flee. "Whatever. I have to go. There is my Number 2 tram." Würmli watches his neighbor go and waves goodbye, and as he does, he looks around to see if other people notice that he has a friend to whom he is waving adieu.

Würmli briskly walks up the street towards the newspaper stand, but then he stops abruptly. He is talking to himself again: "What nonsense was that about the elevator's malfunctioning because the window was not fixed? Sometimes you say some stupid stuff, Andreas ..." And then he mutters, "Brazil, I wish I were there ..."

Back in his small apartment on Florastrasse, he picks at random one of several tea bags dispersed in a drawer. He warms up water, and with a hand that is no longer steady, he pours the hot water, some spilling over the counter. He wonders what will happen when this hand is no longer capable of doing as little as that.

A week ago, he had a strange conversation with a little man, the shoe repair store owner on Kreuzstrasse. He had told this man that Andreas Würmli was not always a lonely drunk. About twenty years back, when he was thirty-six, he was a sober man with a solid job. He was also a good-looking man, athletic as most women and men in this city; his thick silver black hair and a finely cut mustache were attractive. His face was nicely tanned all year round—the effects of sailing his smallish boat on Lake Zurich in the summer and skiing in the winter. If for some reason, he could not engage in these activities, he used the tanning machine at the gym.

He had a few colleagues (after all, calling someone a "friend" is unusual in this society, he tells the shoemaker while thinking how different it is in Brazil), and occasionally they would have an after-work drink at the Three Kings or the Corner Stone, but that was all the drinking he did then. He felt that he was well respected by everyone around him—not liked, mind you, just respected. These were not really buddies, and what was taking place was just content-poor collegiality. His father would have greeted people by lifting his hat. He did not do that anymore; it was not the way people showed respect these days. Still, he was equally respectful and respected, just as one likes to be in this town.

As the conversation continued, Andreas got a bit excited and told the half-stranger that by that time he no longer was in love with his wife. He, of course, was aware that he was supposed to act like a proper family man—a man with a wife and with children still living at home. Sonja, whom he married about nineteen years earlier, his daughter, Ann, who was then seventeen, and his son, Thomas, one year younger.

The appearances of Swiss bliss were all there. Wife and children would greet him respectfully, politely, upon his return from work: "Hello, Papa," or, "Just in time for dinner," or, "I hope you had a good day at work."

After all, explained Andreas to Hans the shoemaker, moderation in love and all other interpersonal relationships was the gold standard in Switzerland. In fact, he, himself, had been raised in this fashion, and from what he could tell by looking around him (his childhood friends, for instance) this was expected. "Not like in Brazil," he seemed to mutter to himself.

Hans looked at him puzzled but did not respond. Andreas explained that somehow, this coolness left him dissatisfied and restless. Maybe, he reflected when things started to unravel, he had been inspired by his exposure to Brazilian culture. As a teenager, he had spent two wonderful years there. His father took on the position of representative of Roche, the big pharmaceutical company in São Paulo. For years thereafter, Andreas spoke with excitement of how outrageously open and warm these people were. Andreas looked at his parents with scorn when he heard them talk derisively about the Brazilians. To him they were not inferior, just the opposite. He had close friends in Brazil. Mario and Humberto were the closest beings in his life, and he had a girlfriend, Laura, who made him laugh. With her he felt uninhibited, just like she seemed to be. With them he didn't feel constrained and required to hold back opinions, feelings, actions of kindness and tenderness.

When he came back to Zurich, Andreas went to the "Uni" and concentrated on math and science to ultimately become an electrical engineer. At the Polyball, the annual autumn ball, he met Sonja and they clicked. She was of Turkish descent and, as such, a bit different from the others: she was not blonde, and she laughed loudly, shamelessly. He thought he may find Brazil in her again. A couple of years later they would have their first child, and soon thereafter, the second. He had gotten a new position with a company that produced special transformers used in the energy industry. His professional life seemed stable and he had reasonable expectations of moving up the corporate ladder.

Now at home, Andreas reflects over that conversation and still wonders why he told this shoemaker his life story. Maybe it was his kind face; yes, he had a kind face. He also seemed to be listening. So few listened to him these days.

Dissatisfied with the taste of his tea, he gets up, takes out a half-empty bottle of Johnnie Walker Red Label, and spices up his drink. "Yes," he mumbles to himself, "few pay any attention to me these days, but not for long."

He sits in his armchair, the one that is in front of the TV, and reads the paper, but he cannot concentrate. His mind flashes a series of pictures, all including Jeanine, and the images are all from a much better past. That train to Horgen, his home when he was a married man, sitting across from a woman who would change his life forever. How he at first did not notice her, but once his gaze met hers, he could not stop looking at those beautiful almond-colored eyes that seemed to smile, smile relentlessly, all the time. Those eyes were so inviting ...

They courted each other without saying a word, just by looking at each other kindly, lovingly. Jeanine returned his smile, and as she did, her nose seemed to produce a little twitch that was totally disarming. Her light-colored skin was sprinkled by a few light-colored freckles which made her look younger than her age. Her demeanor was unequivocally easygoing, an extremely striking appearance in the normally tense environment he encountered on this home-from-work train. In his adulation, he kept on looking at her, not from the corner of his eye, but unabashedly straight-on. She did not move to another seat as many others would around here, but stayed put returning his inviting glance. To his regret, his stop had come too soon. But the next day he made sure to be on the same train and in the same seat. She was there smiling at him, and two years of love and deceit were about to begin. This one incident, straying away from the expected routine, boring life, would eventually bring him down—bring him to the state he was now.

They did speak on this second day, first about stupid, meaningless things like the weather and the beauty of the city (always the standard expression and proof of good citizenship). Eventually they turned to more substantive issues concerning work and the quality of their hectic lives. Throughout the conversation, the underlying theme seemed to be the same—that which engulfs all early stages of a love relationship—do we really belong to each other as we seem to think we do? This was much more than a meaningless flirt, it was obvious to both that there would be consequences. By the time the train reached Horgen, Andreas asked her, "Same time, same train?" and she gave the expected nod. When Friday came, they knew a fair amount about each other and agreed to meet for lunch the following Monday. On the next Friday they decided to start the following week with dinner in town. They would tell their spouses that they had a business engagement. They tried to have dinner together Monday or Tuesday because the weekends were becoming unbearable without seeing each other. After a month, they skipped dinner and went to a friend's vacant apartment so that they could spend time together away from clothes, pretenses, and formalities.

It was pleasing to be together like that, caressing each other, holding each other, making love. They knew that being in this deceitful relationship was difficult on both, but they also enjoyed their togetherness tremendously. The topic "family" rarely came to the fore, as if spouses and children did not exist—it just was easier this way, even if it was consciously artificial in its design.

Andreas closes his eyes; keeping them open is somehow harder on him these days. He remembers how they began engineering business trips that would bring them together, a long weekend in Italy or in France. Deceit became even harder at that point, but it was not impossible. Jeanine was an unusually successful corporate lawyer working for a small firm that was grateful that she worked for them. She could control her agenda, and as a corporate lawyer it was almost normal to have business trips that would include weekend meetings. On Sunday, she would come back to spend some quality time with her kids. For Andreas, the story was always Sonja, she was naturally suspicious and jealous. She asked questions: Why the frequency of trips suddenly? Why were there meetings in Milan; he never had them there before?

Andreas would say to himself, "Her Turkish blood is boiling over." He knows now that he became testy and unkind. "Why do I need to report to her on all my comings and goings? Why did she become so intrusive?"

Ah, those moments of eternal love. Once they felt free of their family chains, the two would plunge into a world of love and lust that made it all worthwhile to them. They would spend seemingly endless time embracing in their nakedness, absorbing each other's flesh until it almost felt like one's own, quietly kissing the mouth, arms, legs, posterior, breasts, and back to every inch of the face. They would make love with great intensity, turning the loving hugs of before into a rush of lust. And once love was consummated, they would stay embraced, as if they were one, as if they were meant for each other for eternity, and this is how they would fall asleep.

With raised eyebrows Andreas remembers the poignant scenes as if they had occurred yesterday. He asked Sonja for a trial separation knowing it would enable him to be with Jeanine without having to answer daily questions. Instead, a week later, he got served divorce papers at his office desk; he was in shock. For the first time in his life he was not in control and it brought him close to a nervous breakdown.

Suddenly his memory flips to his childhood; he recalls how his last name was the source of much abuse, how he had to struggle with kids calling him "little worm" as they piled on top of him punching and kicking. He was toughened by that early experience, however, and as a young adult he could cope with trouble better than most. His stoic nature was a great weapon, but the armor vanished on that day the divorce papers were served; he suddenly felt like his world was collapsing around him.

He now recalls with some lucidity that the worst part of his breakdown was that it made him a much less pleasant friend to, and less effective lover for, Jeanine. His hugs were no longer fully committal, his lovemaking became restrained and confused. Her response shifted too. She became cold and the unraveling was quick; suddenly, she was telling him she could not see him for lunch, the trip planned to Venice would not be possible, she had family responsibilities and she did not want to turn her back to those, she would call back (oh, sorry, she was too busy) ...

More pictures cross his mind: the rush of lust that was gone, the loving hugs which once seemed to whisper eternity and so quickly became history. How he was saddened, bewildered, and unsure of himself. At work people started talking about his divorce, word got out that he had been having an affair. Zurich is a small village when it comes to gossip, and people love to gossip there. He had nobody to talk to. He had rented a small apartment in Zurich and at night he would go to a small bar and get drunk. It was better than going to bed and feeling all the pain. He wanted to go back to his family and could not; the locks on the door had been changed. He wanted Jeanine for himself, but she was not returning the desperate phone calls. He did not want to force her over by making some sort of a scene that necessarily would reveal the deceit to her family; that is why he would not call her at home though he could have. He took on his punishment in silence, like a hero—but he was very confused, lonely, and desperately sad.

His eyes are closed, his mind also slowly closes the drawer of running pictures and allows him to fall asleep. His mouth dribbles as if to display the comfort of the relaxing nap. It is better to sleep than to feel all that pain.

Andreas wakes up in a huff. He must make it downtown, he must inspect the area where the Pope's parade will pass. He runs down the stairs almost falling; and on to the street to catch the tram. It is almost lunchtime and the wagon has more passengers at this hour. From the corner of his eye, he inspects the people in the tram. The older lady, the one with tightly combed white hair, stares at him and grimaces as she shakes her head. He notices how she resolutely launches herself to the row of single chairs, so coveted because they shield one from human contact. He looks around and sees only sour faces. Some kids talk loudly about a crazy teacher at school and the story causes them to laugh wildly. The older passengers issue more disapproving grimaces, and the shaking of heads directed at these kids is quite overt. The disdaining faces seemed to come now from all corners. "Ah … Brazil!"

By the time the tram reaches the main street, Bahnhofstrasse, Andreas vaults out. He must get to the corner restaurant's bathroom. He is having a tough time controlling himself again. He barely manages to reach the downstairs lavatory. In fact, his pants show a few spots which he hopes will dry out in time for him to go back to the fancy street. As he goes up, he pretends to have been a customer and is on his way out. He does not want to linger here and pay outrageous prices for a cup of coffee. He smiles as he realizes the contradiction—frugality is a way of life for most Swiss; it is also appropriate for those who want to make sure they have enough money to last a lifetime. But his sense is that he will not last too long (and he does not even terribly care about that). He also knows he will not take whatever savings he has to his tomb, but stinginess has been ingrained into him like mother's milk. He is as Swiss as they come in this regard.

He passes by a newspaper stand. The headline in one of the main papers reads: "The Power of the Vatican." It riles him into anger. Yes, they have too much money and too much power and the world's misery could be alleviated if they would spend some of it. There is a need to wake up the world about this disgrace, make it clear to these men of the cloth that they are callous, and he wants to be the one who will bring this to their attention. He is uncertain how he will achieve this; he just feels the urge to do something.

Maybe he can organize a demonstration. But who would heed his call to action? He has been marginalized by his own society. He is even ignored by Karamanlis, the neighbor, even by his own children for heaven's sake!

Andreas walks down Bahnhofstrasse and he wonders how he can bring meaning to his life, how he could be noticed again. He smiles at a well-dressed woman whose long blonde hair, tight jeans, and boots make her look extremely desirable in his eyes. She sneers and demonstratively turns her head, clearly insinuating that she wants nothing to do with him. He feels the pain of the rejection, his alienation and isolation, and as he often does these days, he mumbles to himself, "I will show them."

He has been walking up and down the main street for half an hour, aimlessly looking at the trees, the Christmas decorations in the windows, the people bustling by, and he senses a great deal of irritation. He is in a chaotic state of mind, angry thoughts about his present condition, images of the past that include Jeanine in bed naked, his wife and young children at the dinner table, and his bewilderment about the Pope's visit crisscrossing like the leaves swirling in the wind on this cold late November morning. He reaches Paradeplatz and is relieved to see his tram approaching.

He needs to go home, have a drink, concentrate on what actions he wants to undertake about this Pope's visit.

Once home, he grabs a piece of cheese and quickly swallows two thick slices—no bread, nothing else. His appetite is minimal these days, the snack will be enough. Then he grabs the bottle of whiskey and takes it directly to his mouth. He no longer uses a glass to drink his alcohol. No need to dirty a glass when no one else will be drinking from this bottle. As he senses the liquid running through his anatomy, he feels calmer. He sits in front of the TV and turns it on. He wants to stop thinking. They are showing old movies at this hour and sometimes they are good ones. He happens to have missed the beginning, but he recognizes the movie *Taxi Driver*. Robert De Niro talks to himself and holds his revolvers as if he is ready to shoot. Andreas sees the connection. It is not by chance that he came home to turn on the TV, and it is not happenstance that they are showing this movie. The message sent from the heavens is clear to him. This is what he needs to do. The world will recognize him for what he is about to do. He was a good sharpshooter while in the army, he was calm, his hands did not shake, and his aim was good in those days. Could it be that he still has that ability? Maybe if he does not drink for the next two days until the parade, his hands will not shake. He knows he should not kid himself. He will not stop drinking; whatever ability and steadiness he can muster will have to do.

The following morning Andreas goes to a store in the industrial district. He once heard of this backstreet shop where he could cheaply purchase a gun. He will be asked "For what purpose?" and he will tell them it is for his own security; even fancy Bellevue is no longer safe. A good address will make it much easier to buy the gun. There is plenty of respect for wealth in this town.

With the gun tightly packaged inside a shopping bag, he goes back to Bahnhofstrasse and looks for a good place where he can position himself at the time of the parade. He must be able to aim unmolested, without any disturbance. He spots the same beautiful woman he saw yesterday — the one with the boots, the one who dismissed him with a quick turn of her head. He follows her with his yearning eyes and with a quicker step than he has had in some time. He sees her go into a multi-floor shop. He is fairly sure that it is her and he wants to be convinced that she is as dismissive as he thought. Maybe he will dedicate his act to her and to her despising him. He notices that she is going to the fourth floor and he follows her by taking the stairs. He discovers an outdoor cafeteria located on the second floor of this famous store. It is still open, despite it being quite cold by now. It's quite nice up here among the plants and the comfortable, well-cushioned armchairs, when it is not raining or snowing. From the outer edge of this balcony you can see the men and women milling about on the main street through which the parade will pass the next day.

He is now convinced. Thanks to this beautiful stranger which fate must have sent in his path, just like the *Taxi Driver* movie, he has found the perfect place to mount his attack. This act of violence is being directed by stronger forces than his volition, there are clear signs of that. He will come up here, he will be able to see everything, and he will not be bothered.

Satisfied with his success, he heads back home. He totally has forgotten to pursue the woman. No matter. He's lost track of her; she vanished, in sight and in mind. Once back at home he must call his children, maybe he will give them a farewell speech of some sort. He needs to make sure they understand why he will attack an important personality. He should call them now, not much later. He will have to go to bed early; he needs to be rested if this is going to go well.

He picks up the phone to call his daughter first. The phone rings several times, but she does not answer. He calls his son and he does answer.

"Hallo, Thomas, this is your father."

"Father? Well, what a surprise. What makes you call me?"

"Listen, son, there is much that bothers me these days and I am going to do something about this. I want you to know that I am doing this out of a sense of duty."

"I am not sure I understand what you are saying. If you have to do whatever it is you want to do, I guess you must."

"Okay then, I love you."

"Be well, Father."

Andreas is not happy about the tenor of the conversation; it sounded like Thomas wanted to get him off the phone ... "Why did he not ask for any details? He is another one who does not care ..."

There has been a tear in the relationship ever since Andreas was forced to leave the house in humiliation. His son, Andreas believes, has essentially accused him of abandonment, even though Andreas always sought to stay in touch with his children. The relationship is a "correct" one but there is little affinity. It is different with his daughter—she always seemed to have had a soft spot for his crisis, an understanding of why it all happened the way it did.

He reaches again for the phone; his daughter still is not answering. He tries again after five minutes, after ten, and finally on the fifth call he reaches her.

"Hallo, Ann, it is your father."

"Hallo, Father, are you okay?" Andreas produces a faint smile—apparently his daughter cares enough to sense the high-pitched tone in her father's voice.

"As usual, I guess. I wanted to tell you that I am about to do something unusual and I am doing it out of conviction."

"Please, Father, do not harm yourself."

"Don't worry, I am not about to commit suicide."

"Are you okay? I am worried."

"I am going to show the world that there is a need for change."

"I think change is good; just don't hurt yourself."

"I want you to know I love you."

"I love you too."

Andreas was so close to discussing his plans with her, but somehow did not dare, and she did not want to ask. The unfolding of his conversation with her did not lend itself to a more open conversation of his plans or anything else; even if it felt better than that with his son, it felt like his children had divorced him too. He is upset and restless. Will his children ever understand? Will they judge him poorly? Will they change their last names in shame? He raises his voice: "It does not matter; they have their own lives, I have to do something for myself."

After quickly eating some insipid precooked pasta, he sits in front of the TV and is strangely calm. He is not thinking about tomorrow, about his attempt to change the world, about the actual event. He likes watching hockey on TV. He barely can see the puck and that helps him to ease into sleep, the almost empty bottle of whiskey near him. He wakes up well after the end of the game and turns to his bedroom. The parade is at 11:00 and he will not have a problem being there on time.

He loads two bullets into the gun's chamber and carries the revolver unwrapped in his right coat pocket, no hiding bag this time, just his hand over it to make certain it is there and does not fall out. He has decided this morning that he does not care how well he aims, he does not need to kill, he just needs for the shock to wake up the world about the Vatican's hypocrisy. The newspapers will speculate about the reasons. Some will be accurate, some not. He has also decided that he will not put anything in writing as to the reasons for the attack. He does not mind that this event turns into a puzzle; in fact, he sort of likes it.

When Andreas Würmli reaches the building with the coffeehouse terrace, he is dismayed to find out that its entrance is shut down. They gave every employee the day off and closed the store. They put up a sign: "We thank you for your understanding." They love to use that phrase around here. He recalls that he once created a joke in which the pilot of an airplane explains that the engines are failing and he will need to make a forced emergency landing and concludes by saying, "We thank you for your understanding."

Andreas gets restless, angry, and desperate. He looks left and right but finds no easy alternative that will be as good. He also assumes that all other stores are closed and all other buildings with balconies to the street would not let him in, even if he is dressed in nice clothes. Hospitality in Zurich is not written large anyway.

He resolves that he will post himself at the edge of the street, near Paradeplatz, and shoot the bullets through his coat. He will ruin this nice coat, but that will be his personal sacrifice. He gradually nudges himself to a position that is close to the front; the spectators are four deep and the multitude is not happy about people who push around, but these days, with so many foreigners around, they have gotten used to it. That is what this elderly woman tells her middle-aged daughter as Würmli manages to push past them. He is being designated as a foreigner? He, with his slick gray hair and mustache! He whose family history, on both sides, is as Swiss as they come. From Canton Aargau to boot!

It is ten minutes before the parade will start at the bottom of this street, near the lake. One good thing, about Zurich: punctuality is to be expected. Würmli is restless, antsy, and uncomfortable. In order to protect himself against his weakness, he is wearing a special diaper for incontinence. He is happy he purchased it some weeks back. Incontinence is not his current problem, rather it is the anxiety, the extreme nervousness, about what is to happen.

He lightly hops from one foot to the other waiting for the procession.

Suddenly there is a commotion in the crowd. Clearly they are coming, there is applause. He smiles; his opportunity is about to become reality. The world will know the name Andreas Würmli.

He looks in the direction of the lake, where the parade is expected to originate. He sees police cars and policemen on horseback, the usual dignitaries. Probably clergymen will join the politicians, all walking down with dour, stern faces, not a smile to be found on one face (So why have a parade if you can't be happy about it?) It's not exactly your Brazilian Carnival. Andreas spots the odd-looking white vehicle; he has read that for this occasion, since Zurich is a safe city in a crazy world, the vehicle will be without its shielding bulletproof top. He nods: that is good.

The images become clearer with every passing moment. Andreas caresses the gun, and it feels extremely cold to him. He opens the coat buttons so he can more easily maneuver the hand holding the gun. The police cars pass by, the riders seemed bored. In a few seconds, they will become much more excited.

The white vehicle with its famous rider is now in front of him. He raises his coat, his arm in his pocket, he presses hard the trigger. Nothing. No noise, no shot fired, no smoke, nothing. He now presses harder, his arm still extended, still nothing. People shout at him to lower his arm, they cannot see.

The vehicle has already passed him, and he would have to shoot the man's back. He will not do that. He turns and pushes his way out of the crowd that is still standing there cheering.

He walks quickly towards the small river, the canal that carries its river waters to the famous lake. It is two blocks down and there is a little walkway at its banks. He is now running, stumbling towards it. He lightly twists his ankle as he storms down the stairs to the walkway. He vomits a yellowish substance, looks around to make sure no one sees him, and throws his revolver in the water.

He has never polluted the waters of Zurich, and in doing so now feels tremendous guilt.

At this moment of utter despair, the immense burden of correctness and perfection that was inculcated into him from the day he was born, the overarching psychosis that has rendered this society to be so uptight, is crashing down on Andreas and he feels the guilt of immorality, not as an almost murderer but as a polluter.

He collapses on a bench near the walkway and weeps uncontrollably. "How will I be able to tell my children that the big event never happened? How will I ever give meaning to my life again?"

He has brought along a pocket-size bottle of whiskey, the kind they sell on planes, a bottle which he had saved for a special occasion, and he empties the contents in one gulp. He sits there, on the cold bench near the lake that he loved as a youngster, and he contemplates the sad reality—fiction has turned into reality and reality has turned into fiction. His disease made fantastic moments turn into monstrous designs, but failure augments his despair. The subsequent crisis becomes tragedy, and eventually it all threatens to turn into nothingness. Decay follows decay. He screams, "Brazil!"

He half walks, half stumbles through the mostly empty streets of Bellevue to his apartment building. As he takes the first steps of the staircase to the hallway he fails to notice the person sitting there waiting for him.

He is startled to hear a familiar voice call out "Papa!" It is his daughter. She gives him a polite hug as she says: "What happened to you? You look so disheveled and upset?"

Andreas asks her to join him in the apartment. He shows her a chair at the dinner table. He takes the other one across from her and in as clear a voice as he can muster he tells her: "I am planning on moving to Brazil; I want to look up my childhood friends. I want to go to one of those places where they detoxify you and help you stop drinking. I want to be happy again, and I think I can find it among those people there."

His daughter smiles at him and nods: "That is the best thing I have heard from you, Papa, in a long time. I hope it works for you. Please stay in touch."

GRAY MATTER TURNS DARK:

■

DARK: A STORY OF LOSS

Liftoff

While walking across the University of Chicago campus to spend yet another day in the library and fully immersed in thoughts about my dissertation, I was jolted by a swift maneuver perpetrated by a man who speedily but quietly had positioned himself behind me. The man folded his hands and extended his arms; they were placed on my posterior and then lifted quickly and forcefully to bump me upwards. I had not heard Josh coming and his ploy totally surprised me. While shouting, "What the heck!" I flung my arms chaotically in self-defense, and almost struck my friend in the face. Josh's face-expression conveyed a "Gotcha!, C'mon, you must have enjoyed this," and amusement all in one. He was mocking me. I was not pleased and did not enjoy that kind of physical proximity to another man, but I could not get angry at my best friend. Soon we were both laughing heartily. Our friendship had literally been propelled to a new, more haughty status.

121

As if we were two Roman warriors, Josh and I made our peace by holding each other's arms. We decided to celebrate our truce at the Medici, the local pizza joint, later that evening.

It was a beautiful day in Chicago, a rare occurrence. After one of those seemingly endless winters, spring had come briskly. However, I was not enjoying much of this—or anything else. My days and nights, at least until 11:00 p.m., were spent at the Regenstein library accumulating information that would enable me to make a cogent argument about the rise of a new class of bureaucratic-minded leaders in Spain. That was the main subject of my dissertation.

Once in the library, I had difficulty concentrating. I was thinking about my friendship with Josh. We had known each other for about two years, and even though we came from different worlds, and held divergent political views, we tacitly had agreed somewhere along the way to not make those issues insurmountable obstacles to the friendship and disturb the mutual appreciation for each other as individuals.

We met accidentally in one of those chaotic monstrosities otherwise known as university dining halls. These huge theaters held hundreds of people moving in and out at any given time. Mostly students rushed to devour some mediocre sustenance, while others sought to find friends with whom they had planned a get-together.

Josh was working on a math formula while absentmindedly eating his hamburger. I sat across from him—the nearest available seat. Not more than a couple of minutes later, while we both were engaged in our own matters, a huge drop of ketchup fell directly on Josh's math scribblings rendering them illegible. Josh was furious and looked up angrily, but when he noticed this stranger, me, smirking at the situation, he started laughing so loudly that other students turned their heads towards us. Typically, when I laugh hard my whole body shakes, and then my eyes tear up. It was no different this time, and I could see Josh was enjoying the 'saucy' accident too. I told him I was truly sorry that I could not help him with his math problem ("not my forte," I quipped) and we struck up an amiable conversation that ended half an hour later with a simple, noncommittal "See you later."

Two days later I happened to see Josh walking as if in a daze across the quadrangle. I immediately noted his grim expression and ashen face; it seemed to match his agitated nature. Though I was shy and hated intruding, I felt like I needed to ask what was bothering him. Josh told me that he had just heard that his mother, who suffered from depression, had been hospitalized again after attempting suicide. He did not know how to get to her quickly. He was broke and his father refused to lend him money (the parents had divorced years back) by saying, "Instead of running to your mother's bedside every time she has a relapse, you should concentrate on your studies." He was clearly running out of options. I told Josh I would gladly lend him my car. "My mother lives in Washington State, I can't drive out there" was his dejected response.

"Well, then, let me drive you to the airport and lend you the money so you can fly out there." Josh was incredulous.

"Seriously? You would do that? We don't even know each other."

A week later, Josh called me and invited me to come over for dinner. He wanted to show his appreciation. That Friday night we ate, drank a bottle of wine I brought along, and chatted for about five hours. I got the feeling that a special friendship was formed that evening. Sometimes you just feel a lot of empathy for a person. You are willing to jump into the fire to rescue him or her and you are also certain that this feeling is reciprocal.

It was obvious to anyone who cared to look that we shared a special commonality, something unique that differentiated us from the others in the wider circles we hung out. Outwardly we did not look alike. He was unkempt and wore cheap clothes. Even though I downscaled somewhat by buying jeans and flannel shirts like those worn by locals and my new friend, my wardrobe was more of a mix—a reflection of my parents' imprint to look the part of an upper-class gentleman.

Maybe we were seen as bright, intellectually curious and well-read. And indeed, we were. Though this was the second half of the seventies, we expressed significant sympathy for the anti-war youth. We often trumpeted our disdain for conventional behavior as that generation often did. On the other hand, we steered clear of the drugs culture.

Josh was born in the suburbs of Toronto to a somewhat famous economist and a Polish-Jewish immigrant painter. His parents divorced when Josh was fifteen, but he showed no apparent scars from it. Deep down a divorce always affects its children, but he was skilled at hiding the pain. Josh was good looking even though his hair had grayed prematurely. Soon after the ketchup incident, I realized that this new friend was popular with the women on campus. His face portrayed great intensity, which they loved. He was also athletic; his short legs were muscular as could be expected from someone who had been a ballet dancer in his younger years, and his torso was strong enough to lift a ballerina. I imagined female students thought he was a good lay.

Josh was a bit of a globe-trotter. It was a by-product of his travel while part of a Canadian ballet ensemble. Eventually he quit the ballet company and went to college. His father was eager for this to happen and often egged him on about it, ridiculing him for his work.

But he remembered with fondness those ballet years. He often talked knowingly about many European cities I also knew well. It was clear he enjoyed reminiscing about these places with me. I thought the multicultural exposure gave him a more sophisticated understanding, especially about the diversity of ethnicities roaming this world.

This was an important element in our friendship, for I was a foreigner in Chicago. I came from Ecuador and had lived in Spain while attending undergraduate studies at the Universidad de Salamanca. Although my mother was English and I spoke the language well, I was definitely the foreigner in that Midwestern hubris.

My parents, owners of a modern art gallery, used to emphasize European superiority in all matters of taste and culture. I rejected their notions to some extent and revolted with my decision to come to the US ("Of all places?" my parents decried) for my graduate studies.

Once in Chicago and perceptive about my surroundings, I shed some of the 'rich European kid on campus' identifiers. A few weeks after I landed I decided to buy a car. I avoided looking spoiled by choosing a second hand 1972 Pontiac. It was so big I called it my boat. When it turned out that its size prevented easy parking in the congested area of the campus, I replaced it with my 'ugly green' Ford Pinto.

Back at the library, I shook off the dreamy reflections about my friend and started taking notes about the banking oligarchy in Spain during the Second Republic. I could not procrastinate any further. I had been consumed by the research for my dissertation over the last six months and the scope was getting broader and broader. I was worried that it would take ten years to complete. I remembered the story of a student at this university, who in the fifties had written a masterpiece on the link between the arms race and European imperialism prior to WW I. He died of exhaustion two days after defending his thesis. The story scared me so much that every time I was inclined to procrastinate, I would remember him and write without interruption for hours.

Academic Troubles

A few months later, Josh and I agreed to get together. I had to see him to discuss something important. When I entered the Medici, I had an easy time guessing where Josh was seated; he was surrounded by three girls, all undergraduate students working there. Once I got closer, I saw a familiar scene: a cup of coffee, some math scribble on a notepad, a cigarette pack and an ashtray. I quickly moved the ketchup container far away from him, while I sternly shook my head. He let out a big grin. As if by a touch of the magic wand, my appearance caused the three waitresses to say their quick "See you later" and disappear. I pretended to be miffed with jealousy at his success with them (secretly, that was actually the case).

"Josh, I have a huge problem," I said. "No, it is not the women. Well, that too. But right now it is that I am having a colossal fight with my dissertation advisers. I am trying to provide an account of the changes that have been taking place in Spain over the last forty years, since the Civil War. These sons of bitches are saying that my argumentation must position me somewhere in the philosophical spectrum. They claim I am trying to provide a 'value free' statement, and that there is no such thing."

Josh's response came out like thunder; it showed me that he had a razor-sharp mind: "You are telling me that they want you to declare yourself, position yourself as a Marxist or whatever the opposite is?" Even though he was working on econometrics, he quickly understood the nuts and bolts of the debate.

I considered his response. "I suppose that at the end of the day, that is precisely what they want me to do. They argue that any discussion of this kind cannot be done in a void, that I must create arguments that would ultimately be made from a vantage point which places me in either this or that camp. While I understand their argument, I intuitively and ideologically detest it. I want to know why things have happened the way they did in Spain (or, sometime in the future, anywhere else, for that matter). I want to make the argument based on facts and stick to the actual evolution of history, untainted by a loaded ideological bias. Of course, I know that I should not ignore wealth, 'classes' if you, I mean they, wish, but, I am absolutely sure that change was not only caused by class struggle—it was not the only factor that created transformations.

"Suddenly, some younger Spaniards who cared about their country, wanted to do the best they could, by applying more modern tools than had ever been used in that country before. How the hell do you talk about that in Marxist terms? How can you, on the other hand, ignore it? Yet when I speak, let's call it, from both sides of my mouth, these creatures, my advisers, start shaking their heads vehemently—as if I committed high treason. I want to research a topic. I do not want to be a member of a church or a political party while doing so."

Josh agreed wholeheartedly but provided little advice as to what to do. In hindsight, the reasons were self-evident. He was a true-to-its-creed "Chicago economics" member. One of a large majority of believers that Adam Smith and Ayn Rand had it right. He attributed many problems in the social sciences to Marxists and left-leaning academics. He did belong to a religion of sorts. For him, my problem was a by-product of the times, a "decline in civilization" he once called it jokingly. For that simple reason, my problem could not be resolved.

We did not see eye-to-eye on these matters. But I never let it come between us, and I can with confidence say that he felt the same way. Even though I knew he could be ruthless and selfish, I appreciated that he was highly intelligent, passionate, and utterly honest. But, above all, he was the kind of person who would do anything for a friend, just as I was.

It was fun to be around him, hang out at the local bar and talk about a thousand things. I secretly harbored the wish that I might even get lucky and find a girl that would get tired of unsuccessfully chasing after Josh and smile invitingly in my direction. On more than one occasion, I tried to distill in my mind what made us such good friends. Why the strong shared feelings. I said to myself: "this is not a relationship of utility, but of kinship; always remember that." That is the best that I could come up with. Somehow, I managed to survive the testiness of my advisers and complete my dissertation. I sourly contemplated this reality: at that time, getting a PhD in the social sciences had become a measure of fortitude and stamina rather than the ultimate intellectual hurdle it may have been in earlier decades. Universities were becoming industrial machines whose output was to accredit individuals—men and women who would adorn their name with this pedigree as they sought a job in some field, often enough, alien to the one studied. For most universities, struggling financially, the input was students, and their parents, who could shove mountains of dough to fuel that machine.

Josh, on the other hand, struggled mightily to get his degree. Ultimately, his department allowed him to piece together several articles he had written for one or two econometrics journals. The PhD machine seemed to have its modus operandi even outside of the "softer" sciences.

Best Men

It was a pleasant surprise to find out that we both managed to get teaching jobs in the same region of upstate New York; even if the two universities were some 130 miles apart. This allowed us to maintain contact, albeit less frequently. On a late spring day, I got a phone call from him: "Why don't you come over and visit with us?"

I was surprised: "Who is us?"

Josh explained that he had met a woman. She was, in fact, a student at the University of Rochester. Later I learned that she had attended his class; came to his office to discuss something said in that class. This was followed by coffee, eventually a dinner, and soon thereafter moving her belongings to his apartment. They understood and smilingly accepted that going forward she would only be able to get home tutoring.

For a while they kept their relationship a secret, fearful of the possible repercussions and either or both being thrown out of the institution. However, after quietly exploring the possible reactions of his colleagues and the administrative authorities, they were relieved to find out that both bodies were more lenient than fathomed.

I reminisced about the women in Josh's life; the serious relationships I knew about rather than the numerous one-night stands. His women were all significantly younger than he was. They were beautiful, slender women with faces that expressed character and intelligence. He cheated on all of them. Some tolerated it more than others. They always seemed to react negatively to his overt selfish ruthlessness. Or, at least, that was my interpretation.

Ramona, who became his first wife a year after they met, decided to break up the marriage unofficially by moving to Thailand. She was going to do some field study was the excuse; thereafter came the official divorce.

After that came Linda—another young woman he met while she was attending his ballet classes on campus. He always did that to earn a bit of money. I once went to see him teach his class and it was a sight I will never forget: his demanding approach, his presence, their overt adulation.

Linda seemed madly in love with him and I thought he would enjoy the devotion and allow this to last. But, to my surprise, he seemed bothered by the attention and looked for opportunities to extricate himself: he went camping, visited his siblings for whom he cared a lot, and eagerly created distance between Linda and himself.

Beatrice, the beautiful daughter of a famous Nobel Prize–winning economist, never got as far as Ramona. Josh had convinced her to move into his apartment quite quickly, but she left him two months later when it became clear to both that she demanded more fidelity and more tolerance than he could muster. The excuse to break-up was simple: the teaching position he would be offered would take him far away anyway. There was no use to hang out together. He did ask her to join him at the new location, but she declined. "You know it will not work and I will be stuck somewhere I do not want to be," she said. Their expectations differed too much to allow for a successful partnership.

Beatrice sought to understand what was going on by talking to me, and I tried to show compassion, perhaps even more than that. She quickly distanced herself from both Josh and me. I had pointed out my ability to compromise, my bigger heart, to present to her a contrast with Josh. It was treasonous. My excuse was that her heart was no longer wanting Josh. Still, I was trying to exploit a situation for selfish purposes. Deep down I knew friends don't behave like this. My best excuse, today, is that the desires of the flesh took over. But I am not proud of that episode.

In the meantime, I had had a series of doomed relationships. I had left the love of my life in Spain when she decided to stay home rather than join me in the US. The women I met as a student were no match to her in her beauty and intelligence. They never lasted long.

That was all in the past. As I went to visit Josh, I puzzled over the new girlfriend. I was also wondering why my friend had asked, more so insisted that I come early on Friday. Nevertheless, I arranged for a substitute teacher for my class and went. As soon as I arrived, I was dragged to a clothing store that had a large selection of tuxedos.

"You will perform a special function tomorrow," Josh told me. "You are about to be my best man."

I was thrilled, confused, and angry all at once. It was typical of him to pull a stunt like this. Considering that Josh had a brother for whom he cared a lot, and, I assumed, a great number of good friends and colleagues that he held in high regard, I was very flattered by his decision. On the other hand, I was also annoyed with him. A best man performs certain duties before a wedding, and being taken by surprise like this, I feared I could not properly fulfill my duties. Josh's response was anything but surprising: a "poor baby" smirk and laughter. That was exactly the point; he and Julia had conspired to produce a situation that would make me almost helpless. Whatever largesse I wanted to offer would be curtailed by time and space.

Almost. I insisted on hosting a lavish dinner that evening. The family members of both sides were, of course, to share the special moment. Josh shook his head, smiled, and said, "Typical of you! Always looking for a way to usurp my plans aimed at curtailing your spending on me." Years later Josh would reminisce, "That was a weekend of celebration, not only of a marriage, but also of a brotherhood."

I thought that Julia was just what one would expect of a woman marrying Josh: young, smart, long-legged, pretty. It was obvious that when Josh looked for and pursued these barely-of-age women, he was getting older and the gap between their ages was becoming larger. But in comparison to Ramona and Beatrice, she somehow seemed not just younger but less refined. That evening I surmised that she had come from a lower-middle-class milieu in Buffalo. This was reflected in small things that bothered my snobbish concepts. Although I had disavowed my stuffy parents' ideas of "upper class" standards, I could not totally escape my upbringing. I felt that Julia was not the right woman for my friend. But I also understood that class and sophistication in a woman were not the virtues Josh was interested in. When, during our student years we would go camping in Wisconsin, I had great problems with roughing it out. Josh had none. When the discussion was which watering hole to go to, Josh was more inclined to go to the local dive. The demarcation lines between us were clearly drawn and hovered over all aspects of life. He sometimes made sarcastic remarks about my pomposity but appeased me quickly with a strong hug.

Deep down the wedding weekend also produced some sadness for me. I tried to cover this up as well as I could—I was there alone; I felt unloved and in a foreign land. I had had a tempestuous affair with a married woman before I left Chicago. It had been almost a year since I left her, and any efforts to find a companion landed nowhere. Since the college where I taught was in the middle of a social and cultural wasteland, I had great difficulties finding someone with whom I could share my life, or, at least, my bed. Josh's way of hooking up with a student was neither morally acceptable, nor feasible—my looks were nowhere near as good as his. I sought companionship through a variety of new connections and had a few one-night stands, but that was all. There were also a couple of single women on the faculty of the small college. I went to dinner with some of them, but these outings revealed the incompatibility.

From time to time, I was still jealous of my friend. But upon second reflection I would come to my senses and realize that friendship, in its purest form, leaves no room for competition or jealousy. I was clear that

I should not allow myself to draw comparisons between us. Instead, I should appreciate the unconditional friendship shared by us.

Three years later came payback time. I asked Josh to return the favor and act as best man at my wedding. Months after meeting Liana, a woman who seemed to care more about me than my money, my origins, or my family, I decided that this was the right person with whom I could form a lasting union. She was not perfect by any stretch of the imagination. Her sense of humor was limited at best, but she would not harm a fly. Josh, in typical fashion, thought that such decisions were best left to the one whose fate would be sealed, that each person should make them on his own. "If you care for her and she cares for you, I am delighted that you decided to marry her."

I found out years later Josh expressed doubts about Liana to his wife, but he did not share them with me. Friendship was about support, not about dissuading someone from taking the leap. The unknowns, even in the case of a best friend, are greater than what one does know. He would have to hope that it all would work out for the best.

Eventually, Josh regretted not having said something. Years later, I confided in him that I was bewildered by the lack of love, even empathy, shown by Liana. I admitted that perhaps I had contributed to disharmony by being pedantic and demanding. In any case, I felt despondent by the whole mess. The house we moved to, at the end of a cul-de-sac, was emblematic of the stranglehold on the marriage which was getting tighter with every bit of deterioration in Liana's already low levels of self-esteem. I understood much of that intellectually but could not accept her behavior. At first, I hoped change would come with time, but it just did not. Fifteen years after we got married, as the relationship became more and more estranged, and after several visits to therapists and counselors, the marriage would officially break down, but not the way most would have expected. Liana was the one that asked for a divorce. Josh would never find out about that part.

Life Sets Us Apart

In my life, I did not have many friends like Josh: individuals with whom I could discuss sensitive, delicate matters, get the opinion of a bright man whom I considered a brother. However, by the time we reached our late forties, our friendship had been affected by distance, family and work. It got reduced to periodic phone calls and even more infrequent get-togethers. The telephone exchanges were a poor substitute to the warm conversations of the past. They lacked the depth they once had, the intensity, the empathy, the sharing of a story, to its most minute details.

Geography was partially responsible for creating the sentimental distance. I moved to New York and Josh and his wife (she was now a law professor) were able to arrange teaching positions at neighboring universities in the Deep South. A busy workload was no help either. We honored our friendship by checking on each other from time to time. Perhaps, we did so to celebrate our past. Perhaps it was to make sure that we would be there for each other in the future.

Three parents died in quick succession over a span of four years, and we both offered truly sincere condolences via telephone. These deaths were expected to some extent; thus, they did not cause a crisis for the bereaved. The friendship had never spanned beyond us to our families, though our parents sometimes hosted us.

Only Josh's father was still kicking around, despite his heavy smoking and abusive drinking. He still changed "girlfriends" with some frequency. Years earlier, when I visited Josh at his father's apartment in NYC, I concluded that these female friends were more drinking buddies to the old man than anything else.

Liana and I had two children, and while the marriage teetered on the brink of disaster for a long time, I was determined to stick it out so that the children would have a decent enough home.

I was always more the family man than Josh, who apparently was not interested in children. Josh proclaimed to the world that he was doing the responsible thing since he was unsure as to how one could raise a child while in such a fluid job situation as his and his wife's.

Brain Damage

It was a warm spring day in New York when the phone rang; I was alone with the children (my wife was at some professional meeting in California). It was Josh's brother, Jon (all the children in the family had a first name starting with J). At first I had difficulty figuring out who was calling; I barely knew Jon. "I am sorry to tell you, something awful has happened. Josh has had a terrible accident and is semi-comatose. He asked for you."

The staccato sentences left me numb and dumbfounded. Of course, I was totally unprepared for the call. I did not know what to say.

"Can you come down to Alabama?"

I was even less prepared for that. I explained that I was alone watching the kids and that I would have to make plans. Could I have his phone number and call back? I wanted time to regain my composure and make reasonable decisions considering the terrible news.

My first inclination was to call back and say that it would be too complicated to travel because of the kids. It was upsetting to be this unresponsive in the face of tragedy. Maybe I just did not want to face my friend battling death. Maybe I held a grudge for all those times Josh exhibited extreme egotism. But every time I decided that I would not go, I heard the echo of Jon's voice saying, "He asked for you." I said to myself, "At a time of semi-consciousness, with his wife, father, and brother nearby, he chose to remember you and you are not responding?" Finally, I decided that I had to go down. It was Wednesday, Liana would be back the next day, and I could take a day off from work and fly out Thursday night and spend the weekend in Birmingham. I called my wife and told her the sad news (her reaction was stronger than I expected considering she never liked Josh that much, and was not prone to much emotion in any case). I told her of my plans and that she would have to take care of the kids. I was thankful that she did not protest or cause difficulties; she was often much less accommodating. I then called Jon to inform him of the time of my arrival. Jon was thankful; either he or his father would be at the airport. I called twice more to get updates on Josh's health. There were glimpses of hope that he would pull through.

When I arrived in Birmingham, I was greeted by Josh's father. James had aged dramatically. He had sustained his good looks for longer than one would expect, but now his face and hair had turned ashen as if they heralded the coming of death. James thanked me for coming; he told me he was very anxious. "My family has never looked this vulnerable, first Jack dies in a kayaking accident and now this." I did not know if James looked so weak because of his drinking and plain old age or because of the recent traumatic experience, but I felt sorry for the old man. Watching your child die or worrying about it must be the most difficult experience of all.

However, now the concern was Josh. James told me that, as best he could tell, Josh was on his way to visit his wife (she had taken a job in Mobile); he had worked till late the night before and went to the bar and had a few drinks. He took off right after that. Either Josh had had an accident that caused a stroke, or he had a stroke that caused him to lose control of the truck and have the accident. He hit a phone pole. In any case, oxygen had not gotten to his brain for some time. While there were doubts at first if he would survive at all, it now became clear that he was going to live, but there was concern about his ability to function. Was there too much brain damage? James drove directly to the hospital and we walked quickly to the Critical Care Unit and Josh's room.

Surrounded by several medical devices lay a man who looked astonishingly well given the circumstances. He had some lacerations on his face from the accident, but his pale color was not different from the way Josh looked normally (I always thought that his smoking was a cause of that old-age complexion). I definitely expected much worse than what I saw. Josh's eyes were closed when I came in.

Julia came over and hugged me warmly. She also seemed in better shape than I expected. She then guided me to Josh's bedside and whispered in her husband's ear, "Your friend is here." She took my hand and put it on Josh's. Josh grabbed the hand as if he was going to shake it and smiled slightly but kept his eyes closed. He then let the hand go. Julia said, "I think he is glad you are here and so am I." At the nurse's request, we all left the room.

Julia and I went for a cup of coffee. She was quiet for some time but then she broke down, and with teary eyes she said, "I know he will make it, but I don't know if he will ever be able to teach again." She knew how important his professional pursuits were to him. There was little that I could say or do, but I was glad to have come; even though I could not have a significant impact on Josh's health, I stood by him and offered Julia all the support she needed now and in the future.

"If there is anything I can do to help him recover, in his rehabilitation, let me know," I said.

Julia nodded with a slight smile of gratitude. I spent the rest of the weekend in a haze. Like a robot, I went with the family to a restaurant near the hospital. The food was bad, the surroundings strange, as if I was on another continent. I could barely understand these thick southern accents. Everyone seemed to wear clothes bought at Walmart. I followed Josh's family to the hospital, but they spent more time in the cafeteria than in Josh's room. "He needs a lot of rest," the doctor said, "but he will make it."

For me, ever the task-oriented achiever, it would normally have been frustrating to be this helpless; however, that weekend I resigned myself to the notion that Josh's well-being was a matter of not days or weeks, but months.

When Julia took me to the airport (maybe she wanted to relieve James and Jon from driving me, maybe she herself wanted to see something other than the hospital and its nearby surroundings), she drove quietly and I was too numb to say anything. But as she said goodbye, she gave me a big hug and asked me if I would come back.

I knew I could not refuse. This short trip was just the beginning of my journey alongside Josh's rehabilitation. I told Julia that I was ready to help in any way I could. Would his rehabilitation be expensive? "Yes, of course. But he, we, are insured as university staff. Just come back," she responded. I checked my electronic agenda and realized that I could be back three weeks later. "Please call me if you need me sooner," I said as I was ready to pass airport security. "In any case, please keep me informed how things are going. I'll speak to you in a few days."

As I slumped into the airplane seat, I realized that Julia was a much better person than I had thought. She was caring, strong, and what one would want in a life partner. Julia had surprised me, and she would surprise me even more.

When I went to Birmingham the second time, Josh had been released from the hospital and was recovering at his father's home. Once again, James picked me up at the airport and drove home.

"They do not know the extent of the damage to Josh's brain, but it is significant," he said.

I saw Josh in a gown, looking bewildered, as if his eyes could not focus. He no longer was hooked to machines and was ostensibly ambulatory. I had a chance to fully realize the severity of the damage when I saw Julia hurry to walk Josh to the bathroom. "He does not remember how one releases," Jon said sadly.

Josh spoke somewhat incoherently, but he was quickly learning how to do things like grab a fork and a spoon to feed himself. I was eager to hear from Julia the details of his situation and asked her if we could go somewhere to talk in private. With Josh asleep, we went to the garden outside the house. "Josh will have to go to a place that specializes in these kinds of trauma. It's located in Braintree, Massachusetts. We are trying to make the arrangements; they need to make sure that they will have space for him. They seem to produce miracles from time to time. We will see what they can do for Josh. According to the doctor, little is known as to why some people respond to treatments better than others."

I was deeply saddened by Josh's condition. I had not fully recognized what the impact of the stroke had been until I saw it with my own eyes. Seeing this extremely intelligent person learning how to eat and go to the bathroom was simply heartbreaking. When he ate, some of the food would spill from the side of his mouth. He was incontinent and had to wear adult diapers. The trip back to New York was much harder on me than the one taken three weeks before.

During the first two visits, I was made aware that my friend smiled at me in recognition. But the exchanges were so limited that I was not sure as to whether the smiles were because Josh remembered me as his best friend, the best man at his wedding, the person in whom I had confided intimate secrets, and with whom I discussed life-changing issues, or perhaps the smile simply conveyed some confused knowledge of the difficult moments he was undergoing, and some appreciation that there was a person there to lend a hand. Ultimately, whichever version, or combination thereof, was in fact accurate mattered little. My presence there was, in typical fashion, full commitment, no apprehension, no caveats, no excuses. This was what I wanted to do. It felt good to give.

Rehabilitation

Julia called in late September to tell me that Josh would finally be able to travel to Braintree to begin his recovery. "No one knows how far this will take him, but it needs to happen."

I promised to visit them there a week later. During that first visit, I learned about the process of rehabilitation for Josh's brain damage. It was amazing that such matters could even be attempted—a true sign that mankind was making advances despite all the negative aspects of modernity. And yet, no one knew for certain to what extent Josh would function independently ever again, not to speak of teaching at a university, or writing for academic journals. He was making great strides already; he had regained his ability to walk straight, to eat normally, and there was no longer a need for adult diapers. Still, his speech was slow and he lacked the ability to comprehend complex matters clearly.

I was also elated to hear the surprising news that Julia was pregnant with their first child. Without being told so, I was convinced that Julia wanted to have a son with Josh, to have something that would be fresh and intact and undamaged —a young life that would keep Josh's spirit alive. It was clearly an act of heroic proportions given the uncertainties of the moment, uncertainties that engulfed all aspects of life, emotional and spiritual as much as practical.

I recognized that my first partial rejection of Julia was dead wrong, that this woman had performed an act of love that perhaps no other woman in Josh's previous life would have done. I was visibly moved; tears rolled down my cheeks. Julia said that Josh's reaction was much more serene when he was first told. It could be that he did not fully understand what he was told, or maybe he had a subconscious concern about his inability to provide for the child. Could he be able to be a true father to this new being? And if he could, how long would it last? At least that is what Julia and I wondered. If he was not particularly vocal and wordy before the accident, he had become even quieter, more taciturn thereafter.

Braintree did produce the miracle. Josh started reading professional journals four months after arriving at the institution. He would get tired quickly and he would take longer to write a formula, but he could do it. Nine months later, exactly a month after Bruce's birth, he stood for the first time in front of a class at UAB. Most students knew what had happened to their teacher and they were in awe. At the end of the class they gave him a standing ovation which he dismissed with a hand wave. Julia, ever thankful for the support that I had given her (I had also lent her some money during the ordeal), was quick to call me and give me the good news. I wanted to see my friend in such good form and promised to visit as soon as possible.

Lights Out for the Friendship

Two weeks later I made it to Birmingham and Josh and Julia were both at the airport to greet me, a baby stroller next to them. The next morning while drinking coffee, Josh's favorite time on a leisurely day since the time we were students, I reminisced about having breakfast at the Agora near campus. Josh's face went blank. He could not remember a thing. His eyes, always so expressive, emitted a mix of apathy and frustration; I represented to him the large chasm created by his health crisis. Braintree had been able to save his ability to think through difficult math problems, but it was not capable of recovering the memory that had been wiped out by the stroke.

Through his silence and his look, a mix of frustration and anger, he made it clear that our common, shared memories were gone forever. But perhaps what was more disturbing to me was that he silently conveyed to me that he did not care that this had happened. Could it be that the stroke had eliminated his ability to feel such emotions? In fact, it seemed to me that he would rather not be reminded of what was missing.

Suddenly, I felt nauseous. A friendship is built on common bonds, on fond memories, on history. And these were all gone from my friend's mind forever. Through Julia's intervention, and maybe Josh's intuition, Josh knew he had a good friend in me. Old pictures of us camping or horsing around would also tell him that. But this was all floating in amorphous space. The friendship had lost its grounding. Perhaps there was some sadness in Josh's face, but he could hardly be lingering in such emotions given the huge break he had gotten—to be alive, to be able to teach, and to have his wife and child next to him. Right after the accident, at the hospital, he had asked for me, but apparently, these were just instincts. He could not figure out why he had asked for me.

I understood all this intellectually, but emotionally I was unable to cope with what had occurred. How can I relate to a person whose memory of the past is so different from mine? How do I build the trust, the empathy, the warmth that is based on so much common history, when it is lacking in one of us? The task was simply insurmountable. It was like a limb that has been cut off and can no longer be reattached to the body. There was too much that was foreign in the relationship. We had become estranged in the most meaningful, most complete sense of the word.

I used the pretext that one of my kids had come down with mono to leave Birmingham earlier than planned. In fact, I simply had to run away. Maybe I was a coward not to confront this new challenge, but I did not believe I had the strength to face the heartbreak of a vacuous look, an empty face every time an anecdote would surface. Julia called from time to time, and I was always polite, friendly even, but always sought to create distance. I was plainly unable to cope with the way fate had separated us. I decided that it was easier to live with memories truncated by a fatal blow than to face the gulf created by his accident.

A year later I called their house in Alabama but got no answer. I left a message but did not hear back. A couple of years passed, and while hanging out with common friends at a university reunion I was asked about Josh, if I had heard anything. It prompted me to try and reach out to my former friend once more—to no avail. Apparently, he was uninterested in even the most minimal hello. Numerous emails and letters did not achieve any sort of breakthrough. Our friendship had just become an opaque historic incident for him. Certainly, that was not the case for me.

Years later, the opportunity to discuss Josh with my son came up. We were going through the wedding album and Josh was in many pictures: handsome, smiling, and very elegant in his tuxedo. I thought that my son was now old enough to understand. There were two ways to deal with this tragedy: one was to mourn and cry over a lost friendship. The other was to feel blessed by the opportunity to have had such a connection with another human being. It was important for me to convey to my son that I also felt privileged to have the emotional depth that would allow me to experience such a fantastic bond. I told him how I was enriched by the conversations Josh and I have had. That I wished for him, my son, to have such a friend, and feel such deep feelings. And, yes dare I say it, I would want this for my son even at the risk of going through such a tearing experience.

LOBOS LOCOS

∎

"**I** assume the Mouse is also coming,**"** Dahlia smirked as she took a small bite of the terrine she had bought earlier that morning. She knew that when her face contorted into a grimace of displeasure it was unattractive, but she was unable to hide her feelings from her husband. In any case, he did not need to look at her to know her distaste for the man everyone called "the Mouse." She once remarked, "He does not even care that that is his nickname." Forever the businessman, James was more interested in the potential benefits the investors brought, even if with time James learned that they were greedy rather than savvy, small-minded rather than enlightened, and often just downright unpleasant. As he nodded to confirm, James Crown shared his wife's sense of heaviness about the upcoming gathering.

Short, somewhat pudgy, with a small face, a small mustache, and shifty dark eyes, Abraham Silver a.k.a. the Mouse, would fly in from London. He was smart but exuded nervousness, even outright fear—strange considering his intelligence and wealth. Always insecure, when it came to international travel, he turned into a total wreck. It was not about the safety of airplanes, or terrorism, but the deadly fear that one day, the police would apprehend him and start tax-evasion proceedings. He owned a good number of lower-income houses in Camden, a somewhat downtrodden London community, and his company managed these just within the confines of the law. His great worry, however, was the monies he had inherited a decade earlier. He decided to keep them with the same

Swiss Gnomes, where they had been for a long time. He had the duty to report these to the English authorities and pay the required taxes, but he chose not to do so.

Ever since, he lived with this fear of everything unraveling. In comparison to the other partners, maybe his crime was minor, but who is to say what demons dance in our heads and cause us to be frightened? To an earlier gathering the Mouse came wearing a *chullo*, a wool head-cover he ordered from a Peruvian folklore store; they wear these to shield from wind and cold. It covered the Mouse's ears and much of his forehead, exposing a small portion of his Caucasian face with its small mustache. It made him look strange, particularly in the middle of a warm Spanish spring, but he couldn't care less; he felt safer. Dahlia once quipped with sarcasm, "I can swear that the Mouse is enough of a twisted personality that he enjoys playing with the police 'cats.'"

"La Villa de los Lobos Locos," James and Dahlia's mansion, was located just outside the small village with the same name. Nicely situated in the higher terrain above Marbella, it was out of the public eye but not overly distant from the jet-setters having fun in the Mediterranean resorts. Lobos Locos, the village five minutes away by car, was founded by a self-important, albeit lesser nobleman of the sixteenth-century whose name was even longer but no one remembered. Commoners shortened the village's name to Lobos Locos, or "*Doble* L" or "LL." They were quick to smile as they recounted the myth that gave the place its name: the nobleman having recurring nightmares about his enemies dancing around his clobbered, almost lifeless body while wearing wolf masks.

The annual gathering of the group was always held here, ever since the founding of the business in 1998. Knowing that location equals power, James insisted so. With its ample facilities, it was also convenient. It allowed some partners to stay over, the inconspicuous address placating to the more secretive types. The Mouse, for example, demanded one of the three guest rooms. He would not be caught, even dead, in a hotel that required his registration and passport. Other partners stayed in nearby Marbella so they and their female companions could frolic after sunset.

The women who joined the shareholders (all of them happened to be men) were not always the same, nor were they usually the wives. The clandestine couples would go to the beaches, a short trip away, and at night frequent the Marbella bars, restaurants, and discos. This fit well with the more energetic types and their desire for hidden pleasures, away from the home, from suspicious family members or acquaintances.

It was James's entrepreneurial drive, his aptitude to spot people to match a business need, and his abundant joviality that helped him put together the deal, but it was Dahlia's ingenuity and vision that originated it.

James was born and raised in Manchester and still lived there for part of the year. Recently, however, he preferred to spend more than six months in Spain. He loved outdoor activities and sports. In his youth, he was a soccer goalie; those days, he swam for many miles and played tennis. Older now, and often in pain, he replaced tennis with golf. He appreciated the warmer Spanish climate—it was much easier on his arthritic knees.

Dahlia's social networking brought this business opportunity to the couple's attention. In late 1997, Dahlia had chatted with a real estate broker who offered them an enormous piece of undeveloped land, about ten kilometers down the coast from Malaga. The price was attractive (for James nothing was ever cheap), but the sum was still too large to be purchased by them alone. After visiting the site, Dahlia had convinced James that this was an excellent location to develop a members-only golf club with a nine-hole course, a social venue, and a restaurant at its center, maybe even a swimming pool near the main building. She was endowed with a fantastic eye for seeing what was not yet there, and she understood the rich and their proclivity to stay secluded and protected from filthy Gypsy beggars and enterprising young Spaniards peddling cheap wares. She attributed to others her own disdain for the "riffraff." She knew a private club would get a warm response from the growing Northern European seasonal migration to Iberia.

It was up to James to exploit the opportunity and launch the project. Where would the investors come from? He heard about a gathering in London that seemed to be good hunting ground. A new foundation was being started and it needed money. Its purpose was to better the lives of Palestinians in the camps of Gaza. The idea was that peace between the Palestinians and Israel would only come about if their living conditions were improved. It was typical of the attendees to see the solution to problems through an economic lens. Money was something they had learned to respect; more so, cherish—- yes, even venerate.

The meetings extended over three days. They heard speakers who knew, or claimed to know, something about the conflict, and others who thought they knew something about conflict resolution. They established action groups, discussed how much money should be raised, and where it should be deployed. The organizers got some to pledge donations of half to one million euros. James left the meetings with his own little treasure: a decent number of business cards of individuals who at breakfast, lunch, or dinner heard him speak with great excitement about his own new project. Three showed immediate interest to join, three others were eager to find out more, and a couple were more reserved, but all were potential investors. He phoned Dahlia to tell her that her dream of seeing this project launched was a step closer to reality. She should put together an information packet: pictures, maps, and whatever other valuable information she could get her hands on. They would need to send out an attractive brochure to the potential investors.

Dahlia greeted James at the airport with a big smile. James recognized that proud smile, he had seen it before. She had spoken to the broker who represented the Catalan family selling the land and got assurances from this Mr. Grande that they would have two weeks to make a bid on the land. They would also have the right of first refusal if another investor would preempt them. Nothing came easy or cheap in this new, post-Franco Spain. Dahlia assured the broker he would own 0.5 percent of the shares of the development in return for his services and even signed a short memorandum to that effect. In addition, he would become the manager of the club once it was set up. James recognized the stroke of brilliance of the set up organized by his wife and was delighted.

They were a handsome couple even at this stage of their lives, when they already had adult children and a first grandchild on the way. James was blond, with piercing blue eyes. Though he limped slightly because of several knee operations and the screws that held it all together, he still looked like an athlete. Dahlia, of Iraqi descent, had the expected dark, olive brown skin; she was petite and wore only comfortable silk clothes that would dance around her body at the slightest breeze. James was sure that she often got what she wanted because of her self-confident and charming smile. Occasionally, her face would turn sour, her eyes would get small, the lips of a mouth that was slightly too large for her smallish face would turn into tense, thin lines of anger. It was smart to stay far away from her when she was in that frame of mind.

Five days later a kit including pictures, appraisals, budgets, and plans was sent to all potential investors. Putting together the package was not easy in a Spain where even color copiers were scarce. But Dahlia found the way. Now the critical question became: would they join in? Except for the eccentric film producer from Beverly Hills, they were all

European and some were friends who could join together. Eventually six committed to the partnership. James and Dahlia were elated. They would be the General Partners, get ten percent of the shares, receive dividends and additional income for their routine managerial work.

The positive feelings did not last long. Three years later, by 2001, James became intolerant of this group. "Why does Maurice have to smell so badly; why not apply some deodorant?" he complained one night. Dahlia reminded him that he had asked the same question the previous year. James characterized the majority as "second-generation brats." He saw them as forty-year-old men who had tasted the silver spoon since infancy, indulged in all the benefits of the wealth created by their parents, and were certain to be deserving of every bit of it. James was particularly put off by two, Leopold Schwartz and Henry Bauman, friends since childhood, and living in their beloved Vienna. They were revolting as they routinely exhibited a huge sense of entitlement; they were beyond arrogant. These traits were even more striking when contrasted with their faculties. "What justifies their statements? What excuses their behavior? Their intellect is limited, their knowledge of basic facts lacking— probably because they skipped school as often as they attended it. Why this utter rudeness? They so often make no sense and then they annoy with those stupid outbursts." They displayed greed and avarice more than any of the others. Everyone else was eager to make plenty of money from the project, but these two saw their major contribution to be quibbling over expenditures. During one earlier visit in 1999, Leo and Henry had placed a call to another golf club near Lobos Locos to schedule a game. When asked if they were members, they answered that they were not, but that they were playing with James who, of course, was. They would save the additional €30 charge for nonmembers. When James arrived at the club to play with another friend, the club's secretary was confused. "I was told you were supposed to play with your friends Henry and Leo." James instantly knew what had happened; he slipped a €20 bribe to the club official to keep silent and avoid unpleasantness. That night he pulled the two Viennese to the side and sternly addressed them: "If you ever try something like this again, I will have you officially barred from entering the golf club. I had to bribe the club secretary €100 not to throw you out. You each owe me €50." They shrugged their shoulders and smirked; each pulled a €50 bill from their wallets. They had been caught, and instead of being embarrassed, their smiles suggested a "you win some, you lose fewer" attitude.

The fax machine feverishly beeped the arrival of a message; James read it out loud for Dahlia's benefit: "Sorry, too busy to come to the yearly festivities, finishing the biggest movie of my life. Send the dividend to the usual account and fax me the confirmation. If there is something that requires my attention, any important decisions to be made, you better call me on my private line. Regards, Matthew Plummer."

James sighed: "Our big star is, once again, not coming." M.P., as many called him, was an octogenarian with the vivaciousness of a cabaret impresario and the stamina of a man half his age. His life was his work, and although he had amassed a small fortune as a mostly B-flicks producer, he was an equally keen and active investor: real estate ventures, a few biotech companies, and a large bond portfolio. Though quite adept at managing his financial empire, his greatest joy, he would stress, was the production of movies and the squeezing of the actresses' backsides. Because the movie production was so time-consuming, he had learned to master most of what modern technology made available. Financial reports concerning his holdings covered a big part of his desk, and while most of us were sound asleep, he would review them and carefully assess each item. Because he only slept four hours (in fact, ever since he was young, he would get headaches if he slept longer), he would work till 3:00 a.m. Those who knew him were certain nothing would slip his oversight, even at this late stage of his life. He intimidated them all with his excellent mastering of detail.

M.P. knew how to negotiate. His tough bargaining tactics made him less loved by business associates of all walks of life. But James and Dahlia had also seen the humanity in him. One year while visiting California they saw how he tenderly cared for his demented daughter; ever since, they felt close to M.P. If he was intransigent, they smiled; if he was capricious, they humored him. James regretted not having M.P. at this meeting for another reason: his jokes would often relax the typically tense atmosphere. He was a short man with a large gut and a balding head, but he was charming and exuded confidence. That charisma seemed to give him magnetic powers.

The year prior, when he attended the annual gathering, M.P. proved very instrumental. The group was quarrelling and he masterfully brought them back into the fold. The economies of the world were shaken after September 11, 2001, and tourism had declined even in sunny Spain. The year had been financially difficult for everyone assembled there, and when the partners heard about the meager dividend from their Marbella property, they were not pleased. The rumblings started immediately. These wealthy investors were not too keen on getting bad news, especially not that year when they already had suffered great losses in the global stock markets. The spoiled brats chanted, almost in unison, "This cannot be! Maybe someone is stealing from us, maybe we should change accountants." Another partner, Maurice, had inquired how he could sell his shares and bolt out of the partnership. M.P., sensing that the situation was snowballing, rose to his feet, and with a crescendo theatrical voice that could remind you of Jason Robards, implored, "Stop acting like spoiled children who cannot face a normal economic downturn. I have my accountants look at the books every quarter (which was a tremendous white lie) —- there is nothing wrong with the numbers. It is just a normal cyclical downturn." The members immediately calmed down, maybe because of his age, or because he was the celebrity in the group. Maybe it was because they were impressed with the theatrics of his presentation, or perhaps it was because he projected the authority and leadership of an American general rescuing Europe from Hitler. M.P. saved the group from falling apart—- something that would have precipitated the need to find a buyer for the property at the worst possible time.

As always, first to arrive was Gregory Rosenblum. Always accompanied by a woman that was never his wife, they would stay in Marbella. He enjoyed the ambiance, the good life offered by the jet-setters' town. He had no qualms being seen with a different woman every year. He and his wife had not shared a bed for at least fifteen years; both knew they only stayed married for tax and other financial reasons.

Greg, as he liked to be called since his student days at Berkeley, was a Berlin physician whose practice specialized in the cure of rheumatic diseases. He made a good living and spent a good part of it on his hobbies. A friend of Schwartz and Bauman (he went to college in Vienna before going to medical school), he joined this real estate investment due to Bauman's insistence that he, just this once, do so. Even though he was skeptical of Henry and Leo's stories about fortunes made in this or that investment, he went along with the deal. Perhaps his passion for golf influenced him to acquiesce. The doctor was surely the least wealthy of the group. In fact, he borrowed from a bank the capital to buy his share in the development. Greg was also the most easygoing and, to the irritation of many, the best golf player among them—by far.

Even though he usually was relaxed, money matters and nervousness about this venture got him excited. Over a cappuccino at one of his favorite cafés, Greg routinely complained to his friend Peter, the Swiss banker managing his portfolio: "They say they have all this money. I think they have it because they inherited a big chunk and because they routinely manage to escape paying taxes on much of what they have and do; it is not because they are such savvy investors." He would get agitated and begin stuttering, "Th-th-that is the difference between th-th-them and m-m-me. I pay fifty percent t-t-taxes on what I make; they probably manage to hide ninety percent of th-th-their income. Besides, what kind of a life do they have, always on the phone, always t-t-t-t-talking deals, always k-k-k-kounting money ... at least I enjoy my life ... r-r-r-r-right, Peter?"

Greg knew that he had been dealt a good hand by Fortuna. Good looking like an actor, Greg was not a luminary, but he was smart about human relationships. Women were attracted to him, and he always smiled and found a way to charm them. "He is always hunted down by a few women who seem keen to jump into bed with him," observed a friend with a touch of jealousy. Greg, fully aware of his popularity, confessed to Peter, "I can't let any woman into my heart, that way I can enjoy and spread my time among a few."

Greg looked forward to his trip. He would receive his dividend check (a large portion would go towards paying off a portion of the bank loan), and he would enjoy what Spain had to offer. He envisioned that while he was not making any real money on the deal now, in the end he would own the shares free and clear, and once the property sold, it would provide for a nice chunk of his retirement nest egg. He was nearly sixty and needed to think about retirement. When he went to the meetings, he always had a small knot in his stomach. Will the dividend be distributed? Will they finally announce the sale of the property? He had arrived on Tuesday in Marbella and called James, who told him, "If you need anything, call us; otherwise we will see you Thursday."

Greg turned to Martina, his Slovak girlfriend at that time, and attended to what he appreciated most in life. Because she enjoyed Greg as much as he enjoyed her, she put up with the limited availability of Greg, the short trips to Spain, Greece, and Cyprus. She knew he would never divorce his wife and she would never be able to claim him fully to herself. They would spend time at the restaurants near the water, after-dinner hours at his favorite bar where they would pass the time, like everyone else, ogling others and being checked out in return. These had been the ways of the jet-setters forever, only the location changed: Nice, then Cannes, St. Tropez, San Remo, and now Marbella. At around 1:00 a.m., they would finally head to their five-star hotel room, have a loving moment before falling asleep in each other's arms.

If the Mouse irritated James and Dahlia because of his constant paranoia, Maurice triggered feelings of outright hostility. Prior to launching the partnership, the group had come together to see the site, meet the architects, discuss financial and other aspects of the development, and sign the agreement. Maurice was the sole voice expressing opposition to James and Dahlia getting ten percent of the total shares for putting the deal together. James explained and justified it by stating the obvious facts: he and Dahlia had come up with the idea, it was their early work negotiating the terms with the broker representing the seller that allowed the launch of this project, and they would also be the ones visiting the site while under construction. Even the stingy Viennese did not object.

But Maurice thought that a partnership only works if it is a deal between equals. Originally from Lebanon, but now spending most of his time in London. No one knew for sure how he had become very wealthy. Five years ago, a magazine had published an article about arms dealers making a lot of money out of supplying weapons to terrorists; his name was mentioned there. Maurice was well schooled in driving a hard bargain. His view of life was that it was constant war. In a moment of exceptional openness, he had told James that he viewed every business deal, every human exchange, in fact, as a situation with winners and losers. He even commented that after his death he wanted the epitaph to read: "Maurice won many more battles than he lost."

At the closing of the first partners' meeting, Maurice demanded that in the future, James meet with him one day in advance and answer any questions in private. That was the pound of flesh that he extracted. James was none too pleased about this concession. With every year that passed he loathed the man and this early one-on-one meeting more. Maurice would come into the office, an obnoxious odor always accompanying him, and ask James all kinds of minutiae about the development, details that were not described in the financial reports of the partnership. Were all the people frequenting the club really members paying their annual dues? How did he know they were? Could he demonstrate that this was the case, or was he making it up? Why was attendance at the restaurant not higher? Was the chef overpaid?

James lost his normally even temper when two years earlier, at the time of the global crisis, Maurice told James that he was planning to ask the other partners to contribute a portion of their own shares to cause an increase of at least two percent in Maurice's total in the venture; that, he claimed, would be the cost of him agreeing to stay in the partnership. He wanted to get out, but he understood that because of the crisis no one could afford to buy him out.

James, his face red and his eyes bulging, demanded they go to the patio and away from the other partners; once there, he told him, "Look, Maurice, there is no clause in the partnership agreement that allows any one of us to demand from the rest to buy him out. Furthermore, if you come even close to asking for this ransom-like increase in your shares—and this is nothing more than Middle Eastern–style blackmail you are applying here—I will personally guarantee that you will not leave Spain with your body intact. I do not know how, but you will break a few bones before you board that plane." James hoped his voice was not too shaky, that he was believable enough. He disliked using such primitive, violence-threatening language, but he did not know how to stop Maurice from being Maurice. During his childhood, James had firsthand experience with the impact of gruff treatment. He knew that the mere threat of physical violence could strike terror in some hearts. As a tall and strong youngster, he was able to apply force, and he kicked more often than he was kicked. His younger brother, David, in contrast, was a sickly, smallish boy who at least once a week came home with a bloody nose. Abused by classmates. James felt frustrated that he was not able to watch over his brother at all times. When he turned twelve, James swore he would do anything to get out of the violent neighborhood, and eventually he did. When he got his first good-paying job at the age of twenty-two, he was elated he could afford his first house on the other side of violence. That day he pledged not to apply violent force and coercion ever again. Later in life, one could hear him reminisce and say how proud he was not to revert to those methods once he got out of the old neighborhood. He sheepishly acknowledged to himself that this once he had come close to breaking his pledge, even if he had not violated it.

When Maurice would arrive, James had the maid usher him into his office; he would make his offensive visitor wait ten minutes before entering the room. He could not help it, disdain was probably written all over his face. At the same time, he was apprehensive of the next extortion scheme.

That Wednesday James was told that Maurice arrived promptly at 3:00 p.m.; James walked in ready for another round of friction. Yet, to his complete surprise, Maurice appeared calmer and less belligerent: "Hallo, James, all is well with you I hope?"

"Yes, Maurice, all is well. With you as well?"

"Everything is fine. Business is a bit slow, but I am managing. I suppose there is no major news from Malaga Country and Golf?"

"Nothing much out of the ordinary."

"Well, in that case I will go back to the hotel and I will see you tomorrow for the partners' meeting."

James was taken back by the reversal. Why would Maurice have come all the way to leave a few minutes later? Was this his way to say that he had finally relaxed, that he was no longer worried about being cheated out of his interests in the partnership? Was this a ploy? James had learned over the years to be circumspect about the actions and motivations of most of his business partners; in fact, of most people he interacted with, he mistrusted Maurice the most—him and his eyes that never looked directly at you.

"Sure, we'll see you tomorrow."

Through his machinations, Maurice had established the agenda and tone of the interactions between them. James could not stop Maurice from leaving, he could not say, "I am prepared for all your questions; go ahead, ask." He was not in control of the situation, and although he liked nothing better than Maurice leaving, he was uneasy about what had transpired.

Maurice kept a well-guarded secret learned many years ago: as a business school student, he had participated in a course on negotiations, and during those practice sessions he figured out that when negotiating with an equal who needs you, you can employ theatrics and wrestle control of future discussions in your favor. Your counterparts will always be afraid of your temper, of your unstable nature, your "irrationality." Maurice used these tactics when necessary. In his library, he kept a large section dedicated to two topics: the art of negotiation and winning stratagems in conflict. You could find books on game theory, Machiavelli, Chinese writers like Sun Tzu and Mao, Germans like von-Clausewitz and Moltke, military men like Marcus Aurelius, and yes, even several Shakespearean plays.

Later that night while lying in bed next to Dahlia, James described the earlier meeting. Dahlia's reaction was like his: "This guy has something up his sleeve, and I wish I knew what it was."

Perhaps because of the encounter with Maurice, perhaps because these partnership meetings were always stressful, James had a poor night. He had fallen asleep quickly, as he always did, but he woke up at 1:20 a.m. and lay awake for hours. He glanced at Dahlia's naked back, at her still beautifully shaped body. She was petite, but her figure was well shaped; you could see that even when you only saw her back. Her shoulders were round, her buttocks still firm and her legs muscular, but considering her strenuous exercise routine, not excessively so. He was happy with his marriage to her; it was so much better than his first.

Notwithstanding, he found himself strangely devoid of any sexual appetite. Because he was worried, he was flaccid. His instincts told him the meetings would be unusually difficult. His sixth sense was usually sound, and he guessed that trouble lay ahead.

Not having slept much, tired of lying in bed with his thoughts and concerns as his only company, and frustrated by his lack of arousal and lust, James went down to the kitchen at five in the morning. Copper pots and pans hung above the stove; that and other Spanish accents in the room pleased him. Together with the warm, brown ceramic tile, they produced a strong sense of home and familiarity. At 6:00 a.m., James was seeking peace and comfort in this room. He would need to leave and finish his preparations soon, but by spending time in his kitchen, he was reminding himself that he could always come back to this place, regain the strength of purpose that had guided him this far.

He made himself a cup of coffee and sat at the kitchen table to work out how the upcoming meeting would unfold. There would be the presentation from the manager of the club, Grande, who would include the reports from the accountants and from the comptroller. James would then present the overall picture, tying in foreign tourism in Spain, the Spanish economy, and real estate prices in the area. These presentations would be routinely interrupted by those present. The urge to ask questions had more to do with ego, their own need to remind everyone of their presence, as if they were so physically small that one would only see them through their unpleasant voices. A quick lunch (sandwiches and snacks) would be served by the staff of the club and most would leave soon thereafter. The next day they would all have a late breakfast on the terrace of Lobos Locos. It would be a sunny, warm day, but the early breakfast hour would lend itself to be pleasant enough. Later, they would travel to the club to examine its condition and to check out the golf course. James knew it to be particularly important to those who could play the game, even though their airs of self-importance; normally that air would be more powerful than the swings that would give flight to their golf balls.

In the afternoon, they would have a closed golf tourney, the gladiators would engage in their version of a wrestling match seeking to prove a vacuous point. Only the Mouse seemed not to care if he won. And he never did. These men played a game in which most of them were barely above average. They loved the competition and acted as though they were vying for the US Open Cup, the Masters' Green Jacket, or the British Open Championship. They were attempting to prove their manhood, their superiority, their competitiveness. To Dahlia (as hostess she always was around) they looked so glaringly empty and so pitifully weak.

The third and last day, at around 11:00 a.m., they would have a wrap-up session while eating brunch. Many would have to catch flights that same afternoon. As they left, James would give each partner an envelope containing his yearly dividend check. Based on experience, the last session would turn out to be either calm and pleasant, or stormy and difficult. James always feared that its structure-less nature was fertile ground for serious trouble to erupt. As he prepared a second cup of coffee from the espresso machine, he wondered what would happen this year. Just before these meetings James would get the strongest urge to dissolve the partnership. But he was still hoping that real estate prices in the area would peak so that the property could be sold at the best possible price. A long time ago, when he just started investing, a friend recommended a known maxim: "You always prefer to decide when to sell a property rather than have circumstances determine when to sell it." Maybe prices could go up a bit more, maybe it was just time to turn attention to a new project.

Ever so slowly, the rising sun brought light into the kitchen and James had to move away from the glare and the blinding reflection produced by the hanging copper pots. He liked Spain but he also felt that much like its shameless, total, uninhibited sun, Spain could bring people to acute agitation and trigger nefarious thoughts. He praised calmness, but he was being pushed to a state of great unease with no obvious relief in sight. Maurice had something up his sleeve. James's intuition was often right and he relied on it heavily. How would he deal with it? How could he deal with it? He had threatened him once before, but that was not the way he wanted to go. He had promised himself not to resort to violence. He had told Dahlia of this commitment and he did not want to disillusion her. She was too important to him. He had once heard about a shady situation Maurice was involved in; maybe he could fight fire with fire.

He briefly called Grande to discuss some details and went upstairs.

Back in his bedroom he saw that Dahlia, already awake, was lying naked on one side, as before, reading a book. As was often the case, James enjoyed making love to Dahlia in the morning. He gently took away her book and kissed her on the lips. It was an invasion of her space, and she could have refused James's intrusion, but Dahlia enjoyed the abruptness of morning lovemaking; it brought all her senses to a prickly wakefulness and she liked that. Thereafter, they rested, holding hands, each one staying within the confines of their early morning thoughts, not talking. Dahlia was thinking about the beauty of lovemaking when it all fits like the two hands holding each other so perfectly as if they were made for each other. James was still extremely worried about the upcoming meetings, and although he had been totally devoted to Dahlia a few minutes ago, and although his hand holding Dahlia's reflected his love for her, his mind turned to the mundane worries that had brought an early end to his sleep.

Eventually the hand followed the mind and disengaged from Dahlia's. She was annoyed by James's behavior: why could he not have extended the intimacy longer? How could he be so affectionate and warm one moment and so detached and cold a few minutes later? She got up without saying a word and let the shower pouring down her back soothe her. James knew what bothered Dahlia, but he could not, did not even want to, stray away from his concern about the upcoming meetings. He needed to be fully alert and aware of all contingencies, he needed to think about all eventualities.

While in the shower Dahlia reflected on how upset she was about James' distance just before. She could make a fuss about it, but she was smarter than that. She had a good marriage and she understood that this was a difficult and stressful moment for James. Dahlia finally broke her silence: "How will you deal with Maurice? There has to be a way to match his nastiness and his subterfuge. You are smart, James, my love— find that way."

James was moved by Dahlia's insight and her plea. He went down to the kitchen and made one more call to Grande. James spoke quickly and in a low voice about an idea he had.

As soon as Dahlia was done with her shower, James headed that way. They crossed paths without saying a word, without touching each other, expeditiously, purposefully, machinelike. "How quickly great love can turn inside out in the modern beast," thought Dahlia. "Unfortunate is the person who wishes to extend a moment of unity of souls and have it carry lasting love beyond its own delightful apex; unfortunate the soul who is not satisfied with basking in the short-lived essence of sexual intimacy."

Wearing his usual outfit: blue pants, light yellow shirt, and blazer, colors that made his blue eyes dance, James checked himself in the mirror with approval. At least his face looked alert and his eyes did not reflect the nearly sleepless night. A tired face would invite much more harassment from his partners. Sex also had an invigorating effect on him. He had heard friends say that they would have sex to sleep better at night; he could not understand what they were talking about.

Ten thirty in the morning, prompt as always, the Mouse steps out of a taxi that had driven him directly from the Malaga airport. He is wearing the largest sunglasses James has ever seen; his clothes appear oversized and that is likely to be purposeful as well. Underneath his mustache, James can divine a thin smile. The Mouse had made it one more time. There had not been any police interrogation, no interruptions, no hindrance. Thank goodness EU membership made continental travel much easier. Dahlia does the courtesy of showing him to the guest room where he would stay for the next couple of nights. He is thankful he can stay at Lobos Locos; no hotel registry will have his name. The meetings will start in half an hour and he needs to wash up, so he is reminded where the towels are and that the bathroom for his use is next door. "Do not wander about and mistakenly use ours" is what Dahlia is thinking.

Soon thereafter, the others arrive in quick succession. First the two Viennese, then Greg. They already are talking about the usual themes: golf and girls. Henry describes in much detail and with fanfare how he had arranged the services of a black call girl, and he explains that "he just had to have this experience once in his life." Greg asks if it is different, if they have three breasts or two vaginas. He is goading Henry, but this flies by unnoticed, perhaps as unremarkable as the night may have been for that prostitute. Greg remembers what his friend Peter had told him: "Our generation of men has a hard time getting old, cannot accept the decay, the declining sperm count, and the ultimate fallout of circulation." Greg thinks that Henry's is another way of fighting the demise. He says little more. In fact, if you look into his eyes, it seems like he is enjoying the crowing of the rooster. He is used to hearing Henry talk about his sexual exploits and his feelings are mixed. He doubts half of them took place, but he is also aware of his own sexual appetite and so he delights and is aroused while listening in.

Five minutes before the meeting starts, Maurice arrives. Everyone else is there, except M.P. of course. In the meantime, the officers of the club have also arrived, and their presentation begins. The seating around a large oval table that was bought by Dahlia during the company's second year, and at its expense, is partially informal, partially formal. James and Dahlia are always at the head of it, the rest take chairs randomly; except that Greg, Leo, and Henry always take one side of the table, the Mouse, not particularly liked by anyone, sits at the other end, and that leaves Maurice to occupy the side that is closer to the kitchen door. Maurice always leaves a bit of distance from the others. He most often is out to make a point and does so here as well. He likes the notoriety.

The room sees little usage during the rest of the year. Few host lavish dinner parties anymore. Help has become expensive these days and no hostess would want to break her nails washing a ton of dishes. In any case, it was meant to be a formal dining room and is appropriately located near the kitchen. It has a large window which covers a significant portion of the wall and allows a view of the countryside. The beautiful landscape almost looks like a painting, and so the window was framed as if it were a painting—Dahlia's unusual taste coming to the fore.

James welcomes the guests briefly and embarks on a presentation about the general business conditions affecting the club. It has been a decent year, membership is slightly up, but, because of necessary improvements and upkeep, expenses were unusually high and the dividend payout will remain unchanged. James states the facts in a businesslike manner. He has learned that his delivery must not show the slightest signs of failing confidence. The political environment continues to be positive for real estate investments in Spain. That raises hopes that the development can be sold for a substantial gain. The shareholders would have to decide whether this is the year to call it quits. James surprised himself. There it was. He had said it. Maybe they will react, maybe they won't. In any case, it will be important to convey the message to M.P. as well.

Maurice interrupts him, his French accent heavy: "The issue of selling the club should be left to the end of the discussions. There should be a professional presentation on its expected value, and it should not come from James, even though he has a significant percentage of the shares." Maurice is already at it, thinks Dahlia. Maybe the bastard should be reminded who laid foundations for this venture.

James pulls himself together, he continues stating facts about the continuing influx of northern Europeans (especially English and German) coming to Spain to hibernate. It is critical to the future of the exclusive and more expensive club that they come. Foreigners represent sixty-three percent of the club's membership. He passes out the schedule, pretty much the same as the one of years before. He does not ask if there are any questions. He knows this group does not need to be asked; he simply sits down.

The manager of the club follows with his presentation. Carlos Grande had traded in his half percent, promised to him by Dahlia, for this sinecure of managing the business. He is paid handsomely, and his contract includes a special bonus when the property gets sold. Grande explains that prices were raised slightly, and the restaurant had good income because it hosted and catered a few weddings. But expenses were up: a new roof was put over the restaurant, the pool upkeep became more expensive, and the tiles around the pool had cracked and needed to be replaced. All in all, the net result is a dividend distribution that is

154

equivalent to a 6.35 percent yield, the same as last year. James expects the silly remarks and questions to start pouring in: "Why wasn't the new tile less expensive? Why did the old crack? Who was responsible for the purchase of the bad tile?" Henry, Leo, and Maurice enjoy hearing themselves torture *Ingeniero* Grande; they all chime in, and they smirk as they always tend to do. These fellows smirk way too often, thinks James as he sits impassively at the head of the table. He would like to put a stop to it, but he can't. He is incapacitated by the present amalgam of mediocrity and wealth, and while he is aware of their limitations, he is frozen. He finds this ironic and produces a strange, twisted smile.

The men were as noisy and as raucous as in years past; James is getting exasperated and resolves that the property should be sold. He has had enough of all this. Dahlia had also gotten used to it, but she notices that her eyes are turning smaller, the smile is vanishing from her face, and she suddenly feels a light twitch of the muscle on the lid of her right eye. It's a nervous twitch she interprets resolutely: she is getting too old for all of this. Her thoughts are interrupted by the Mouse's voice. He rarely speaks and the high-pitched sound brings her back. "I am in real estate. I manage properties. We buy tile and it lasts fifteen years at least. I do not understand this." Even he has turned into a renegade, but his face contorts apologetically for lashing out.

Because of the multitude of questions, the session that usually takes an hour extends to almost two. By the end, everyone's nerves are brittle, and the adrenaline is flowing fast and furious. Maurice mockingly raises his hand as if he were in school; he, somewhat theatrically, asks for permission to speak to the group. James knows that lightning is about to strike. "I have been with this group from the beginning, and in business even longer. I have never seen such incompetence in management. We have a couple that brought us the property, a nice property that has potential to make good money for us, but afterwards they ran this business like it was their personal business. They have put in place this person whom we cannot even remove." He points at Grande. I suggest that we nominate a new management board, that we ask Mr. Grande to step down and go home, and that we reduce the share owned by Mr. and Mrs. Crown."

James senses that Maurice's bombshell has exploded with exquisite timing. The group was sounding more and more like a bunch of rebels ready to pounce on James, Dahlia, and Grande, and he is exploiting the situation fully. It is clear that Maurice would like to nominate himself dictator, just like Gaius Julius Caesar did. What Maurice lacks in finesse he makes up for with audacity; what Caesar lacked in political wisdom he made up for with ruthlessness. James closes his eyes, and as he does the room spins dizzily. He notices that several of the partners' faces start spinning as well, just the faces and their mouths contorted in unusual grimaces; they are all caricatures, grotesque and unfriendly. At first the Viennese are noticeably nodding their heads in approval of Maurice's statement. Then they start shaking their heads when he speaks of actions to be undertaken. But James senses that this has more to do with their instincts telling them that they are seeing danger in Maurice. James is sure that if they have the opportunity, these two will exploit the situation to benefit themselves from the crisis.

Is this all a planned conspiracy? Did they raise all these questions to set the stage? Has Maurice promised them something in return? The questions are pounding through James's mind, like his heartbeat. He looks around to see if the group's eyes convey dismay or pleasure, surprise or callous readiness to pounce on the carcass. He can't tell whether these are wolves or sheep, and this annoys him almost more than the actual battle he is now facing. He is boiling inside.

Not a single man stands up to defend him and Dahlia. He looks around again to make sure he sees the real faces, not the masks he saw a few seconds earlier. Furthest from him, the Mouse's face seems to say, "See how it feels when you get trampled?" Greg, good old Greg, he is shaking his head; he is unhappy about the turn the meeting has taken. Is it because of loyalty to James and Dahlia, or because he just wants his check and to run to his girlfriend? It is hard to know. Greg does not say much except mutter, "Nonsense, nonsense."

James is furious as he continues to canvass the table. His investors—the ones he so painstakingly courted years ago—are ignoring the same couple who brought the investment opportunity to their desks, the two who engineered a special deal with the broker so that they could get the property, the ones who hosted the meetings for so many years, tolerated this bunch of egocentric mediocrities, and showered them with pleasantries. Henry and Leo are talking in hushed tones. It is not clear to James if they are plotting to exploit the situation for their own benefit, but he knows that ultimately that is what they care about.

It is time for him to act, resolutely, with impunity, but without showing them his disregard:

"Friends, not only did I bring a good deal to you when I met you in London. I also have served you well. In fact, Maurice, who wants to take over, is the one who wanted to rob you of a percentage of your shares until I stopped him. This, as you remember, was a couple of years back, and it appears he is at it again now." He looks around. No one is asking questions, nor are they wooed, not yet. "In any case, no decision of this magnitude can take place without the full partnership voting on it. We must pass on the information to M.P." James feels like he has regained a measure of control. He has raised some doubts about Maurice. He hopes that the group is puzzled by his comment about Maurice trying to gain something at their expense. Above all, they really respect M.P. and this is crucial. James has gained time, and time is an important element of control that he can also use to his advantage. He quickly follows through:

"M.P. is still asleep now. We will be able to speak to him in a few hours. I suggest we adjourn until 4:00 p.m., at which point we will call him. In fact, we can video-conference him in."

It is subtle, but nonetheless important. This group of shallow characters will be much more impressed by seeing M.P. than by just hearing him. After Maurice's surprisingly peaceful visit the day before, James had decided to set up the possible videoconference with M.P. He figured that since the man is in the film business, this was not going to be a technically difficult issue at his end, so all James had to do was organize it on his side. The day prior, he spoke to M.P. at some length about his uneasiness with Maurice's visit. M.P. promised to be helpful, but at a price. The old man would fall in line and give something, but he also asked for something in return. James expected this much, so it was all right. M.P. needed the golf club's restaurant for a location for his new film, and he wanted to get it as cheaply as possible, maybe for free. "We always have budget problems," he reminds James.

James assured him: "You will get it for free, as long as the name of the club can show in a couple of places of the movie. If they do that with cigarettes and beer, why not with the club?" The partners would understand it was for the club's benefit. Maybe this once they would not ask for something in return. After striking the deal with M.P., James called Grande, who arduously worked on getting the instrumentation for the video feed.

Maurice carps that James is just buying time and that he is acting out of self-interest. It is Henry, surprisingly shallow, pleasure driven, sex-obsessed Henry, who butts in and says, "We all need time to consider what you have proposed here, Maurice." It is not a conspiracy after all. There is a quick nod from others. When James glances over, he feels that their minds are hard at work trying to decide where they want to place themselves on this issue. They can gain a few percentage points of ownership, they can get rid of Grande, whom they never chose nor ever fully trusted. But after that, what? Will they leave it all in the hands of Maurice? Can they trust the usurper? Leo chimes in, "This is too complicated a matter; we should also listen to M.P. We should reconvene at four this afternoon."

As the meeting adjourns, it is now well past 1:00 p.m. Dahlia can see that Maurice is feverishly working on Greg to support him. She moves over with a tray of sandwiches and a fake smile; she is delighted to interrupt. The other side of the table is talking about golf and girls again, as if nothing of consequence had just transpired. The Mouse has turned toward the terrace and no one knows where he stands on these matters. There is not much of a luncheon as most tapas are left untouched. It is as if all are looking to exit the theatre at once. Grande looks angry, but when James gives him a light nod, he smiles.

James and Dahlia eat their lunch in the kitchen. They are alone and they do not say much. Maybe they could talk about perfidious behavior, about associating with strangers, about salvaging what can be salvaged. They are probably thinking about the same things, but they do not say. They know that business is like this; they are not rookies. Dahlia also knows that James will somehow pull this off. It is a quick lunch, just a couple of bites, and James says he wants to go for a swim to relax. Dahlia figures he wants to be alone and she is mature enough not to ask further questions. She watches him take the BMW a few minutes later. She is worried but not overly anxious as she mutters to herself, "I hope he is doing the right thing." The last thing she can see is that he has grabbed his cell phone.

James comes back at 3:30 and he looks relaxed. It puzzles Dahlia, who expected him to be much more agitated. She has tried to take cover from her thoughts by keeping busy. She has spent the time arranging some pastries for this unplanned meeting. Grande's people have set up the large TV screen to be used for the videoconference, and Dahlia also made sure they would not scratch the walls while setting up. They all come in as close to 4:00 p.m. as possible. They don't want to be in the room that is packed with uneasiness, and postpone lingering in the tense atmosphere for as long as possible.

James stands. "Unless someone has something to say, I will call M.P. right away." They all nod. "One more thing, Mr. Grande, would you please leave the room?" Grande does so without a comment, like a dog that is sent to do his business outside.

The link is established quickly and M.P. is seen in his short-sleeve shirt, two buttons open, a thick gold chain around his neck, and a broad smile on his face. His hair is colored brown, but at least what limited hair is on his head is natural. Even so, he reminds Dahlia of the "impresario" in the movie version of *Moulin Rouge.*

"My European friends, how are you all?"

James takes the lead. "M.P., I am sorry you are not here, and I am glad to see you are as well as always. An important issue has come up and we need to talk to you, if you don't mind."

"I suppose it is important for you to want to go through the trouble of video-conferencing me and bothering this old mate."

"Maurice has essentially proposed to kick out the management, including Mr. Grande, Dahlia, and me. That is the gist of it, but I thought I should let him speak for himself. Maurice, please come over to this side so the camera can focus on you."

Maurice looks unusually shaky as he moves over to the head of the table. He does not have the air of certainty he had in the earlier meeting. He clears his throat.

"Hello, M.P., good to see you. I proposed this morning that we dismiss Mr. Grande. Once again, expenses are too high and our dividend will remain the same because of that. This is the only business I have where my income never increases. However, I have also thought it over, and if we can sell the property with a nice gain in the coming year, then the expenses have been worth it, and since Mr. Grande was the broker who introduced the property to us, maybe we should commission him with procuring the sale. As for Dahlia and James—our nice hosts"—his voice is now truly shaking—" we should discuss all my suggestions next year if the sale does not go through."

"Well, Maurice, it looks like over the last two hours you have done some thinking and cooled down a bit, my friend." M.P. is usually diplomatic and has a good poker face, but here the old man has slipped up; it is now crystal clear that a discussion with James about the content of the upcoming conference call had taken place earlier. M.P. is using that Jason Robards voice again. It always works for him. "I think it is wise to sell the property in the coming year. I approve, and I also think that since Mr. Grande will be busy finding a buyer, he will be less available to run the place. I have a good friend who can do the job for one year. He runs a Beverly Hills hotel—I mean, used to run it until he recently retired—and I probably can get him to do it. As for James and Dahlia, they brought us the deal, it will make a nice profit, and since they are such a nice couple, why don't we stop bothering them?" He says that with a wink as exaggerated as that of the mistress of *The Weakest Link.* "I wish you all a very nice evening. Regrettably, I need to go and shoot more film, and this damn director is giving me lots of trouble, like always. How do you Europeans say it? *'Comme toujour'*."

In his usual way, M.P. has been the defense lawyer and the judge all at once. He states things as if there is no room for further discussion or argument. This is how it works for him in the Hollywood jungle, and how he expects it to work elsewhere.

"Thank you, M.P. I am sure you will produce another masterpiece; you have done it before." Dahlia gets the sense that James means M.P.'s speech now. But she is rather shocked about Maurice's turnabout. What happened over the last few hours? How is it possible that Maurice, the proverbial attack dog, changed his mind and agreed to a much less radical move? Leo speaks out: "I think it is settled then. Grande will only stay as manager of the club until the new man comes. If he ran a hotel in L.A. he cannot be too bad. Make sure his salary is the same. He is retired, and even if he is American, he cannot be more expensive at his age. After that, Grande looks for a buyer and I sure hope he finds one fast. His bonus, originally part of the contract with him, should be part of his compensation as the broker for the sale. I sure hope this happens before the next annual meeting. I have grown fed up with the heat of Spanish summers and with their women." Dahlia is nauseated by the childish laughter this last sentence elicits. She is also fed up, but with these partners.

They all agree quickly. Relief is written over all their faces. Leo makes one more suggestion: "I think we have spent enough time together as a group. I do not think more meetings are necessary. If someone wants to play golf at the club, let them do it on their own. We already have the financial statements. I suggest we adjourn. If it is okay with all, I would like my dividend check and to get the hell out of here."

That night in bed, Dahlia suddenly turns to James and stares at him with the biggest eyes he has ever seen. "What happened, James? Why did Maurice change his mind? Why was he less adamant to kick us out? Did you use violence, James? Please don't tell me you broke your pledge."

James is slow to respond. He is thinking it over: should he tell her the truth and perhaps become a lesser man in the eyes of his best friend and lover? Or should he lie and conceal as he may do with a business associate? He ultimately decides that he cannot lie to her.

"I paid a visit to Maurice after I left the house. I did not go for a swim. I took along a friend—actually, it is Grande's friend—someone you don't know. He is a journalist. A couple of years back he traced a story about a drug related scheme that was hushed up in corrupt ways. A judge was bribed and the culprits went free. Maurice was rumored to be part of the scheme. My new friend and I reminded Maurice that this story could do him much harm if it were revived. I suggested that we sell the property this year. The rest of what you heard from Maurice this afternoon was him working out the details. Poor Grande had to be the sacrificial lamb. It all came out reasonably well, and I am looking forward to getting rid of the club."

A few minutes later Dahlia starts crying and James holds her tight. All he can hear through her sobs is: "You did not break your oath. My love, you did not break your oath!"

After a short while, James sat up in bed, his torso straightened up, his legs were crossed lotus style, and he asked Dahlia to do the same and face him. This position was much easier for her than him with his knee problems. He knew this, but he wanted the moment to be special:
"My love, I know how you feel, and I am so proud that I decided not to resort to force. I did it as much for me, and my pride, as I did it for you, for the love I feel for you. In a few months, when we sell the club and dissolve the partnership, we will be proud of what we achieved, not only in the monetary sense but that we built a beautiful company, we managed a gathering of some rather strange bedfellows and shepherded them to a successful finale. You, my love, you were a very important partner in this endeavor. I could have used force, or threatened to use violence. But I could never look you in the eye ever again and say I love you and have you believe me."

"You and I will often laugh about this group of people with their strange habits and ideas, we may even visit our film producing friend at some point. Above and beyond everything, I know I care for you today more than ever before."

JAMMING

■

My name is Carl Horak and I am twenty-four years old . I just celebrated my birthday last week. Maybe that has caused me to turn pensive and reflect over the tension in my relationship with my father for the better part of my life. I was always a loving son and so very proud of his public role as a professor and an author. But I also was painfully aware that often enough I did not measure up to his expectations. For a long time, I had great difficulties reconciling both truths.

I am thinking about the times I was a confused adolescent—it made perfect sense to want to escape my overbearing father. Nonetheless, my rebellion was just bluster leading to further frustration. I now realize that any attempt to escape him, or even his shadow, was bound to be hopeless. Beyond the financial dependence, I was, after all, genuinely proud in carrying the same last name.

Over the years, when I would talk to friends, I often found myself proudly advertising that my father had been lauded in a professional magazine (my mother made sure I always knew about those). Often, my buddies could not care less, but I ignored that.

Walking around the room he used as his home-office, while he was at the university, I would look at copies of his book, look at the name, our name, touch them and feel my chest swell. I knew that while I was pushing back against his demands to strive for excellence, deep down I wanted nothing more than to gain his admiration and respect. All along, I had no siblings to share feelings and vent whatever frustrations I harbored.

I remember I was about fourteen, one February afternoon, I came home from school, my Mom gave me the expected hug and asked me to sit next to her as she opened the *New York Times*. She put her index finger on a line. There it was: in the second paragraph, our last name, "Horak." The article was referring to my father's involvement in Czech literature. Mother, always very reserved and quiet, making sure she was on the sidelines, that her family, and foremost her husband, was well fed and able to do his important work, told me how proud she was of Dad and what he had accomplished over the last two decades. I asked her what the article was about, and she responded that it was about a new generation of Czech writers; it mentioned Father as an authority on anything related to that country's literature.

Of course, by then, I was already somewhat aware of my father's importance. The Washington Square apartment was frequently visited by men and women of all ages. From the tone of their voices, very serious conversations were being held. During those early teenage years, I did not know what they were discussing. I eavesdropped, but the words were almost foreign to me. What I did notice, however, was that often my father was the lone speaker, and I concluded that they had great respect for his opinion, stayed quiet listening to him.

I was also made keenly aware that he thought I should follow in his footsteps. Even then. From the time I was very young, whenever I wanted to go to a friend's house and play games or if I wanted to hang out with classmates, he would tell me that there were more important things in life. I can still hear him say: "I know you like I know the palm of my hand; you want to go and play." My recollection is that his voice sounded strident and persistent, even if those words were always accompanied by a smile.

I suppose he could not help it, but his stern eyes made me wonder if I was misbehaving. I could hear his mouth saying, "I love you, son," but those piercing light blue eyes were foretelling of a sermon exhorting, a caring parent pushing, a father demanding. Early on, I would hear, "You should do your homework." In my teens, it was, "Study harder," and, "You ought to be thinking about these important subject.," After I turned sixteen, it was "Carl, try harder, give more, push yourself until you sense that you gave it your best, go the extra mile."

I remember that one afternoon my mother told me that she knew Father was very demanding and that I felt stressed because of that. "But," she explained, "he means well and wants you to become as famous as he is." I went to my room, closed my eyes, and wondered whether my frustration was without merit. Here it seemed that I would never be able to please him, but maybe I had gotten it all wrong; maybe my intuitive rebellion, my anger, my great desire to flee the man who gave me life and a big portion of my biological (we look very much alike) and psychological makeup was neither wise nor respectful. I went back to Mom, and with what was probably a sad voice, said, "I just wish he would show more pleasure with my good grades, would show some pride in my good report cards."

Today I am in awe of Martin Horak because he is considered one of the world's foremost experts on Czech literature, and even more so because of his philosophical insights. The Columbia University professor of comparative literature was also the author of a book focused on understanding titled *Meaning*. It was a book that, one review noted, had gained world acclaim. Even if his expertise was in areas that were somewhat obscure, not exactly at the center of human concerns, I prefer to note that among the cognoscenti he was a well-respected academic. My earlier internal revolt has turned to admiration; that voice that pushed me harder was not just that of my father, but also of a man respected by a much broader circle of people. How could I ignore it? Take for example my friend Andy, whose father was a chronic alcoholic, and in Andy's own words, "a loser." He could not possibly feel the same pressure to perform when the words exhorting performance were coming out of such a drunken soul.

The subliminal struggle, I already realized by the time I was in high school, also had something to do with the fact that I felt a tremendous urge to compete with him, and maybe not necessarily with him, but with his fame. Today, years later, I know that, in effect, I was trying to prove Dad wrong of whatever criticism he voiced by gaining my own notoriety and matching him in the societal-status game of life. That became a major preoccupation for many years after I turned sixteen.

If the early years (during elementary school) showed that I was talented enough to get good grades in most study areas, these results brought limited satisfaction to a father who was quick to praise me but always asked for more. In the later years, thinking that I was smart enough to broaden my perspective, he felt encouraged to pass on his knowledge on a variety of topics in his expertise. I was merely an adolescent when I started hearing about Deconstruction and Derrida, about Kundera and Jaroslav Seifert. I was barely a teenager when he started telling me about his thoughts about "meaning." He even would use the German word *Verstehen* to point out the gravity of the subject; philosophical arguments were being drummed into me even then. But I was not particularly inclined to absorb the dense material; if fully understanding meaning was a controversial philosophical subject, to me it sounded a bit foreign and weird. Instead, that crusade of his became a perfect opening to rebel. In fact, I took the rejection a step further by showing interest in sci-fi literature, which Father considered utterly superficial, even irrelevant. Why he could not understand that his stuff was close to incomprehensible to me at that age, and that Czech literature was as distant and foreign as the small country itself, is beyond me. Such a bright man but, all too often, so far removed from reality.

Obviously, I was aware of our cultural lineage. My father had stressed his, our, European origins (he firmly believed that they made us intellectually superior), but to me that heritage, in and by itself, was not good enough a reason to give priority to the material he was trying to push on me. The rejection of my father's teachings was full-fledged. I would listen to him, or rather, pretend to listen to him, but my mind was shut off. Once, I vividly remember, I was recalling scenes from *Star Wars* while he spoke. I looked attentive (at least, I thought I did), but barely heard a word and internalized none. The rejection was instinctive, natural, unrehearsed, unplanned, and undistilled by any consciousness; therein was its strength, its totality. I was convinced that Father did not notice, but notice he did. He was not pleased at all and admonished me, "I know you like I know the palm of my hand, and I also know what you are thinking even if you are not saying it. Do you think your father is a fool spending time and effort teaching you about concepts like 'meaning'? Do you think that all those who respect your father's academic work in this area are idiots? Why would they listen to what your father has to say and you, my son, remain oblivious and so distant while I give you the best of what I know?" It sounded like that man, my father, was trying anything, including sounding very haughty, to try to get my attention. I would look at him and remain quiet, and that was even more irritating for him. He knew, because he did know my inner thoughts. There was never going to be submission. But Martin Horak was not the kind of man who was willing to give up quickly, and he would seize many opportunities to discuss philosophy, epistemology, and "meaning" with me.

In an effort to lessen the tension in the house, around the time I turned fifteen, my mother convinced Dad to buy a piano and have me take lessons. "He has these wonderfully big hands, and I bet he can play well." I soon discovered that my hands, in fact my long fingers, were capable of gliding with great facility over the piano keys, and eventually I enjoyed spending hours playing known pieces like Beethoven's *Moonlight Sonata*, or a Bach étude. The lessons were fine, but I had more fun trying out my own little compositions and exploring the effect of some chords. Maybe it was that I started classes late, maybe it was part of my rebellion, but I was a lot less interested in classical music, which my parents loved (Bartok, Brahms, and Beethoven were their favorites). My preference was jazz. While I was informed enough about classical music (what European household would not inculcate that Eurocentric musical universe?), jazz was what would get me excited. Its free-floating nature, the ability to break the mold and improvise, fit my character to a T.

Father was not enamored with his son's new dedication to music. "You are spending too much time on that stuff. Sure, I want you to have fun, and music, any music, even jazz, brings joy to the heart, but every hour you spend listening to that music or improvising on the piano, you are not spending learning things that you will need later in life, once you go to college and hopefully, graduate school." I would listen, nod, and grab a book, but my earphones would go back to where they had been, and my head would rhythmically bounce to the music of Stan Getz and the Modern Jazz Quartet.

Time passed, and I was set to go to college. I needed to—but also wanted to—discuss with my father my options of colleges that would accept me. My grades were good but not phenomenally good. He tried to influence me to stay in New York. Columbia would surely accept me. But for me it was obvious. I had to get out of New York City, the place where my father had established his little empire. At the end, the compromise was to stay on the East Coast and go to Amherst. The geographical distance, 165 miles, seemed far enough and was a welcome factor in my new life.

After an unremarkable freshman year, and one semester of the following year, I went to my advisor to discuss a semester abroad. The discussion broadened to my general plans until graduation and beyond. Suddenly a strange thing happened—I had to confront my own and other people's questions about what I was going to do with my life, this time without having to listen to my father egging me on. I had to figure out how to become a well-respected human being on my own, and how I would end up showing Father that any misgivings he might have had were unfounded. I had to find a path in my studies. My advisor, Dr. Pet, as students tended to call him by shortening his name (Petkovich), knew that I was the son of Martin Horak and tried to push me in the direction of comparative literature. I refused to follow in Father's footsteps. Then Dr. Pet tried the geographic link: "How about getting some expertise in Eastern Europe? I seem to recall that you like political science, and there is a revolution of sorts going on in Eastern Europe... " And so it is that I, Carl Horak, the son of a Czech immigrant, the son of an authority on Czech literature, got interested in the region that included and engulfed Czechoslovakia.

Even today I wonder if this became an area of interest by accident or by design. Was it that I chose it because other things were less interesting, or because my father's large shadow was still hovering over me? I began to learn Russian. If there were to be a revolution, it would have to involve the Bear that dominated the region. I was doing so even though I felt nothing but disdain for almost all things Russian (vodka, which I fell in love with, excluded, of course).

When I went home for Christmas, Father asked me what courses I was taking and what plans I had for the future; I told him about the new direction in my life. Lately he had become visibly older and somewhat of a misanthrope. He started berating me about these being easy choices, gut courses, and the need to pursue deeper philosophical questions rather than listening to some guy interpreting Russian history.

That Christmas visit made me very unhappy; for the first time in my life I felt that the father I knew and secretly admired was fading. If before there was a schism caused by his pushiness, I thought we would eventually bridge it; that Christmas I felt that the gap was widening beyond repair and that it would last forever. Winter was always a special season for us two. We used to spend time playing chess and watching football (when the Giants played he used to act like a kid; I enjoyed watching him screaming at the TV screen). Neither of us was inclined to do so that year and it made me want to go back to the quaintness of New England. After being away from home for some time, I wanted to feel again that sense of belonging. When it went missing, I decided that my life had turned a new leaf.

For spring break, I did not even go back to New York. Instead I hung out on campus splitting my time in four places that were becoming central to my life. One was my girlfriend Anna's bedroom in an off-campus apartment she shared with two other girls. From Anna, I learned that sex was not just about the physical act (what other creatures roaming the planet do), but was also delightfully comical, (especially that one time we reached climax just as the classical station was blasting the *Hallelujah* hymn). I spent the rest of my time at the local bookstore where I worked seven days a week so that I could have enough money for vodka and Anna; at the library, where I would spend hours listening to tapes in the language lab; and in the basement of Charles's fraternity where three friends and I practiced our music as we were trying to put together a jazz band.

It was a great time in my life. A time during which, I must confess, I gave little consideration to Martin Horak. Anna and I ate together, slept together, loved together; I was thrilled to see her enjoying the band. My time in the library was efficiently spent—get the homework done, go to the lab and become better at speaking and understanding Russian, and when tired, borrow a jazz music tape and listen to that. The band was clearly amateurish and we felt we were a work in progress; maybe we never would become good enough—but we had fun and laughed a lot. The bookstore made me eventually the one responsible for scheduling, which meant making sure things went smoothly despite the frequent shifts and changes in personnel. Pretty much those four concerns remained with me for the next two years. Naturally, coursework and classes had to be added to the schedule, but there was only limited pleasure derived from those, and I often took them to be a necessary chore.

There was, however, an important interlude. Even before I went to college, Dad and I decided that he would financially support my spending extended time during my junior year on some European campus. "It will be good for your formation," he had said. I took that to mean in his way of thinking, that without that experience, I would be a deformed, incomplete human being. The notion of spending time even further away from him had great appeal and remained an attractive proposition even after we had become more distant during the Christmas of my sophomore year.

And so it was that I spent the junior spring semester in Aix-en-Provence taking courses at the "Sciences Po." The university was near the center of town, and I loved taking long walks in the old city with its little squares, cute fountains, bells ringing from churches left and right. I missed Anna and the band but adapted well to the changes: I replaced vodka with good, thankfully cheap, red "house wine"; Mireille took Anna's place in my bed (but never really in my heart); and I accepted that listening to jazz was a tolerable substitute to playing (maybe because

I never was very happy with the performances of the band). Obviously, it was much harder to find people with whom I could play, and getting access to a piano, or even an electronic keyboard, was beyond my budgetary constraints.

In hindsight, it was all too strange that this beautiful part of the world, a place where artists like Cézanne and van Gogh found inspiration for their transcendent art, would become the place where I first would learn about multinational corporations, international business, new ventures, and the multiple efforts by Western companies to expand and seize on opportunities in what was fast becoming a fact: the opening up of, once-closed, Communist Eastern Europe.

Moreover, I was really attracted to the material I was reading. At the university, the only course that had an Eastern European focus was being taught in the economics department and dealt with all these new developments. For someone whose upbringing and molded general outlook were so far removed from mundane issues like making money, I was flabbergasted to find out that this stuff actually interested me and inspired my curiosity. Once or twice it did cross my mind that Father would be totally appalled by this turn of events, but his influence seemed as distant as the geographic gap of the moment. There were a few times when I reflected: how can the son of Martin Horak be interested in such topics as the potential riches involved in privatizing the phone company of Hungary or setting up a laundry service company in Poland that would cater to the needs of hotels in nearby Berlin? But I rejected these troubling thoughts and remained intrigued about what I was hearing and learning. It seemed peculiarly relevant to me; suddenly heritage, Czech literature, Dr. Pet and Russian history merged and offered a solution to the question that preoccupied me most: What will Carl Horak do after graduation?

Once I got back to Amherst, I found out that questions about the immediate and more distant future were also preoccupying most of my graduating class. Graduate school? A year backpacking through South America? Some Wall Street firm's training program like Anna wanted? The dispersion was confusing and distracting. All these people, so close to me at one point, were going off in different directions like cosmic creations after the Big Bang. My old group of friends did not seem to give me the same comfort of past years; even Anna had become an "estranged girlfriend" of sorts.

It had been a while since I had been in New York and the old place at Washington Square. When I returned from Europe I called home and found out from Mom that while I was away, Dad had suffered another (his second) mild heart attack. He was fine, she said, but I should come see him. Of course, I would go that weekend. Honestly, I felt a bit bad about my selfishness and lack of communication with home. I had focused solely on life in Aix and how to exploit Eastern European opportunities; I was suddenly worried about my father, about his health. Furthermore, I was still looking for an anchor and a compass, and travelling to New York at that time was both the right thing to do and possibly even useful.

He looked grayer than I remembered. From Andy, the childhood friend I stayed in touch with, and whose father had died last year, I recently heard, "Heart attacks change people, and it is not only the physical appearance but the scared outlook of a life staring at its impending end." Father seemed hesitant, nervous, and bad-tempered. But at one point, he took my hand and with a soft voice and even softer eyes told me earnestly, "You will be okay." Even though that was just after we had had one more argument about my plans for the future.

Those words will be etched in my memory. He shook his head disapprovingly. He was disheartened and unhappy about my choice to move to Prague and seek employment with one of the many foreign corporations that were sprouting like mushrooms after the rain; they all wanted to tap into the new opportunities. "Business? You, Carl Horak, son of Martin Horak, you want to go into business? What about graduate school? What about the important matters of the soul? You are not an ordinary, superficial businessman!" I am ashamed to confess today that I deviously used heritage and what by now was a fair knowledge of Czech to point out that he had given me tools I could use to my advantage. He would have none of it and continued to argue that business was for the common folk. But then he took my hand.

I went off to Prague with little more than my clothes, a few books, and some jazz sheet music, including a few musical notations of compositions of my own. I was not sure what I would be doing there and how I would feed myself, but I was confident that I would find acceptable solutions to whatever obstacles I encountered.

In the Prague of 1992, I found a city that clearly was going through an historical spring. Youngsters were demonstrating in favor of democratic change and against attempts to turn to the more recent past. The beautiful city with its bridges to the old, medieval buildings, was full of political posters; renewal was as much in the air as foreigners were rampant throughout the city. There was plenty of excitement and lots of hustlers— most foreigners and many locals thought that quick riches were available for the picking. At JFK I met some people on the way over; they wanted to launch a new internet site that would bring foreigners and locals closer— they offered me a temporary position because of my language skills. It was a suitable beginning even if the pay was paltry. It would allow me the time to look around for bigger and better things without starving.

They say that no new beginnings are easy, and this one was no different, but I was young and carefree and found a way to overcome the minor and major obstacles to a fairly happy life in the new setting. My new quarters in the outskirts of the city, where rent was cheapest, were shared with three other Americans (one was the new acquaintance I met at JFK). I slept on a mattress on the floor, but it was okay. While making friends with "locals" of my age was not easy, there was a wonderful assortment of foreigners whose circumstances were akin to mine and who felt the need to bond and make friends as much as I did. Soon enough we had a network that would help each other out, who religiously met at cafés and bars around Legorova Boulevard. Granted, we were mostly men, but some of us knew enough Czech to attract local girls into the circle—many of them thought we were comic and bizarre. "You eat funny and laugh funny," said one, but they did not care. I concluded that we offered them an alternative to the barren (economically limited) life they used to live before the Berlin Wall fell. I will never forget that my first after-sex conversation with Jana included her diatribe in which she blamed all Czech men for leading a very boring sex life. I wondered if I had offered anything that was different.

About five months after my arrival, I found out about Prague jazz. One of the buccaneers looking to make it in the new land had discovered this group of musicians that were looking for a keyboard player; he told them about me. I started spending a lot of time with these three men. They were so much more adept than my Amherst band! The first day, we spent several hours barely saying a word but playing lots of jazz. We nodded contentedly as we discovered that we actually jelled musically; we were making music from a very similar point of view. We would mix classical jazz (what they played in the thirties and forties) with modern jazz (like the new wave of Brazilian *bossa nova*). We fully intended to be international in our sourcing ("Politics has nothing to do with music" affirmed the lead guitarist). We decided to form the "Prague Jazz Musicians" and chose to celebrate this by going to the one jazz club that had been around for decades: Redutta. The oldest among us was forty-five and knew everything and everyone in Prague jazz. He told us that we must go to Redutta to hear Marek.

I inquired about Marek and was simply told: "He is the Godfather of Czech jazz." I knew better than to ask for more details like his last name.

After a couple of months, we got a few gigs in small venues throughout the city and were getting a few koruny for our efforts (food and booze were included to make it even more rewarding). We seemed to agree the music we played was good and were encouraged by the recognition we received. Though I was the youngest, and the only foreigner, I did not play a minor role in the quartet's music making; I was getting my fair share of solo segments to show off my technique, and my compositions were getting played as well.

The most positive aspect of the city, other than its beautiful setting and gorgeous women, was how much any kind of music was appreciated, how knowledgeable the audiences seemed to be. In that context, to my surprise, jazz seemed very important in this city. I was ecstatic! It felt very good when one newspaper called us the new revolution in Prague jazz.

Bids for our performance at jazz venues started streaming in and our appearances were now to packed audiences. All three best jazz clubs, per the tourist magazine that just came out with its first edition, were asking for us to perform. When we performed for the first time at Redutta, I saw Marek in the audience; the man was in his sixties but did not show it. I focused on him a bit and noted happily that he followed our music and seemed very animated. At the end, he came over and talked to Jacek, our lead saxophonist and the founder of our group. We were, of course, eager to find out what he might have said. "The Godfather suggested that we produce a recording," said Jacek with a big grin. We were jubilant! For me that signaled triumph, making it, being someone. "Wow!" I told myself, "People will play your music at home, read your name on the cover, know you."

Though I had to work during the day to make sure that I survived financially, the new position I took at Colgate's corporate relations department mattered little. This band was it! We went to a recording studio for five consecutive weeks—we had to make sure the record would be a hit.

On a cool September Saturday night, our favorite club, the NUJAZZ Club, threw a party to honor the launch of the new CD. When I arrived at the club, I noticed that the place was packed and a long line had formed on the side. I was puzzled, but Jacek calmed me down: "They are lining up to buy our record, man!" These were locals, foreigners living here, and tourists. I had not seen bottles of champagne since I left New York, but it was flowing here. I noticed Jana sitting with some of our common friends at one of the near-stage tables and we smiled at each other.

When we started playing, the audience was cheering us on, but when Jacek told the crowd that Marek would join us for the rest of this set, they went crazy. Amazing Marek, the best-known jazz musician in town, the one everyone called the Godfather because of his efforts to popularize jazz in Prague, was going to join us to play our music. Because he is also a keyboard player, we put on stage a piano and an electric keyboard and we would alternate playing the two instruments. I tried to be impartial, but his playing was absolutely fabulous. If I had any doubts, the smiles on the faces in the audience confirmed this.

I had special feelings for the older man from the first time we crossed paths, with his bald head and casual look. That night I felt closer to him than ever. He took one look at the notes of this version of Ray Bryant's *Sneakin' Around* and started jamming like he had been practicing with us for hours. How he lived and displayed his passion! He was fully consumed in the music, in the moment, in what was happening onstage. While he exchanged looks and nods with all members of the quartet, as any jazz musician would, he would "converse" with me more—he would smile and inspire confidence, he would vigorously nod as he delivered an entry note that would allow me to take over and show off my skills. And it is at that point that I had this strange vision of Marek and my father merging into one. They were not the same age, nor did they look alike, but at this stage in my life I loved them both without reservations.

As we finished the first set, two more would follow. I went over to Marek and shamelessly embraced him. At first, he was taken by surprise and pushed back a tad, but then he quickly reversed himself and warmly accepted the full hug. He gave me a big smile and patted my cheek with his palm.

ABOUT THE AUTHOR

Dr . **Michael Ranis has lived in five** countries, visited more than fifty, and is fluent in six languages. Life's uncanny ability to toss you around, curiosity, and the impulse to excel are largely responsible for the creation of *Opaque Blue*. This book is a literary exploration of Ranis's odyssey.

Born in La Paz to German Jewish emigres who met in that city, Michael was exposed to all the beauty of Latin America and all that is so attractive about Jewish ethical traditions. He chose to migrate to Israel at the age of fourteen (1966). His interest in political matters being a direct consequence of that decision. He received his B.A. from Tel Aviv University (Philosophy and Science of Developing Countries being dual minors) and a Ph.D. in Political Science from the University of Chicago.

Michael taught several courses involving European politics, the Middle East, and Public Policy at Hamilton College and Swarthmore College. He taught for four years before turning his interests to finance, obtaining an MBA (New York University) and entering that industry. He was active in investment banking and portfolio management from 1986 to 2016. Most of his employment was in New York, but he also spent five years in Switzerland and almost as long in London.

Michael has two children. Ethan and Sophie (Julia) Ranis. He also has a beautiful baby granddaughter.

Though interest in arts and music play a significant role in his life, Michael is an avid and accomplished bridge player. He has achieved a number of good results in national and international tournaments. He has embarked on a literary career late in life to challenge himself to write like those he admired.